Velvet
on a
Tuesday Afternoon

VELVET ON A TUESDAY AFTERNOON

AN EDDIE COLLINS MYSTERY

———◆———

CLIVE ROSENGREN

coffeetownpress

Seattle, WA

coffeetownpress

Coffeetown Press
PO Box 70515
Seattle, WA 98127

For more information go to: www.coffeetownpress.com
www.cliverosengren.com

Cover design by Sabrina Sun

Velvet on a Tuesday Afternoon
Copyright © 2017 by Clive Rosengren

ISBN: 978-1-60381-625-0 (Trade Paper)
ISBN: 978-1-60381-626-7 (eBook)

Library of Congress Control Number: 2017948563

Printed in the United States of America

Acknowledgments

———◆———

STARING AT A COMPUTER SCREEN AND putting words in some form of a story oftentimes makes an author feel as though he's in a vacuum. To blunt that feeling, I once again tip my hat to the members of Monday Mayhem, my writing group. Carole Beers, Sharon Dean, Michael Niemann, and Tim Wohlforth provided invaluable guidance in the formation of this third Eddie Collins story. Thanks, guys.

Thanks also to my early readers, Karen Olson, Brad Whitmore, brother Larry Rosengren, and sister-in-law Kathy, who keeps me on the straight and narrow with respect to commas and other such nagging punctuation quagmires.

A special thanks to Paisley for the title. Who knows when an offhand comment will resurface several years later?

And finally, thanks to Catherine Treadgold, Jennifer McCord, and the rest of the crew at Coffeetown Press for providing a new home for Eddie Collins. He is deeply grateful for their welcome.

Also by the author

Murder Unscripted

Red Desert

CHAPTER ONE

———◆———

HOLLYWOOD BOULEVARD IS LIKE A KALEIDOSCOPE you put up to your eye and rotate. Every turn gives you a different perspective, a different arrangement of colored glass, never to be repeated.

On this particular early Tuesday afternoon, my kaleidoscope was tainted by two factors. The first was rain. Serious rain. Umbrellas bobbed along the boulevard, tourists jumped over puddles, and street people huddled in doorways, challenging anyone who dared to invade their turf.

The second factor was my hangover. I couldn't do anything about the rain. I did have a remedy for my hangover, thus the fourth cup of coffee in my hand as I stood on my mini-balcony watching the rain-dampened kaleidoscopic view below me.

I was glad for the rain. Not only was it helping to wash away the smog and the germs here in La La Land, it was ruining the day for one particular advertising agency that had stiffed me yesterday. Besides running Collins Investigations, I work as an actor. Whenever I get the chance, that is. Yesterday I'd had the chance, briefly.

I had booked a television beer commercial and was out in Santa Monica for the wardrobe call. This event gave the ad executives and production people—the "suits"—an opportunity to peruse their actors' wardrobe options on the shoot. They sat behind a long table eating their catered lunch of burgers, ribs, and corn on the cob while we actors, stick people on their story boards, strutted and posed in front of them.

It was a funny spot. A baseball umpire and a manager argue about a call at the top of their lungs. Cut to the two of them having dinner in one of their homes. The only way they can communicate is by shouting. I was perfect for the umpire. At least I thought so. The "suits" didn't agree.

After the wardrobe call, I was filling my car with gas when my agent, Morrie Howard, called, telling me the agency people had decided to "go another way." Apparently one empty suit hadn't bothered to look at the audition tape, nor the callback tape, so when he saw Eddie Collins dressed as his umpire, he must have thought I had sprinkled sugar on his corn on the cob.

I don't know what they saw in that tape, but just ask my agent Morrie: I make a credible umpire, cowboy, salesman, whatever kind of character actor you need to fill out your cast list. If you need a guy in his early forties with a full head of brown hair, a pleasant-enough craggy face, capped teeth, and a body that wouldn't fail a physical but which no gym would take credit for, I was your guy.

I sipped coffee as I watched a truck plow through a puddle and douse two young guys standing by the curb. I was feeling pretty smug, due to the fact that rain was ruining the empty suit's infernal commercial. Morrie had gone on to tell me that I would still get paid for the day, but that wasn't the point. Actors don't do television commercials because of the fee they'll collect for the filming. By the time taxes and an agent's ten percent are shaved off, what's left won't pay the rent. No, they do them for the residuals. A beer commercial would likely get good air time, and the payoffs could be substantial.

After the car was gassed up, I had trouble making it home. A certain bartender sought my opinion on whether or not 3D movies would last. Yet another mixologist and I debated the ineptitude of Congress and what should be done about it. Despite a lot of liquid help, we couldn't come up with an answer.

This morning I was paying dearly for my dalliances. An earlier trip to a greasy spoon had helped, but not completely. Four cups of coffee seemed to be doing the trick. In any case, it was a lousy, gray Los Angeles Tuesday in February, perfect for playing hooky.

From behind me I heard someone knocking on the door to my outer office. Mavis Werner, my secretary, was spending the day at a flea market out in Pomona. She supplements her salary by buying and trading antiques and collectibles. She was on a mission to find a pair of salt and pepper shakers in the form of Tonto and the Lone Ranger. No word on who was salt and who was pepper.

I set my coffee cup on the counter of my studio apartment kitchen and pawed my way through the beaded curtain separating my living quarters from my office. Another knock sounded.

"Hold your horses. I'm on the way."

I shoved a chair to the front of my desk and went into Mavis's office, flicking on the overhead light. Flipping the dead bolt, I pulled the door open to find Larry Wilkerson, my mailman, dripping water on the threadbare carpet of the hallway. He was lanky and covered with a poncho and sodden rain hat.

"Hey, Mr. Collins. Your secretary's day off, huh?" He handed me a clump of letters and a small package.

"So she tells me. You staying dry?"

"Well, you know. Neither snow nor rain nor heat and all of that stuff. Have a good one."

He moved off down the hall and I shut the door. Sitting at Mavis's desk, I sorted through the envelopes. A few bills and a couple of residuals caught my eye; the rest went in the circular file behind me. I walked into my office, turned on my desk lamp, and slit open the envelopes from "SAG-AFTRA, One Union," the moniker chosen in the wake of a merger of the two organizations. The net from the two checks amounted to enough for a matinee movie and dinner. Two reasons for playing hooky.

Then came another knock on the front door.

"Hello," a sultry voice said.

"In here," I replied. "Come on in."

She was gorgeous, tall, and had legs that didn't stop. A cascade of raven hair caressed her shoulders, framing a face with dark eyes that searched the room as if someone were following her. She wore a black leather coat and had a tote bag draped over one shoulder. A short dark skirt and a red blouse completed the ensemble. She carried a small black umbrella flecked with drops of rain.

Her name was Carla Rizzoli.

"Hello, Eddie," she said in a throaty half-whisper that conjured up memories of company on a cold night.

"Been a long time, Carla." I rose from behind my desk, walked up to her, and gave her a hug. She wrapped her arms around me, their grip making me think my plans to play hooky could conceivably change. After a moment she released me and we looked into each other's eyes.

She ran one hand over my cheek and said, "It's good to see you."

"Likewise." I gestured to a chair. "Have a seat." I walked back around the desk and sat down.

She wrapped the little strap around the pleats of the umbrella and sank down, setting the tote bag on the floor beside her. Staring at me, she crossed one perfect leg over the other. The whisk of nylon on nylon reverberated through the small room.

"I didn't think you'd remember me," she said.

"You're not that easy to forget. You look good, Carla."

"Thanks," she said. Her smile formed just the suggestion of dimples on each cheek. "So do you."

It had been several years since I'd crossed paths with Carla Rizzoli. We'd met doing a television show, a legal drama by the name of *Justice Denied* that managed to hold its own for a few seasons. I played an attorney on a two-part episode. There had been talk of making my character a recurring regular. Then the writers had the brilliant idea of having me lose the case, one in which Carla was my client. I went from potential recurring regular to has-been one-shot guest. Notwithstanding my legal ineptitude, we'd started going out. Just when the relationship seemed to be getting serious, she took a walk on me. No reason, no explanation.

She reached into a pocket of her coat and pulled out a ragged envelope. "I found your name in the Yellow Pages. At first I didn't think it was you, but then I googled you and found your website."

"My secretary's responsible for that," I said, as I sat down. "I'm afraid websites are beyond my pay grade."

"So, no more acting?"

"Yeah, now and then. Mostly then. This is my day job, so to speak." Her small chuckle was as provocative now as it had been when I was playing her attorney. "And how about you?" I continued. "How's the career going?"

"Oh, you know, ups and downs. But I've got a shot at a part in a movie. I'm waiting to hear."

"That's terrific. Good luck."

As I looked at her, I recalled the scenes we had done together and remembered being impressed by her talent. She'd been fairly new to the business at that time, but it was evident she could deliver the goods.

"Can I get you anything? Coffee? Something stronger?"

Laying the envelope on the desk, she stood up, removed her coat, and draped it across the back of the chair. Reseating herself, she said, "Thanks. I'm good."

"I can't imagine you needing a private investigator, Carla. What brings you through the door of Collins Investigations?"

"I want you to find someone." She pulled a letter from the crinkled envelope and handed them both to me. "This was delivered to me at work yesterday."

"Where's work?" I asked as I took the scraps of paper from her.

"Uh … well, it's on the envelope."

I looked down and saw her name and the address for a place called Feline Follies on Century Boulevard. She reached across the desk and handed me a business card. It was bright red. On it, embossed in gold letters, was the name Velvet La Rose.

"That's my stage name. I'm working as a dancer, Eddie."

"Really? For how long?"

"Couple of years."

"And you need your own business card for that?"

She heaved a big sigh. "The owner had them made up for all of us. I don't know why. It's not like we're hooking or anything."

"Velvet La Rose. Nice ring to it."

"You're not offended that a stripper wants to hire you?"

I shrugged my shoulders. "Not my place to judge, Carla."

"The tips are good and they let me go out on auditions. I hope it's only temporary."

"Hey, listen, you don't have to explain to me. This whole Hollywood hustle thing is tough going. I once knew a guy who made ends meet by juggling chainsaws out on Venice Beach. You gotta do what you gotta do."

She chuckled and said, "I hope they weren't running."

"Matter of fact, they were." I opened the letter she had handed me and smoothed it out. The letterhead was from the Los Angeles Mission downtown. Scrawled across the page were the words "I'm in trouble. Watch your back. Frankie."

"Who's Frankie?"

"My brother. His birth name is Francis."

"Why the letterhead from the Los Angeles Mission? Is he homeless?"

"I don't know. I haven't seen or heard from him for a while."

"Then how does he know you're working at Feline Follies?"

"I've no idea, Eddie. We had a … I guess you could call it a falling-out. I haven't seen him since."

"How long ago was that?"

"Seven years and eight months."

"I don't get it. And yet he knows you're at Feline Follies?"

"He must. You've got the letter in front of you."

I looked at it again and said, "Can I keep this?"

"Sure."

I opened my notebook and jotted down the address and phone number for the mission. "What kind of trouble is he referring to?"

She started to reply, but choked on the words. She reached into the tote bag and pulled out a handkerchief, then dabbed at her eyes and cleared her throat. "I'm not sure. Could I have some water?"

"You bet," I said, and went into Mavis's usually off-limits closet and grabbed a bottle of water. She twisted the top off and took a swallow. "You all right?"

"Yeah. I didn't think this was going to upset me. I thought wrong." She took another swallow of water and set the bottle on the edge of my desk.

"Frankie joined the army right after 9/11. Our parents were against it. So was I."

"That's the falling-out you mentioned?"

"Yeah. He really ticked us off. But he went anyway. He stayed in until seven years ago. Then he was discharged and disappeared."

"How do you know he was discharged?"

"My dad found out."

"How?"

"A guy by the name of Phil Scarborough called him looking for Frankie. Said he'd mustered out with him."

"Any reason why Frankie would disappear?"

"Not that I can think of."

"What did he do in the Army? Was he infantry?"

"He was an MP." She pulled a photo from the tote bag and handed it to me. "At least he looks like it in this picture he sent me. That's him on the left."

The snapshot showed two MPs in full desert camo posed in front of the main gate of a military installation. Her brother was a buck sergeant. The one on the right, a black man, wore a lieutenant's insignia. I turned the photo over but didn't see a date. "When did you get this?"

"Four years after he enlisted." I started to hand it back to her, but she said, "You better keep the picture, too. It's the only one I've got of him."

I looked at the photo and said, "Is the other guy this Phil Scarborough?"

"I don't know."

"Okay. Tell me why Frankie told you to watch your back."

She said she didn't know and couldn't think of any enemies who would threaten her. I made some notes for myself and Carla went on to give me the phone number for her parents, who lived in Henderson, Nevada. She confided that she wasn't on the best terms with her folks in the wake of them learning she was dancing at Feline Follies. She also hadn't told them she'd received this note from Frankie.

I prepared one of my standard contracts. She filled it out and we exchanged all the relevant phone numbers, after which she wrote me a check for my retainer. She then finished her bottle of water, stood, and put on her coat. I came out from behind my desk and stuck out my hand. She grasped it with both of hers.

"I don't know how to do this, Eddie, other than just saying it."

"What?"

"I'm sorry for taking a walk on you back then."

"Hey, no worries."

"My head was messed up and I didn't deal with it very well."

"Well, if I'd won the damn case for you, maybe you'd have had second thoughts." We both laughed and she gave me a hug. "I'll try to do better as your PI," I added.

She smiled as she buttoned up her coat. "So, have you been in front of the camera lately? Anything I would have seen?"

"I doubt it," I said, and filled her in on my brush with the beer commercial.

"Idiots," she replied. She picked up her tote bag and slung it over a shoulder. "Thanks for your help, Mr. Private Eye, Sometime Actor. Even though Frankie and I haven't gotten along, he's still my brother and I'm worried about him. He wouldn't have reached out to me if he weren't in trouble."

"What about you? Are you going to be safe, to be able to 'watch your back,' as he put it?"

"I'll be okay. I've got pepper spray and this." Reaching into her tote bag again, she pulled out a small automatic that looked plenty lethal despite its size.

"I hope you have a permit for that?"

"The Follies' owner insisted that all the girls have one. It's legal."

"Remind me not to mess with you," I said.

She replaced the gun in her bag and gave me another hug. "Well, I'm not really that tough. You should drop into the Follies sometime."

"I'll probably have to. Consultation with my client, you know."

She smiled and I saw her to the front door. I told her I'd be in touch soon and watched her walk to the elevator. She looked back at me before the door creaked open and she stepped inside.

As I walked back into my office, I mulled over the prospect of having a client who was an exotic dancer with a permit to carry a concealed handgun.

Philip Marlowe should be so lucky.

Chapter Two

———◆———

"You need a GPS, Eddie."

"Why is that?"

"I've got better things to do than print out maps for you." Mavis pulled another sheet of paper from the printer and slapped it on her desk. "I thought you had a Thomas Guide."

"I do, but it's hard to read it and drive at the same time."

"Ergo, GPS." She sat down and held out her hand. "Give me those before you break them." She was referring to the Lone Ranger and Tonto salt and pepper shakers I held in my hands.

"There's not much of a likeness here," I said. "They should have gone with the Johnny Depp and Armie Hammer version."

"Oh, for Pete's sake. Tonto with a dead crow on his head? You're going to use something like that to pepper your scrambled eggs?"

She had a point. I picked up the maps and headed for the front door. "I'll check in with you later."

"If you don't want to fight the Hollywood Freeway, I'd take Vermont down to Wilshire and hang a left." She pointed to the papers in my hand. "It ends at Grand. You'll turn left to Sixth, then a one-way to your right. It's highlighted in yellow."

"What would I do without you, kiddo?"

She sipped from her coffee cup and said, "Well, considering the fact that while I was gone yesterday you were hired by a pistol-packing stripper, I shudder to think."

At a loss for words, I shut the door behind me and walked to the elevator. Already waiting was one of my neighbors from the floor, Dr. Leonid Travnikov.

He was a small, stocky man, dressed in an overcoat. A flat cap sat on his head. Over the years, we've rarely engaged in conversation, no doubt due to his thick Russian accent.

"Morning," I said.

"Good mornink, Mr. Collins. Everything iss all right?"

"So far, so good."

He nodded and we stepped into the elevator. The door closed and we started our creaky descent. After a couple of floors the good doctor harrumphed and shook his head.

"This elevator make me scared. Every day I go up, down, and think it will be my last ride."

"Well, I guess we could always take the stairs."

He harrumphed again. "You take stairs, then come see me. I need patients." He looked over at me and grinned, more emotion than I'd ever seen him display.

I SELDOM VENTURE DOWNTOWN. HENCE, THE MAP. It's a curious section of the city with two distinct personalities. Between Temple and First Streets, government offices loom. At lunchtime the buildings disgorge lawyers and very important people with very important jobs. Huge entertainment centers like the Dorothy Chandler Pavilion, the Ahmanson Theatre, and the cookie-cutter Disney Concert Hall sprawl nearby. In the evenings those very important people sip cocktails and tell each other how cultured they are before popping in to see the opera, the symphony, the latest Broadway hit.

Several blocks south, where I was headed, it's a vastly different story. There are no important people with important jobs. There are no jobs at all. These people cower inside cardboard boxes and tell each other that tomorrow's going to be better. And where a free hot meal can be found.

A few years back I booked a film job that shot in the seedier part of town. Off-duty cops worked as security on the shoot and had their hands full keeping the homeless from raiding the catering trucks. I remember that when darkness fell, the neighborhood took on the appearance of scenes from *Blade Runner*. Needless to say, I didn't tarry getting home.

I found a parking spot on San Julian around the corner from the Los Angeles Mission and made certain the car door was locked. The street was cluttered with trash of all kinds. Paper, garbage, clothing, it didn't matter. Small encampments were set up, fortresses defined by shopping carts, tattered tarps, and mangled cardboard boxes. A grizzled old man leaned against a light pole and pushed himself upright when he saw me coming.

"Spare me some change, sir?"

I shook my head and continued walking.

"C'mon, man, shit."

Dressed as neatly as I was, I knew if I stopped to give him money I'd be a target. Better to drop a donation inside the mission.

One half of a wrought-iron gate was open and I walked into a small courtyard. Several older men sat on concrete benches. Another occupied a wheelchair. Two flagpoles were to my right, the U.S. and California banners hanging lifeless. I entered the building and went up to a craggy, middle-aged man wearing a beard and glasses and sitting at a reception desk. An ID badge on his shirt said his name was John Pederson.

"Can I help you, sir?"

"I hope so. The name's Eddie Collins," I said, handing him my license. I took Carla's letter out of my pocket and unfolded it. "I'm looking for a guy by the name of Frankie, or Francis Rizzoli. Is this handwriting at all familiar?"

Pederson looked at it and shook his head. "This Mr. Rizzoli in some sort of trouble?"

"I'm not sure. Is that the mission's stationery?" I asked.

"Yes it is. From time to time someone will ask for paper to perhaps write a letter to a friend or loved one. We gladly provide it."

I showed him the photo of Frankie in the Army uniform. "Does the man on the left look familiar? This was taken a few years ago. He might have put on some weight. Might even be wearing a beard."

Pederson looked at the picture for a long moment and then shook his head. "Boy, there's a trace there, but we've got so many men coming and going, I'd be hard pressed to give you a positive identification." He pushed his chair back and went to a file cabinet. "Let me see if there's anybody by that name on our emergency rolls." He extracted a file and scanned the contents. "Sorry, Mr. Collins, we don't have a Francis Rizzoli listed anywhere."

"Thanks for your help," I said, and started for the door. "By the way, I'd like to make a donation. How do I go about that?"

"I'll give you an envelope, sir."

I reached into my pocket and separated a C-note from my money clip. "Why don't I just give this to you, John?"

He looked surprised, but took the bill. "We appreciate your generosity, Mr. Collins. Let me get you a receipt."

"No need," I said. I handed him one of my cards. "If you happen to run across Frankie, let me know, would you?"

"Indeed I will."

I went outside to the front of the mission and looked right and left, wondering if Frankie Rizzoli was to be found among this sampling of the disadvantaged. And if so, what the hell was he doing here? It's no secret that a large percentage of veterans wind up homeless, on the street. Maybe Carla's brother was indeed among them.

I walked toward San Julian and stopped in front of two men sitting against the wall of a building, passing a bottle of wine back and forth. They looked to be in their fifties, although it was hard to tell. Both faces were covered with beards and grime. Each man wore frayed jeans, one a stained hoodie, the other a torn field jacket. A shopping cart loaded with bundles sat next to them.

"Excuse me, fellas. Either one of you know a guy by the name of Frankie Rizzoli?"

They squinted up at me, and the one wearing a black watch cap said, "You a cop?"

"I'm not a cop. Just looking for a friend of mine. Frankie Rizzoli. You know him?"

"You look like that cop." He pointed at my porkpie hat. "That Popeye guy. You Popeye?" His companion burst into laughter and grabbed for the bottle.

This wasn't the first time my hat had reminded someone of that Gene Hackman character. I sometimes wondered if I'd be better off going hatless. I pulled out the picture and thrust it in front of them. "The guy on the left. He look familiar to either one of you?"

They leaned forward and peered at the photo, shading their eyes from the sun. Field jacket leaned back and said, "Nah, he don't look familiar. 'Course, I never hung around buck sergeants too much." He took a pull off the bottle and handed it to his buddy.

I continued down the street toward San Julian and my car. My question directed at several others yielded nothing, except more comments about my hat and overpowering whiffs of body odor, booze, and despair. My appearance seemed to make everyone feel they were being rousted by some kind of authority. I kept going down San Julian toward the Union Rescue Mission, another outpost for relief.

Two young men sat on a broken-down sofa, one of them black, the other Hispanic. They passed a joint between them. A wrinkled blue tarp stretched between two shopping carts provided a little shade. I knelt down and lifted up the edge of the plastic. They made an attempt to hide the joint, but not the aroma. The black guy wore an LA Dodgers cap and a greasy leather jacket. His Latino companion was hatless and had on a zippered hoodie. Suspicion washed over their faces as I lifted up the tarp.

I showed them the snapshot. "I'm looking for the white guy on the left. Either one of you seen anybody that looks like him?"

"Who the fuck are you, man?" the Hispanic said. "You *La Migra*?"

"Come on, I'm not immigration. I'm just looking for this guy. His name's Frankie Rizzoli. Either one of you know him?"

The black guy slapped the picture out of my hand and kicked at me. "Get the fuck outta here, man."

I picked up the photo and showed it to him again. "What's the matter? You know Frankie?"

"Yeah, I knew him. The guy's bad news."

"What do you mean 'knew'? Is he dead?"

Dodger cap inhaled a hit off the joint and then shook his head as he held in the smoke. After a few seconds he exhaled a cloud in my direction and slurped from a plastic bottle of water held between his legs.

"I don't know if Frankie's dead, but if he ain't, he will be pretty soon."

"Why's that?"

He stared at me for a long moment, then finished what was left in the bottle and tossed it into the street. He folded his arms in front of him. "I'm done talkin'."

I turned to his companion. "What's goin' on, *amigo*? Help me out here."

The Latino man took a hit off the joint and passed it back. "There was a shooting a couple of weeks ago. Over on Crocker. A guy we know said Frankie saw it go down, man. Maybe he was even in on it."

"Manny, shut your fuckin' mouth!" the black guy shouted. He kicked at me again and tried to get off the sofa, but I backed up and he sank down. "We don't know nothin'. I don't know who the hell you are, mister, but you'd best be on your way."

I stuck the photo back in my pocket and started walking toward my car. I'd struck a nerve with the guy in the Dodger cap. Frankie Rizzoli had come out of the shadows. Someone knew him. He'd been spotted at the scene of a crime. Something had gone down on Crocker Street. I needed to know what it was.

CHAPTER THREE

---◆---

I WAS ON WILSHIRE, HEADING OUT OF the downtown area. Just before Vermont I spotted a parking meter and pulled over. Some generous soul had left me forty-eight minutes. The Austin Lounge Lizards had been providing the drive-time concert. Ejecting the CD, I fumbled my cellphone out of my pocket and found the number for Lieutenant Charlie Rivers, my LAPD conduit, who'd helped me out a time or two in the past. It rang three times and he picked up.

"Rivers."

"Hey, Charlie, it's Eddie Collins."

"Eddie-the-Actor Collins? Who never invites me to sample that vast movie collection of his? I keep asking, but no dice."

"Soon, Charlie, soon. In the meantime, how long's it been since you dropped into Pink's?"

"Pink's? My mouth is watering as I speak." There was a pause and I could hear him talking to someone in the background. "But my cop's instinct tells me my chili dog comes with a condition. Am I right?"

"Guilty as charged. A couple of weeks ago, maybe a month, there was a shooting on Crocker Street downtown. It'd be great if you could give me details."

"Yeah, I think I remember something. Is this client-related?"

"Always, Charlie. Can you also run a name through the system for me?"

"This is gonna cost you another lunch, Shamus. I haven't been to Philippe's in a while."

"You got it."

"Who am I looking for?"

I gave him Frankie's name and the spelling. "One o'clock good for you?"

"I can smell the onions. See you there."

I feel very fortunate. Every private eye needs a cop friend with a good appetite. Charlie broke the connection and I flipped open my notebook to the page where I'd jotted down the number of Carla's parents out in Henderson, Nevada. Ruth and Benjamin Rizzoli. After two rings, a woman answered in a small, faltering voice.

"Hello?"

"Mrs. Rizzoli?"

"Yes?"

"My name's Eddie Collins, ma'am. I'm a private investigator. Hired by your daughter Carla."

"Carla? Is she in trouble?"

"No, ma'am. She's asked me to find your son, Frankie. He may be the one in trouble."

"Oh, good Lord, not Frankie. What's he done?"

I heard someone talking in the background. Mrs. Rizzoli took the phone away from her mouth and I could make out her saying, "It's somebody calling about Frankie."

After some rustling, a voice boomed, "This is Benny Rizzoli speaking. Who is this?"

I repeated my name and the reason for my call. "Have you heard from Frankie recently?"

"I ain't heard from the kid in years. What's he done now?"

"That's what I'm trying to find out."

"Is Carla all right?"

"She's fine. As a matter of fact, she told me she's up for a part in a movie."

"Yeah, well, she's said that before. Meantime, I s'pose she's still at that damn club."

"Carla told me a Phil Scarborough called you at one point looking for Frankie. That right, sir?"

"Yeah, I think that was the guy's name."

"Did he by any chance leave a phone number?"

"Ah, lemme think." Benny did so, then continued, "Seems to me he might have. Hang on a minute." He dropped the phone and I heard him speak to his wife, then some more rustling on the other end of the line, and he came back on. "Yeah, here it is." He read off a number with a 310 area code. Phil Scarborough was somewhere in LA.

"I thank you, Mr. Rizzoli. You've been a great help."

"Listen, Collins, if you find the kid, tell him his mother worries about him."

"Will do, sir."

I didn't ask if he shared the worry. He broke the connection, and I put the phone back in my pocket. The 9/11 attack was a pretty distant memory. One would think resentments between father and son had cooled by now, but apparently not. *Not my problem*, I thought, as I fired up my car and headed back into Hollywood.

PAUL AND BETTY PINK ACQUIRED A fifty-dollar loan in 1939 and turned it into a Hollywood goldmine. For seventy-five years at the corner of Melrose and La Brea, the famous and infamous have been scarfing down Pink's hot dogs. Charlie Rivers was one of them. He stood in front of the eatery surveying the menu. I beeped my horn at him and was lucky enough to find a parking spot in the back. When I opened the car door, I was greeted by the irresistible aroma of chili and onions.

Charlie's shirt was open at the neck and his tie hung askew. Aviator sunglasses perched on his nose. He had a folder in his hand. "I'll grab us a table. Since you're buying, you can stand in line."

"Fair enough. What tickles your fancy?"

"Given the fact I'm dining with an actor, I'll have the Marlon Brando and a diet soda."

"You got it." He meandered back to the patio and I grabbed a place in the queue. Fortunately it wasn't long. Ten minutes later, I balanced two dogs and drinks up to a small table. Charlie was looking over some papers.

He shoved them to the side and contemplated the nine-inch wonder in front of him. "What do you think? Marlon had a few of these in his time?"

"The pictures don't lie, Charlie." I'd opted for a pastrami Reuben, and the first bite put me right with the world. Between mouthfuls, I said, "Did you get a hit on Frankie Rizzoli?"

"*Nada*. Just the fact that he was in the Army. Why you looking for the guy?"

"My client got a letter from him. He's her brother and she's worried about him."

He wiped a sliver of mustard from his chin. "So why doesn't he pick up a phone?"

"The letter came from the LA Mission. He may be on the streets." I took another bite of my Reuben and watched a limo glide up next to the building. Two young suits and an even younger woman wearing a skirt short enough to embarrass even me climbed out and got in line to order.

I drew Charlie's attention to them. He turned and shook his head. "This goddamn town. I swear."

"Young Turks gotta eat, Charlie."

"Yeah, right. And I suppose she's their secretary."

I dabbed at the corners of my mouth. "So what went down on Crocker?"

He wiped his hands on his napkin, took a swallow of his soda, and flipped open the folder. "Ten thirty p.m., two weeks ago, the twentieth, Central responded to a report of shots fired at Crocker and Eighth. Officers arriving at the scene found one gunshot victim. A witness said an altercation took place in front of a black SUV. Two shots were fired, three men jumped in the vehicle and sped off."

"Who was the witness?"

"One Elmer Billingsley. On a beer run. He couldn't get a plate, and wasn't much help in describing the suspects. Two street people, male, refused to speak to officers and fled the scene."

"Drugs involved?"

"Could be. Paraphernalia was found on the shooting victim."

"You got a name for him?"

Charlie took a bite of his sandwich and chewed as he flipped a couple of pages. "Yeah, here it is. Guy's name is Phil Scarborough."

I stopped mid-bite. "Say that again."

"Phil Scarborough. Why?"

"He was in the Army with Frankie Rizzoli."

"So?"

"I rousted a homeless guy this morning who said he thought Rizzoli saw the shooting go down. Might even have been involved."

Charlie took a bite off Marlon and chewed for a minute. "So at least your guy isn't a ghost."

"Right. If he hasn't disappeared into Skid Row. You been down in that scene lately?"

"Nope. Not my bailiwick." He flipped through some more pages. "No address for this Scarborough. But EMTs took him to California Medical over on Grand. They should know."

"If he's even still there."

"True. They probably wouldn't hold him two weeks." He polished off another morsel of his Marlon Brando and wiped his mouth. "I can give you a name down at Central if you need more info." He gave me the address of the hospital and the name of a detective in the Central Bureau.

The two young men and their "secretary" got their hot dogs to go, climbed back in their limo and glided off to do their business, whatever that might be.

While we finished our sandwiches, Charlie asked how my acting career was going. I recounted the beer commercial debacle and he sympathized, but he didn't offer to pick up lunch.

CHAPTER FOUR

---◆---

A S I DROVE UP LA BREA back to my office I pushed pieces of this puzzle around in my head. Two former army MPs are discharged. MP #1 possibly disappears into a homeless jungle. MP #2 winds up a victim of a gunshot on the fringe of that same jungle. #1 might have witnessed #2 being shot. Common sense told me the two of them had to be connected. Phil Scarborough had a phone number, making it possible for Mavis to locate him. Frankie Rizzoli, on the other hand, was a different ball of wax. I needed to drop my Mr. Clean image and do some more rummaging around Skid Row. And I knew somebody who could help me.

Mavis was on the phone when I came through the door. She didn't sound pleased.

"You're not listening to me. I had a long phone conversation with you people last week. You quoted me a price, so I ordered the pieces. Now I come to find out you charged me more than we agreed."

As she listened she rolled her eyes, then made a fist and held it next to the receiver. I heard a garbled voice on the other end and she said, "Fine. I'm sending them back COD. You can keep the damn things. And you better refund my money." She slammed the phone down, took a deep breath, grinned, and said, "Well, hello there, Mr. Collins. How was your trip downtown?"

"Trouble in e-commerce, kiddo?"

"Idiots. Everywhere." She crumpled a slip of paper and threw it in the wastebasket. "So, did you find your guy?"

"Not yet. I've got a phone number for Rizzoli's Army buddy. Think you can find me an address?"

"Lay it on me, boss man." She wrote down the name and number and turned to her computer. She was clicking keys as I walked into my office.

I dialed the number for Scarborough and got a generic message, which I decided to ignore. No sense in spooking him before I had the opportunity for a face-to-face meeting. Next, I punched in the number of the hospital. After listening to an electronic menu, I finally got a live person.

"I'm calling to inquire about someone who was admitted a couple of weeks ago."

"Are you a relative, sir?"

"Yes, he's my brother. I'm from out of town and just learned that he was injured."

"What's the patient's name, sir?"

"Phil Scarborough," I said, and gave her the spelling.

"Please hold." I did, for what seemed like an eternity. Finally she came back on. "Mr. Scarborough was released on the twenty-third."

"Thank you, ma'am." I hung up and looked at the calendar lying on my desk. Scarborough had been in the hospital for three days, meaning he was probably convalescing at home. That convalescence apparently didn't include answering his phone.

I thumbed through my Rolodex and found the number for Reggie Benson. Some months back, I'd come across him on the Santa Monica Pier. His friends called him Tired Reggie. I'd been in the Army with him, ironically, as an MP. He'd saved my life one hot summer night in a Korean village. I figured I owed him, and got him set up with a job as a security guard/night watchman at a funeral parlor, of all places. My goal was to eventually get him back on his feet and rely on him for help in cases when I needed it. Trying to find Frankie Rizzoli on Skid Row might be just the ticket.

He picked up after three. "Reggie, it's Eddie."

"Hey, man, how you doin'?"

"I'm good. How's things over there in the land of the non-living?"

"Great."

"Nobody going bump in the night?"

He laughed and said, "Nah. Hey, this Bernie's a super guy."

Bernie was Bernie Feldman, a friend of mine who gave Reggie the job and the rent-free apartment. "That he is. Say, listen, does he ever give you time off?"

"Yeah, he said he'd give me a night in case I wanted to go out and do something. A movie, maybe."

"And when is that?"

"Matter of fact, Eddie, it's tomorrow."

"You're kidding. Outstanding. I've got a little project. Let me run it by you.

Maybe you can give me a hand." I filled him in on what I had in mind and he said no problem. I told him I'd touch base with him tomorrow and hung up.

Mavis stood in the doorway with a slip of paper in her hand. "This number matches an address on Larch Street down in Inglewood."

"Where in Inglewood?"

She slapped the piece of paper down in front of me. "Mavis's map-printing only provides one set per day, per customer." Reaching for the Thomas Guide on the shelf behind me, she placed it next to the address. "Here you go." She flounced back into her office, knowing damn well she had scored a point.

I had no recourse but to look up the address. Scarborough lived a few blocks west of the former Hollywood Park racetrack. I studied the Thomas Guide grid and decided the best way to get there was to take the 110 down to Century Boulevard and head for the ocean. Then I realized Carla Rizzoli's place of employment would be in the vicinity. We hadn't talked since our initial interview, and I thought it might be a good idea to check in with her. The simple truth is I'd been thinking about her constantly since she'd walked into the office. I found the business card she had given me and called her cell. It went to voicemail, and I told her to call me back.

Mavis was putting the finishing touches of tape on a package as I walked into her office. "Has Fritz got any old clothes lying around he doesn't wear?" I asked. Fritz Werner is her husband and drives a city bus. "Threadbare, dirty, beyond Goodwill?"

"I'd have to look. Why?"

"He's about Reggie's size, isn't he?"

She ripped off a piece of tape and stuck it on a seam of the package. "Pretty close, I guess. What are you up to now, Eddie?"

I outlined my plans for tomorrow. She looked at me with her head cocked to one side, a hand on a hip. I could tell this operation wasn't getting rave reviews.

"That's a little dangerous, don't you think?"

"Maybe. But I have a hunch Frankie Rizzoli is down there somewhere."

"And maybe doesn't want to be found."

"Could be. But he's going to have to say that to my face."

"Okay, I'll ask Fritz tonight." She sat in front of her computer and stuck a sheet of labels in the printer. "Where you off to now?"

"I'm going to knock on Phil Scarborough's door."

"And then?"

"Thought I'd drop in on my client and give her an update."

She stopped what she was doing and looked at me. "Don't tell me you're going to a strip club?"

"It's a gentlemen's club."

"Yeah, right. Then try and act like a gentleman, would you?"

"I'll give it my best shot, kiddo." I hit the hallway before the lecture could continue.

CHAPTER FIVE

———◆———

L OS ANGELES TRAFFIC IS BAD ENOUGH to try the patience of a parish priest, and getting through the downtown convergence of the Hollywood and Pasadena Freeways might make him renounce his vows entirely. I finally accomplished said task and found free sailing heading south. Century Boulevard appeared and I glided down the off-ramp and headed west.

After a few blocks, a construction site popped up on my right. The landmark Hollywood Park Racetrack had been demolished. After seventy-five years, the erstwhile stomping grounds of Seabiscuit, Citation, and Seattle Slew had disappeared to make room for three thousand housing units, a hotel, parks, and of course, a cinema with probably a dozen or more screens showing two or three movies.

My cellphone went off, and law-abiding citizen that I am, I pulled over, put the car in park, and looked at the screen. It was Carla Rizzoli, my client.

"Hey, Carla. Thanks for getting back to me."

"I'm glad you called. I've got some great news."

"What's that?"

"I got booked on that movie I told you about."

"Well, all right. Congratulations."

"Thanks. I start on Monday."

"That's terrific."

"Any news on your end, Eddie?"

"A little, actually. Where are you?"

"At the Follies. I'm between sets."

"Well, I'm in the neighborhood. Thought maybe I could swing by and bring you up to speed."

"Absolutely. You know where it is, right?"

I told her I did and said I'd see her in a bit. Popping into a gentlemen's club in the middle of the day wasn't something I was accustomed to, but hey, business is business, right?

I nosed back into traffic and continued west on Century. At La Brea I turned right, did the same on Hardy, and then a left on Larch. The street held a mix of apartment complexes and single-family dwellings. Phil Scarborough's address was on the left. I parked across the street. The house was small and painted egg-shell blue. A front yard was neatly trimmed, and a set of rose bushes ran along an open porch. A red Toyota RAV4 sat in the driveway.

I walked up to the threshold and noticed an elderly black man next door. He was on his knees, working on an array of yellow flowers surrounding a small tree in his front yard. When he saw me, he sat back on his haunches and wiped the sweat off his forehead.

I knocked on the aluminum screen door. Venetian blinds covered a window and the only sound I could hear was a plane approaching LAX from the east. I knocked again and turned to look at the Toyota RAV4, locking the license plate digits into my head. A third knock also resulted in nothing, so I turned to go and saw a small gap appear in the Venetian blinds. Someone was inside but wasn't about to answer the door.

As I started heading back to my car, the gardener next door got to his feet and stepped to the edge of the driveway. "I ain't seen the guy lately."

"Phil Scarborough, right?" I said.

"That his name? You got me. Never really met him."

"Is this his Toyota?"

"Don't rightly know. I seen another fella show up a few days ago. Could be his."

"Thanks," I said. "Nice-looking yard you got there."

"Whatchu lookin' for him for? You police?"

"No, sir. Publishers Clearing House. He might have won some money."

"Sheeet, man. You yankin' my chain. Crawl back in your fuckin' car and skedaddle outta here." He shook his head and started walking down his driveway.

I got behind the wheel, picked up my camera and zoomed in on the Toyota RAV4. I took a couple of shots and then focused on the license plate and got all the digits. While I was at it, I aimed the camera at the window with the Venetian blinds. This time the gap was bigger and a person's face was clearly visible.

CHAPTER SIX

———◆———

A T THE END OF LARCH STREET, I took a left and pulled over to the curb. Charlie Rivers answered his cell after two rings.

"Twice in one day? Gonna parlay that hot dog into as much as you can, huh?"

"Are you anywhere near a computer?"

"As we speak I am walking back to it with a cup of burned coffee in my hand. Instinct tells me I should sit my ass down and boot it up."

"Can you run a plate for me?"

"Hang on." I heard him slurp some coffee. "What have you got?"

I gave him the license number from the Toyota RAV4 and listened to background chatter in the precinct.

"This gonna be that Scarborough guy?" Charlie asked.

"That's what I'm hoping."

I heard another slurp and more cop noise. "Oops, hang on. That ain't your guy's car. This plate is registered to a James Curran. A Chula Vista address."

I wrote the name and address in my notebook as he rattled them off. "Where the hell's Chula Vista?"

"South of San Diego. Just north of the border."

"Let me give you Scarborough's address. Can you match him up with a vehicle?"

"No problem."

I relayed the info and heard him clicking keys. After a moment he said, "Phil Scarborough, Larch Street address, has a Hyundai Veracruz registered to him. Here's the plate number."

I wrote down the digits beneath the address for James Curran. "Do you get a description of the Hyundai?"

"Appears to be an SUV. Black."

"Like the one supposedly seen at that shooting on Crocker."

"Yeah, you're right. What the hell are you getting yourself into, Eddie?"

"I don't know, Charlie."

"Well, watch your back. I'd hate like hell to lose out on more free lunches."

I thanked him for the help and we broke the connection. I pulled away from the curb and caught a red light at Arbor Vitae and La Brea. As I sat in the left turn lane, I couldn't help but wonder about the face peeking from behind those Venetian blinds. Was it Phil Scarborough? Or this James Curran? Hell, it was the maid, for all I knew—if the maid was a man. I glided through the light, followed La Brea as it morphed into Hawthorne, then turned right. I hoped Carla could elaborate on who her brother Frankie ran with.

IT WAS AFTER 5:00 WHEN I spotted Feline Follies on my right. The sun had sunk below cloud cover over the Pacific and twilight was descending. Despite the early hour, the parking lot was almost full. As I pulled in, two men in suits piled into the rear seat of a taxi. It pulled off and I found a spot next to an extended-cab pickup.

The building housing the gentlemen's club was constructed of concrete blocks painted red with black trim. Over the front door loomed a red, neon-bordered sign that displayed a cat wearing a bustier and a top hat, a cane tucked under one arm and a come-hither look on its face. Two rows of blinking lights gave the impression that the cat's tail was swishing.

I'm not sure who frequents these places, but the close proximity of Feline Follies to LAX leads one to believe that it serves as a refuge from a canceled or delayed flight. Perhaps it offers a guy a final fling in the big city before he boards and heads home to the little woman and boredom.

Once inside, I immediately noticed the aroma of air freshener. Something with a floral note and a little too prevalent. The walls of the lobby were red and displayed paintings of the same top-hatted cat in various provocative poses. The carpet consisted of black and red squares, like a checkerboard. Spotlights focused on pictures of the dancers. To my left was a small alcove where a payphone was attached to the wall next to an ATM. Entry to the club proper was gained through a black-velvet curtain. The door next to it was designated "employees only." Speakers pumping out rock music hung from each corner of the ceiling; below one of them was a surveillance camera.

Standing behind a podium on my right was a bouncer. Given the size of him, I had no doubt he could bounce tractor tires. He was black, bald as a cue ball, and had a scar running down his right cheek. I couldn't detect a neck, and the red blazer he wore bulged under his left armpit.

"Good evening, sir," he said in voice that would put Darth Vader to shame.

"Evening."

"There's a ten-dollar cover charge with a two drink minimum."

"I'm just here to meet someone. One of the dancers."

"I see. And who would that be?"

"Carla Rizzoli." He consulted a list in front of him. "She goes by Velvet La Rose."

"I'm aware of what she goes by," he said. "Velvet is currently entertaining our guests."

"Can you get a message to her?"

"After you pay the cover charge, I'd be happy to call backstage and tell one of her colleagues you're in the audience. She can then join you when she's finished."

"Can't I just wait out here?"

"There's still a ten-dollar cover charge."

I nodded, separated a sawbuck from my money clip and handed it to him. On his left pinkie, a single key dangled from a small ring. Pulling the key off, he used it to open a drawer in the podium.

"You don't have anything on your person intended to bring harm to anyone, do you, sir?"

"Nope."

"Nothing with a trigger or a sharp blade, for instance?"

"No, sir."

He deposited the ten dollars in the drawer, locked it, and replaced the key ring on his pinkie. "Who shall I say is meeting Velvet?" he said.

"Eddie Collins."

He gestured to the black-velvet curtain and punched in a number on a cellphone. "Enjoy, Mr. Collins."

I parted the velvet curtain to find a spacious oblong room, dimly lit with red and blue lights. On the right was an L-shaped bar with stools scattered along the length of it. Two bartenders wearing white shirts and red vests presided. Small tables fanned out from a three-sided stage, most of them occupied. To the left hung another black curtain. Next to it sat a smaller version of the bouncer, only he was white and had blond hair pulled back into a ponytail. Another bar circled the stage, this one more like a ledge, or shelf. A dozen men of various ages sat on short stools, hunched over drinks and piles of loose currency. Their attention was focused on a brass pole in the middle of the stage, not unlike the kind found in a fire station. Draped around this pole was no fireman, however, but rather my client, Carla Rizzoli, aka Velvet La Rose.

She wore red, mid-thigh stockings, black stiletto heels, and little else. A red rose was pinned above one ear. On her lower back was a tattoo, also a rose. Dollar bills—and no doubt higher denominations—protruded from the tops of the stockings and more of the same were wedged in the waistband of a G-string smaller than my pocket handkerchief. She was topless and slid up and down the pole. At one point she maneuvered herself so she was upside down and then slowly sank to the floor and slithered to the lip of the stage, receiving applause and more bills for her efforts.

My attention was diverted by a waitress who sidled up to me carrying a tray with napkins on it. Her work clothes were more substantial than Carla's, but not by much.

"Can I show you to a table, sir?"

I pointed to an empty one near the rear of the room. "Back there would be fine," I said. As I followed her, I glanced in the direction of the stage. Carla recognized me and pointed. Her fingers curled, indicating she wanted me to come closer. Fortunately a lack of empty seats near the stage helped remind me that she was, after all, my client, and that I needed to maintain some semblance of professional decorum. I wondered how long that would last.

I took a seat and ordered a double bourbon with a water back. I looked around and saw the bouncer standing just inside the black curtain at the rear. He fixed me with an impassive stare, nodded slightly, and retreated through the opening.

Carla was on her hands and knees in front of two drooling young men. She shook her breasts at them, then sat on the edge of the stage and placed a stiletto in each of their laps. They stuffed more currency under the elastic of the stockings and she reached over with both hands and tousled their hair.

I found myself feeling a bit voyeuristic. This was a woman I'd once dated. I'd shared her bed, and now she was my client. She'd been in my office only yesterday, and here I was, watching her in an entirely different context. I almost felt like I was invading her privacy in some weird sense. But I certainly wasn't going to retrace my steps and walk out the front door.

The waitress deposited my drink in front of me. She took a twenty and left me two ones and a few coins. At these prices, gentlemen would have to learn the fine art of sipping. I glanced around the room again. The clientele consisted of mostly men in suits and ties, others in jeans and casual clothes. I must confess the gentlemen looked like gentlemen. I also spotted three ladies with male companions. Wannabe dancers? Wives or girlfriends? No way of telling.

Carla continued her contortions onstage, doing things to that pole I wouldn't have thought possible. When my drink was half-full, she finished her last number and struck a coquettish pose. Then she picked up articles of clothing from the back of a chair farther upstage and disappeared. A healthy round of applause floated after her.

A few minutes later, the lights changed and an announcer's voice boomed from the loudspeakers: "And now, Feline Follies is proud to present one of our newer attractions for your enjoyment. Ladies and Gents, give it up for Sissy Santana."

A voluptuous Latina with waist-length black hair stepped out from a center curtain. Unlike Carla's, her long legs were encased in black stockings. She wore a red corset with her G-string. Lacy black garters circled her wrists, and perched on her head was a jaunty red bowler. Generous applause greeted her as she sashayed downstage to the brass pole.

I sipped from my drink and looked around the room. Sissy obviously had her followers, judging by the whistles and hoots emanating from the crowd. She undulated to music with a salsa beat and pranced along the lip of the stage. One exuberant fan stood up and flung out his arms, then lost his balance and collapsed back onto his stool. He was obviously over his two-drink minimum.

I glanced to my left and saw Carla emerge through the curtain next to the ponytailed bouncer. She was wrapped in a diaphanous short robe. Beneath it I could see the G-String and a black bra. As she made her way to my table, several hands reached out to her. She playfully slapped them away and paused to plant a kiss on the bald head of an elderly gentleman. After she moved off, he exchanged high-fives with his buddies.

I stood up as she approached. "Do you have an ambulance on call? You're going to give that poor guy a heart attack."

"Oh, they love it. All part of the show."

I got a kiss on the cheek, along with a hug. She exuded a perfume with a delightful hint of lilac. Coming on the heels of what I had just seen her do, the kiss actually sent a rush of heat to my cheeks. Good thing the lighting was dim enough to hide my heightened color.

"Hi, Eddie. You mind if a stripper kisses you on the cheek?"

"Not in the least. Especially one with those kinds of moves. I'm impressed. How often do they have to paint that pole?" She laughed and we sat down. "Tell me something. I get the rose above the ear, but how did you come up with the name Velvet?"

She parted her robe, nudged one of the stockings down and placed my hand on her leg. "What does that feel like?"

My hand was no stranger to that placement, but it had been some time. I tried to ignore the warmth creeping up the back of my neck. "You better be careful. Wouldn't want to violate our private eye-client relationship."

"Why not?" she said, as she batted her eyelashes at me. I was caught off-guard, but for obvious reasons I wasn't bothered by the feeling. "I mean, there wasn't a problem when you were my attorney."

"Except for the fact that I lost the damn case."

"True that," she said, and we shared a laugh.

I removed my hand from her thigh, and she took it in hers, giving it a healthy squeeze. "I really did enjoy being with you back then, Eddie."

"As did I," I said. My response kind of took me by surprise, but for crying out loud, I'm only human, right? Show me a guy who would say something different under the circumstances, and I'd venture to say he's got ice water in his veins.

"Gosh, it's good to see you. My own private eye. I am so pumped with good news."

The same waitress came up to the table and laid a napkin in front of Carla. "Can I get you something, hon?"

"A Coke, Amy."

"And you, sir?"

"Double bourbon," I said, raising my glass. Amy moved off and I finished the last sip. "The hunk at the front door kept insisting there's a two drink minimum."

"Oh, that's Junior," Carla said. "Isn't he adorable?"

"I hate to think what Senior looks like."

"I can get the drinks, Eddie. They give us some freebies."

"Oh, no. Not when you're paying me top dollar."

She uttered that infectious, throaty laugh again and squeezed my arm. "So, what about Frankie?"

"Your good news first. Tell me about the movie."

She scooted her chair forward, leaned over the table, and grasped my arm. "It's called *Festival of Death*."

"Obviously not a comedy."

"No. I haven't gotten a script yet, but it takes place during one of those Renaissance Festival deals. My character is Helen Burrows. Two kids, husband, the whole nine yards."

"That's terrific, Carla. How long are you booked?"

"Two weeks, maybe more."

"This place all right with that?"

"Yeah, I worked it out with the boss."

"Who's making the film?"

"I auditioned at an office up in Valencia. Some industrial park. The sign said 'Enigma Productions.' You ever heard of them?"

"No, doesn't ring a bell."

"It's a low-budget thing, but that's cool. I'm dying to get in front of a camera again."

"How long's it been?"

"A year and a half. I mean, this job is all right. You know, with the tips and all. But I am not going to give up on that damn acting career. Does that make sense?"

"Absolutely. This could be a good break. You never know."

Carla gave my hand another squeeze as Amy, the waitress, showed up and put our drinks on the table. She ambushed my money clip again, left meager change, then handed Carla a fifty-dollar bill.

"This is for you."

"Fifty bucks?" Carla said. "From who?"

"Those two again. The black guy and that one with the sling." She turned toward the front curtain. "They're right over there. Oh, shoot, they just left."

"Nice," I said. "Obviously a couple of fans."

Carla slid the fifty into her bra. "They've been coming in here for several days. They just sit and stare. I can't get a rise out of them." Realizing what she had said, she giggled. "Uh, no pun intended."

Amy laughed and sauntered off. I raised my glass. "To Velvet La Rose and the movies." We clinked glasses and sipped.

"So, Eddie, tell me about Frankie."

At that moment the music segued into an ear-shattering song for Sissy Santana, who had by this time loosened the corset and dispensed with the two wrist garters. Carla shifted her chair so we were sitting next to each other, hunched over the table like a couple of conspirators. We bumped knees. I couldn't tell if it was intentional on her part. If it was, I didn't do anything to dissuade her. I filled her in on what I'd learned down on Skid Row and my plans to go back there tomorrow. I told her about my call to her parents and getting the number and address for Phil Scarborough.

"You ever heard of someone called James Curran?" I said.

"No. You think he's friends with Frankie?"

"I can't say. He must know Scarborough. His car was parked in his driveway."

"Maybe he's the guy in the picture with Frankie."

"Could be. Listen, can you give me any details about your brother? Height, how much you think he weighs? Any distinguishing marks? Scars? Tattoos?"

She sipped her Coke and thought for a moment. "He's five feet nine. Probably weighs one-sixty or so, unless he's put on weight. I don't remember any kind of distinguishing …. Oh, wait a minute. Yeah, he told me he got a tattoo."

"Did he tell you where and what it was?"

"He said it was on his left forearm. Some kind of lightning bolt."

I jotted down the details as Carla watched me over the rim of her Coke glass.

"A real-life private eye. I'm in awe, Eddie."

"Yeah, well, let me find your brother first, and we'll talk about awe." She reached out and squeezed my hand again. I was starting to get used to it. The music segued into another number and Carla glanced over to the stage.

"Oh, crap, I better get back there. I've got to get ready."

"What does that entail? You obviously don't have to get dressed. Not much, anyway." The question was offered with a half-assed smirk.

She reached out and pinched my cheek. "I have to do my stretches and 'freshen up,' as it were. I'll leave that to your imagination." She leaned over and kissed the cheek she'd pinched, then stood up. "I'll text you and you can let me know what you find out, okay?"

"You got it." She wiggled her fingers in my direction and headed for the rear curtain. This time she stopped and polished the top of the bald guy's head with the hem of her robe before disappearing backstage.

I finished off my whiskey, picked up my hat from the chair next to me, and started for the lobby. A guy in a blue Hawaiian shirt stopped me with his hand.

"Hey, buddy, what's your secret?"

"It's the porkpie hat, pal. You should try it sometime." He shook his head and turned back to his drink as I walked off.

The bouncer stood behind his podium, flipping through a magazine. "Carla says you go by the name Junior."

"That's correct. And you go by Eddie Collins. Did I get it right?" I nodded, and he continued, "Mind if I ask you a question, Mr. Collins?"

"Shoot."

"Are you famous in some manner? Movies, sports, anything like that?"

"Nope. Why?"

"Two gentlemen on their way out asked who you were. They saw you talking to Carla. I hope I wasn't out of line when I told them your name."

"No problem, Junior. Who were they?"

"I don't know their names."

"What'd they look like?"

"One of them is a brother. The other gentleman was wearing a sling."

CHAPTER SEVEN

———◆———

THE NEXT MORNING I WALKED INTO my office and found a shopping bag full of soiled and torn clothing sitting on my desk. I set my coffee cup down and picked up a pair of jeans that at one time might have been blue.

"Is Fritz the mechanic on his bus, in addition to driving it?" I said.

Mavis walked in, carrying a pair of beat-up tennis shoes. "You said you wanted dirty. You got dirty." She plopped the sneakers down. "I don't know if these will fit Reggie, but you can give them a try."

I pulled out a plaid shirt that looked like its owner had spent a day working in a landfill.

"Fritz helped a buddy overhaul a transmission," she said. "That's the result."

"Yeah, these'll work just fine."

"And what are you bringing to this Halloween party? You're not exactly Armani material, but homeless you ain't."

I stuffed the jeans and shirt back in the shopping bag with the tennis shoes on top. "I'm going to pick up Reggie and we'll hit a couple of thrift stores. I think my makeup kit will provide the finishing touches."

"Why do you still have a makeup kit?"

"I'm the comeback kid. You never know. I could be the next matinee idol."

"Yeah, right, and I could be Betty Crocker." She rolled her eyes and went back into the front office.

Mavis had a point. Keeping a makeup kit would lead one to conclude I still did stage work, when I hadn't done a play in quite a while. On the other hand, several times over the years I've gone on film and TV auditions where I've put on a false mustache or added some texture to my face. Today's undertaking could be such an occasion.

In my apartment I set my coffee cup in the sink, grabbed a porkpie hat and the shopping bag, and headed for the front door. Mavis was behind her desk looking at her computer screen.

"I've got to leave early today," she said. "All right with you?"

"Sure, no problem. But could you do a couple of things for me before you go?"

"What?"

I handed her the photo Carla had given me of her brother and the unidentified MP in Iraq. "Can you scan this and make me three or four copies?"

"Sure." She looked at the photo. "Which one's the brother?"

"The white guy."

"And his buddy?"

"Still to be determined."

"Okay, boss man. What's number two?"

"Do a computer search on Enigma Productions. A Valencia address. My client got booked on a movie with them."

"The same client you visited yesterday?" she said, as she wrote the name on a pad of paper.

"You got it."

"And how did that go? You behave yourself?"

"I was a perfect gentleman." The look on her face was a mixture of skepticism and curiosity. "What can I tell you? She's a nice girl."

"I'm sure she is."

"Besides, it's not like she's a stranger. We do have a bit of a history."

"Okay, go for it." She grinned and starting hitting some computer keys as I turned to go. "But hey, listen … is Reggie okay with what you're planning? I mean, it hasn't been that long since he was on the streets. Is he going to have a problem being back in those kinds of surroundings?"

"I don't think so." I opened the door, then turned back and added, "But your point is well taken. I'll make sure he's all right with it."

"Both of you, be careful down there. You're not exactly going to a garden party."

"Will do, kiddo. Catch up with you later."

I walked to the elevator, punched the button, and waited for the car to make its labored ascent. The mention of Carla triggered a flashback to my meeting with her yesterday at Feline Follies. Truth be told, I'd been thinking of not much else. She had flirted with me, and I'd made no effort to discourage her. Nor would I in the future. I'd welcomed the relationship we had a few years ago and if it was to pick up where it left off, so be it. After all, nowhere was it written that a PI couldn't welcome the overtures of a female client. Besides, who the hell was going to tell me differently?

I PARKED ALONG THE CURB ACROSS FROM Bernie Feldman's funeral home. It was a two-story, pale-yellow stucco building with a lawn of serious green grass and luxurious beds of flowers flanking the front door. Sculptured hedges surrounded the lawn. Red adobe tiles covered the roof. It struck me as being an overly elegant place of business, considering what went on there. But then, I suppose the elegance is for the living relatives, not those in the coffins.

A driveway ran along the left side of the structure. Across from it was a ten-space parking lot for customers only. I crossed the street and saw Bernie polishing a sleek black hearse in front of a double garage at the rear of the drive. I guessed Bernie to be in his sixties. He stood about five feet six, was thin, gray-haired, and despite his occupation, always a hail-fellow-well-met sort of guy. I walked up the driveway with my shopping bag full of clothes and received the expected greeting.

"Well, well, well, if it isn't Eddie Collins, Hollywood shamus, protector of the weak and downtrodden. How are you, sir?" he said as he stuck out his hand.

"Good, Bernie. How's yourself?" We shook and I gestured to the hearse. "Someone's funeral?"

"No terminal taxi ride today, fortunately. Just keeping up appearances." He looked at the shopping bag in my hand. "You carry a change of clothes with you? Perhaps an audition? Unless you've abandoned your search for fame and glory?"

"Not yet, Bernie. Reggie and I are going undercover. This is the wardrobe call."

"I see. Skullduggery in the making, eh?" He flicked his polishing cloth at a spot on the hood. "Speaking of Reggie, thanks for bringing him to my attention, Eddie. He's a fine gentleman, and is working out splendidly."

"I'm glad to hear it."

Bernie's cellphone went off and I climbed the rear stairs leading to Reggie's apartment. He must have heard me coming, because he met me in the doorway with the customary broad smile on his face.

"Hey, Eddie, how's it goin'?"

"Good. Got some things for you to try on."

"Yup, yup. Come on in."

I'm not exactly sure how the moniker "Tired" got attached to him, but it didn't fit. He was eager and good-natured, two qualities that served as a basis for our reignited friendship. I stepped through the door and saw that he'd added some personality to the place in the few short months he'd been here. A small rug lay in front of the kitchen sink, another one under the coffee table. Curtains covered the only window in the living room.

"Looks like you're settling in pretty well."

"Yeah, kinda fun lookin' for stuff." He pointed to a small boom box sitting on a shelf. "Got a good deal on that radio."

"At least you won't have anyone complaining about playing it too loud."

He gave me a quizzical look and then grinned. "Oh, yeah, right. Gotcha." He laughed and popped me on the shoulder.

I set the bag on his dining table and pulled out the clothes. "Mavis requisitioned these things from her husband. I hope they fit." He slipped off his shoes and started unbuttoning his shirt. "But hang on a minute, Reggie. I want to make sure you're okay with what we're doing today."

"Yup, Yup. We're lookin' for this guy Frankie, right?"

"It's Skid Row downtown. Might bring back some bad memories."

"Naw, I don't think so."

"You sure?"

"Heck yeah." He finished unbuttoning his shirt and I tossed him a grimy tee. "And I been thinkin', Eddie. I might run into somebody I recognize, ya know? So what about this? I'll say I'm lookin' for my cousin. Maybe there's been a death in the family. One of his parents is sick or somethin', and they want him to come back home. What do you think?"

I looked at him, marveling at his instincts. A few years ago he'd washed out of the San Diego Police Academy. He'd told me he had trouble dealing with the regimen and the authority. But some of that academy training had rubbed off, enough so that I had harbored thoughts of helping him get a PI license, if he was so inclined. He pulled the dirty tee over his head and I handed him the landfill shirt.

"Sounds good," I said. "And how do I figure in?"

He looked up at the ceiling for a moment as he began buttoning the rumpled shirt. "You're my buddy, helping me look for Frankie."

I nodded in approval. The shirt fit reasonably well. It was even a little baggy. He pulled the jeans on. They were too big, but he cinched a belt and rolled up the cuffs. The result looked like he definitely didn't get them off a clothing rack somewhere. Exactly the effect we wanted.

"Try the tennis shoes."

He sat down and slipped them on. "Perfect," he said, as he tied the laces. He took a few steps around the apartment. "Good thing they're white. Or used to be. Makes them look even more beat up." He stopped and struck a pose like he was a model on a runway. "What do you think?"

I laughed and said, "Fabio, stand back."

"Who's Fabio?"

"A male model that drives all the chicks wild."

He rolled his eyes and said, "Yeah, well, forget about that. I ain't gonna be findin' any of them down there."

"You're right about that. Okay, let's hit a couple thrift stores and find you a jacket and something for your head. Stuff everything back in the bag. We'll put on the finishing touches over at my place."

He took off the clothes and started folding them.

"No, just cram everything in. We're going for the wrinkled, Skid Row look."

"Yup, yup, I gotcha." He appeared almost gleeful as he rolled the jeans and shirt up into balls and filled the bag.

"Okay, you ready?"

"Ready, Eddie. Better take my phone, right?"

"Good idea. In case we get separated."

He grabbed his cell off the table, hit the light switch, and we set out. Operation Find Frankie was underway.

I CONFESS TO HAVING FURNISHED AN APARTMENT here and there over the years with a piece of furniture from Goodwill or the Salvation Army. However, with the exception of one particular porkpie that hadn't had its style knocked out of it, I'd never struck gold by pawing through their clothing racks. Reggie and I made up for lost opportunities. We found a well-worn camo baseball cap and an Army field jacket for him, with the nametag "Osborne" still attached. I latched onto a pair of khakis and a sweatshirt. A wrinkled, worn trench coat fit perfectly. Footwear would be a scuffed-up pair of combat boots in my closet. That left my headgear. An old canvas rain hat completed the ensemble.

A bored clerk at the front register took my money and told us to have a nice day. It didn't appear he was having the same. We put our purchases in the trunk of the car and I made a stop at a liquor store, then swung into the drive-thru of an In-N-Out burger shop. Fortified with a bag of what may be the best burgers in Los Angeles, we headed back to my office.

A construction site on the other side of the alley behind my office building had been dispensing noise and disrupting traffic for months. Next to a pile of lumber, I spotted a small bucket that was nearly full of bent and rusty nails. I dumped them out and scooped up half a pail of dirt. Reggie pulled the bags of clothing from the trunk, slammed it shut, and gave me a curious look.

"I s'pose there's an explanation for the dirt?"

"All in good time, Reggie, my man. All in good time." We filled our arms with the various parcels and started for the elevator.

Mavis had already gone, but she'd left behind some computer printouts on Enigma Productions and six copies of the photo Carla had given me. I pilfered a can of soda from her coffee alcove for Reggie and pulled a beer out of my mini-fridge for myself. We sat at my desk and tore into the burgers and fries. I showed Reggie one of the photos of Frankie and his MP partner. "Our guy Frankie's the one on the left."

"What about the black guy?"

"I don't know. Not yet, anyway. Matter of fact," I said, as I rummaged in the center drawer and pulled out a pair of scissors, "we're going to cut him out of the picture." I snipped two copies of the photo in half and gave him one with just Rizzoli's image. "See if you can rough up that thing. We want it to look like it's been in your pocket for a while."

I popped a French fry into my mouth and watched him roll the photo into a tube, unfurl it, and roll it up in the opposite direction. He bent and crimped, then held it up for my approval.

"Terrific," I said. "Now do this one." I handed him the other half picture and went back into my apartment. My makeup kit—contained in a fishing tackle box—sat on the top shelf of my closet. I pulled it down and went back to the desk. Reggie had accomplished wonders with the photos. I wondered if he'd ever done origami.

He pointed to the makeup kit. "We goin' fishin', Eddie?"

"In a manner of speaking. Tools of the acting trade, Reggie." I put the tackle box on the floor beside me and set a small jar on the desk.

"What's that?"

"Texas dirt."

The look of bewilderment on his face was world-class. "Oh, man, you are losin' me." He laughed and shook his head.

I opened the jar. It was filled with brown powder. "Look at this," I said. He leaned forward and watched me rub a pinch of it into the back of my hand. "I played the Gravedigger in *Hamlet* years ago. Went through almost a jar of this stuff. You don't need much. Looks like dirt, right?"

"Yeah." He dipped a fingertip into the jar and rubbed it on his hand. "Wow. That's cool stuff, man."

"What do you say we finish off these burgers and start suiting up?"

As we scarfed down the rest of our food and drinks, I told him to be on the lookout for the tattoo Carla had described on Frankie's arm. Our bellies full, we began making ourselves look like Skid Row inhabitants. I added a little water to the pail of dirt and smeared touches of the resulting mud on strategic parts of our "costumes." Cuffs, necklines, and knees. The ID strip on Reggie's jacket came off, leaving a bit of a rip, which he gladly enlarged. We tore small holes in both our trousers, and generally had a field day. Reggie got the hang of the Texas Dirt in short order, and before long, he definitely passed muster. I found a bushy mustache I'd used at one time and attached it with spirit gum. I thought about donning a rag of a wig I had, but decided against it. If somebody grabbed at me and the mop came off, the ruse would be blown.

Finished with our makeovers, we looked in the mirror and burst into laughter.

"Hey, buddy, got some spare change for a vet?" Reggie said, as he yanked on my arm. I pushed him away and he came at me again, pulling on my trench coat. Still laughing, we got into a good-natured shoving match.

"You haven't lost your touch," I said.

"I got pretty good at it after a while. Hit this one guy up for twenty bucks out on the pier. I think he was trying to impress his girlfriend."

"See, there you go. Fabio in disguise."

"Tired Fabio. I like it."

I took my liquor-store purchases out of their paper bag. First there were two half-pints of cheap whiskey and a large bottle of more expensive bourbon. I dropped two packs of cigarettes, two Bic lighters and several books of matches on the desk, then looked at the label on one of the bottles.

"How long has it been since you've had any of this stuff, Reggie?"

"Oh, man, quite a while. You gonna drink some, Eddie?"

"Despite the fact that it's almost rotgut, I'm going to have a taste when we get downtown. Just so I have it on my breath."

"Yup, I can handle that."

"In the meantime, let's make these cigarettes and lighters look like they've been in our pockets for a while."

He followed my lead as I opened the smokes, emptied half of them on the desk, slid the cellophane wrapping off, and crumpled it and the pack. I replaced some of the cancer sticks and the pack looked anything but newly purchased. I reached into my makeup kit, found an emery board, and tossed it across the desk to Reggie.

"Scuff those lighters up. We'll no doubt have to bribe people with some cigarettes, along with the whiskey."

"Man, you got all the bases covered, Eddie. Sure you never lived on the streets?"

"Came close to it once." I cracked open the fifth of bourbon as Reggie finished with the lighters. For good measure, he bent and tore some of the matchbook covers. "As much as I hate to waste good sipping whiskey, let's smear some of this stuff on us to give the impression we're two steps the other side of sobriety. It should dry by the time we get down there."

"Gotcha," he said. I handed him a paper towel, poured a little of the bourbon in it, and watched him dab it on the back of his neck. Then I did the same to myself. Satisfied that we were ready, I switched off the lights and locked the door. We made our way to the elevator. While we waited, a door opened at the end of the hall and Lenny Daye, another one of my neighbors, stepped out. He locked his door and spotted us waiting by the elevator.

"Hey, guys, what are you ...?" I turned to him and he stopped in mid-sentence. "Eddie? What the hell are you doing?"

"We're on a mission, Lenny. This is Reggie Benson. Reggie, my neighbor, Lenny Daye. A good guy to get to know."

"Pleased to meet you," Reggie said, sticking out a grimy hand.

"If you say so," Lenny said. He stared at both of us, not quite sure he wanted to pursue the matter.

The elevator door opened and we stepped inside. "You coming, Lenny?" I said.

He leaned against the wall and pinched his nose. "You go ahead, honey. I'll wait for the non-drinking car."

The door slid shut and we started our descent. "I think we just cleared the first hurdle, Reggie."

Chapter Eight

W E'D PICKED THE WRONG PART OF the day to get downtown. Despite avoiding the freeway, we were still trapped in the traffic jungle. But then, what else is new in Los Angeles? By the time we drove through Skid Row, it was mid-afternoon, and the jockeying for overnight turf was underway. One couldn't escape the despair and grittiness that filled the sidewalks. Reggie was silent as he gazed out the window at the tarps, cardboard boxes, and other ersatz building materials these people used to create some semblance of shelter.

"Did you ever hang out down here?" I asked.

"Yup, for a few weeks," he said, as he turned back to me. "Got tired of it. Some of these guys can get real nasty. Women too."

"Well, you let me know if it gets too uncomfortable for you. We'll pull the plug."

"Nah, it's okay, Eddie. Might even be kinda fun, knowin' I don't have to stay here."

I parked several blocks from the Mission. I wanted us to be far enough away from the center of the squalor to give us a haven—a place to regroup, as it were.

I pulled out the half-pint of whiskey and took a swallow. Reggie did likewise, only he swished the booze around in his mouth, even gargled it, then opened the door and spit it out.

"I'll drink some if I have to."

"Well, don't worry. You'll probably have volunteers to help you."

He grinned and got out of the car. I locked the doors, checked to see if my mustache was still anchored, and we set off down the street. I started to settle into a slow shuffle, slightly dragging my feet. Reggie saw what I was doing and instinctively followed my lead.

Near the first intersection, we encountered three men slouched against a wall, their feet splayed out onto the sidewalk. One guy with a thick black beard had a shopping cart sitting next to him bulging with plastic bags and remnants of clothing. He'd attached a piece of tarp to one of the wire holes and taped the other end to what looked like a refrigerator carton, giving him a makeshift lean-to.

Inside the box sprawled his two companions, one an elderly black man, the other also black, but younger. The carton had holes in it and one seam was torn and patched with duct tape. The younger of the two black guys wore a filthy Los Angeles Dodgers stocking cap. His box-mate was bald and with two scabs on the top of his head.

We shuffled to the end of their legs. It took a moment for them to acknowledge our presence. Black Beard finally looked up and growled, "Well, why you standin' there, fools? What the hell you want?"

I squatted in front of him and pulled out the picture. "Tryin' to find someone, pardner. You seen him around?" I handed him the photo. "Guy's name is Frankie Rizzoli."

Black Beard took the picture and squinted. "Shit, man, why don't you give me some glasses? Or blow the damn thing up?"

"That was taken a few years back when he was in the Army."

"I can see that, fool." He tilted the photo and looked at it for a long moment. Finally he handed it back and said, "Naw, man, he don't look familiar."

Reggie squatted in front of the two men in the carton. "What about you guys?" he said, as he handed them the photo.

The bald-headed guy said, "How the hell you expect me to see that thing in here with no light?"

Reggie pulled out his lighter and handed it to him. "Here you go, man."

"Well, gimme a cigarette then." Reggie gave him his wrinkled pack. Baldy pulled one out, lit it, and held the lighter next to the photo. "Why you looking for him?"

"He's my cousin. His mom died and the family wants him to come home for the funeral."

"You sure you ain't no cop?"

"No, man, I hate cops."

"Me too. So I don't wanna be snitchin' on somebody."

"You ain't gonna be. What about the picture? You seen this guy?"

Baldy examined the photo and finally said, "He don't look like anybody I seen." The lighter went out and he handed the picture back to Reggie, then started to put the Bic in his pocket.

"C'mon, man," Reggie said.

Baldy chuckled and handed him the cigarette lighter. "Just seein' if you was on your toes, dude."

"What about your buddy here?" Reggie said, gesturing to the guy in the stocking cap.

"Oh, shit, man, Fuzzy here's damn near blind. He ain't seen anybody I haven't." In confirmation, his companion nodded his head and chortled, revealing a mouth with no teeth.

Reggie stood up and we thanked the three men and shuffled off. Around the corner was another small encampment. This one also didn't recognize Frankie. We continued wandering among the homeless for another hour. A young man in a wheelchair thought the figure in the photo looked familiar. The offer of a couple of pulls from Reggie's bottle of whiskey prompted his memory. On second thought, he didn't know the guy. We got a lot of requests for money and cigarettes, even joints, and our half-pints were running low. It was frustrating. I started to think we weren't going to have any success, that any information offered wouldn't be reliable, only fueled by handouts. Maybe we needed a break. We walked down 5th and spotted a roach coach. I paid for four tacos and Reggie carried two cans of soda over to a small retaining wall.

We sat down. "Hell, this isn't working," I said. "Are we just wasting our time?"

"Hard to say, Eddie. Sometimes these people build up a pretty good sense of community, of stickin' together, ya know? Most of 'em like to stay private. I knew a guy out in Santa Monica once who never talked. Everybody called him Murray the Mute. I hung out with him for a few days, and he never said a word. Not one damn word."

I munched on my taco, which had all the appeal of a piece of cardboard. "What if we split up? Maybe two of us intimidates people."

"Yeah, that might work. Wanna try it?"

I washed down the cardboard with the rest of my soda. "Might as well. We've got nothing to lose."

I told him to walk Maple back to 6th, then take it over to San Pedro. I'd head back down 5th and check out San Julian Park, then meet up with him somewhere along San Pedro. We knuckle-bumped and parted ways.

San Julian Park was short on grass, but long on concrete. The small patch of downtown real estate was surrounded by a fence made of metal bars. It had a sliding gate and was locked overnight. Several homeless sat slumped on concrete benches, looking for something to brighten their day. I didn't have it. I flashed the picture at each of them, getting nothing but blank stares.

Nobody had seen Frankie Rizzoli, or if they had, they sure as hell weren't about to tell me. I took a sip from my half-pint and flipped what remained to an old gent sitting against a light pole. He gave me a small salute as I walked off.

Up ahead I saw the sofa where I'd encountered the black guy who'd told me to get lost. His Hispanic friend Manny had told me of the shooting on Crocker and Frankie's possible involvement. I hoped the two of them wouldn't recognize me, but my concern was moot. Manny and his buddy were gone. They'd been replaced by a man and a woman. At least that's what I thought. With all the grime that caked their clothes and hair, I couldn't be sure. I knelt down next to the man.

"Excuse me, sir. What's your name?"

"Henry. And this is my wife Eloise," he said, as he turned to the lump of tattered clothing lying next to him.

The woman stirred and struggled to sit upright. She looked up at me, squinting against the sunlight. "Have you come to take us home?" she said, her voice so soft I could barely hear her.

"No, I'm afraid I haven't, Eloise."

"Oh," she whispered. "I'm sorry. I thought maybe you were an angel come to take us home."

I've been called many things in my life, but that wasn't one of them. As I watched her lay her head back on a tattered pillow, I suddenly felt very helpless for not being able to bring this poor woman some semblance of peace.

Henry reached over and adjusted the shawl covering her shoulders. "She gets confused sometimes."

"I wonder if you can help me."

"Well, we'll certainly try. Won't we, Eloise?"

Eloise uttered something unintelligible. Henry reached over and clasped her hand.

"I'm looking for a man by the name of Frankie Rizzoli. Does that name sound familiar, Henry?"

After a moment of staring into space, he said, "No, I'm afraid it doesn't. Have you come to take him home?"

"Yes, as a matter of fact, I have." I handed Henry the photo. "This is a picture of him taken several years ago. Does he look at all familiar to you, Henry?"

He looked at the photo. "What did you say his name was?"

"Frankie. Frankie Rizzoli."

"A nice-looking young man. And in the Army too. I was in the Army. Quang Tri Province. A long time ago, wasn't it, Eloise?"

She bobbed her head and I took the picture back. Clapping him on the shoulder, I moved off, leaving Henry and Eloise with a long wait for their ride home.

Halfway along the block, I stopped and peered down a set of two steps to a door plastered with graffiti. The entry smelled of urine and vomit. A shapeless hulk sat on the bottom step. "Hey, pal, can I ask you a question?" I started down the steps, but the hulk jumped to his feet and shoved me into the corner. My feet slipped on whatever was on the floor and I lost my balance, ending up on my knees. I almost retched from the smell that flooded my nostrils.

I stood up and brushed off whatever the hell it was that clung to my pants. As I turned to start up the steps, someone slammed into me from behind, jamming me into the same corner. My face collided with the cinderblock wall. A left arm went around my throat and my feet were kicked apart. The right hand yanked my hat off and pulled my head back by my hair.

"Listen, asshole, quit looking for Frankie Rizzoli," the voice snarled in my ear. "He's dead. Got it?" The arm around my throat tightened.

"His sister Carla's looking for him, man, not me."

"You tell his sister to forget about him."

I pulled on the sleeve covering the arm that was about to choke me. It felt like a sweatshirt. The fabric snaked up his arm as I continued to try and get my breath. Then I saw it. A tattoo of a lightning bolt. It pointed toward his wrist and was blue with a red edge, similar to the 25th Infantry's red and gold bolt on a taro leaf. The arm loosened, then pushed me forward so my face was scrunched against the concrete wall. I felt a trickle of blood roll down my right cheek. He punched me on one of my temples, kicked my right knee, and disappeared. I collapsed again, dazed by the blow to my head. After a moment, the stench made my taco revolt and I staggered up the stairs and fell to the sidewalk.

Frankie Rizzoli wasn't dead. Why did he want his sister to think otherwise?

CHAPTER NINE

———◆———

IT WAS ALL I COULD DO to keep from throwing up on the sidewalk. For a couple of minutes I stayed on my hands and knees, taking inventory. A knot was beginning to form on the side of my head. I gingerly touched my right cheek and the fingers came away bloody. My right knee throbbed. As I started to think I was getting too old for these goddamn dust-ups, Reggie trotted up and helped me to my feet.

"You okay, Eddie?"

"Yeah," I said. That assessment didn't ring true when I tried to put some weight on the knee. I flexed it as I leaned against the wall. Limping looked like a distinct possibility for the near future. "Did you get a look at the guy?"

"I saw him running away. Had a flat cap on, a down vest, jeans, and a gray sweatshirt."

"He also had a tattoo on his left arm," I said. "A lightning bolt."

"Hey, that's our guy, right?"

"That'd be my guess." I hobbled a few paces, trying to work out the soreness in my knee. The hulk that had been sitting on the steps wasn't Frankie, but I didn't rule out the possibility that he was a decoy. "Did you see where he went?"

"He took off down San Pedro, heading south. Then he turned left. I don't know what street that is. I was gonna chase him, but then I saw you on the ground. Thought I'd better see if you were okay."

"I'll make it."

"That's a pretty good scrape on your cheek there. We better get something to put on it."

"You have any of that booze left?"

"Yeah, a little." He pulled the half-pint from his pocket and handed it to me.

I tilted my head to one side and poured a drop or two on the cheek. The soreness of my knee gave way to a scorching sting from the alcohol. I upended the bottle, drank the rest of it, and tossed the empty in a trash can.

"I hope you didn't want that."

"Gonna do more for you than me."

"Let's get the hell out of here," I said, as I began limping down the street. I could now tell Carla that I'd found her brother. The problem was I also had to tell her he wanted her to think he was dead.

THE BUMP ON MY HEAD AND the soreness of both my knee and face kept us company as we threaded our way through rush-hour traffic back to my office. Our Skid Row duds filled two trash bags. We took turns washing up in my bathroom. Thankfully I had a few large Band-Aids and hydrogen peroxide. When the Texas Dirt was gone from my face, Reggie helped me put a bandage on my cheek, which would certainly provoke questions from Mavis when she came to work in the morning.

I fixed myself a healthy drink and told Reggie to get himself another soda from Mavis's mini-fridge. As we sat at my dinette table, grins broke out on our faces. We clinked glasses, comrades in arms. Both of us were exhausted, but at least we were wearing clean clothes.

"I don't get it, Eddie. Why would someone want his sister to think he's dead if he's not?"

"Beats me. Maybe he's into something illegal."

"Or the guy isn't Frankie."

"True. But it's more than coincidence he had the same kind of tattoo Carla described to me." I sipped on my bourbon and looked through the French doors to Hollywood Boulevard. Darkness had settled in; neon had taken over. "How do you think he found us?"

"Well, there's a kind of network with street people. Word spreads. Sometimes for blocks."

"Their own social media, huh?"

"Somethin' like that. No Facebook and Twitter down there."

I finished my drink and put the glass in the sink. Reggie handed me his soda can and I dropped it in the recycling bag. Mavis suggests I recycle. Actually, coerces may be the more accurate verb.

"What do you say we get something to eat? I think we both deserve some good chow." Reggie agreed. We left the apartment and found a Sizzler nearby. Two nice rib eyes and baked potatoes made us feel better.

After I pulled into the driveway at Bernie Feldman's Funeral Home, I handed Reggie a folded bill. "Thanks for your help today. Get something for your digs. On me."

He looked at the money. "A hundred bucks? Oh, man, Eddie, you ain't gotta do that."

"Yeah, I do."

"You sure?"

"Yeah, I'm sure."

"Wow." He unfolded the bill and looked at it like it was gold-plated. Who knows the last time he'd seen a picture of Ben Franklin? "Maybe I can get a toaster oven or somethin'." He slipped the bill into his shirt pocket. "What's your plan now?"

"I'm going to fill Carla in on what went down. See what she wants me to do. I mean, we did find her brother."

"Yup, yup. But in a sense we kinda lost him again."

"There is that." I clapped him on the shoulder as he opened the car door. "Get some sleep. I'll be in touch."

"Okay, Eddie. Thanks for the money."

I watched him climb the stairs to his apartment. After he closed the door, I backed out and drove to my office, wondering how Carla would receive the news about her brother. There was something else that stuck in my head. When Frankie pushed me against the concrete wall, he'd kicked my legs apart, much like a cop would do. Granted, he'd been an MP in the army, but that was a while back. A conditioned reflex? Well, maybe. But it struck me as odd.

Back in my apartment, I felt the need for isolation. I debated whether or not to call Carla, but decided I'd get in touch with her tomorrow. It might even warrant another visit to Feline Follies. That prospect alone sealed my decision to wait on the call to her. So I turned off both my landline and cellphone and wrapped my knee in a cold pack. After building a healthy dose of Jim Beam, I collapsed into my only comfortable chair. Mavis's printouts on Enigma Productions consisted of several pages. I settled in to read.

She'd found their website and printed out the pertinent pages. The profile of Enigma Productions fit that of countless small, independent movie companies scattered throughout Los Angeles. Its address put it on Sand Wedge Lane up in Valencia. I'd been in that vicinity in the past for one reason or another and remembered the area as being chock-full of new office parks, evidence of the urban sprawl moving north from LA.

Splashed across the home page of the site were graphics pertaining to the company's current high-profile project, *Flashpoint*, a cable television series concerning U.S. Border Patrol agents. I'd heard of it but had never seen an episode.

The "about us" page provided a short history of the company. The names of several owners were listed, and one caught my eye: Fred Curran. I pulled my notebook from my shirt pocket and flipped a couple of pages. The owner of the red Toyota RAV4 that had been sitting in the driveway in front of Phil Scarborough's house was a James Curran. A common enough name, but curiosity got the better of me.

I lumbered to my feet and fixed myself another drink. The cold pack on my knee needed adjusting. I picked up the file and limped into Mavis's office and booted up the computer. Los Angeles White Pages revealed some ninety Currans in Southern California. James Curran's address was Chula Vista, out of LA proper. I couldn't come up with any connection between the two names, which, I suppose, is why we have coincidences.

I sipped some whiskey and looked at the IMDb profile Mavis had provided. The film Carla had been booked on was indeed called *Festival of Death*. IMDb's breakdown was incomplete, listing only a partial cast. The director was someone by the name of Lester Wells, a name unfamiliar to me. An original screenplay by Mort Simmons also didn't ring a bell.

I printed out all the breakdown pages on *Festival of Death*, then put my feet up on the desk, nursed my drink, and took inventory.

For all practical purposes, Frankie Rizzoli had been located. True, he hadn't identified himself, but the fact that he wore the tattoo Carla described and knew I was looking for him told me that he wasn't dead. He was alive and kicking but didn't want her to know. His note to his sister had told her to watch her back. From what, I hadn't a clue. According to my homeless informant, Frankie might have been involved in a shooting incident downtown on Crocker, where a Phil Scarborough was wounded. This same Phil Scarborough just happened to have been in the Army with Frankie. Scarborough lived in a house where a James Curran's car was found. Now the name Curran had surfaced in connection to Carla's new movie gig. These tufts of information swirled in my head, drawing attention to the bump that had now become noticeable, not to mention the aching knee and sore face.

I polished off my drink, shut down the computer and the printer, and limped back to my apartment. Mr. Murphy's bed never felt better.

Chapter Ten

——— ◆ ———

Y SECOND CUP OF COFFEE SAT in front of me as I slumped behind my desk reading yesterday's *Hollywood Reporter*. I heard Mavis come in, and after a moment she stuck her head into my office. Naturally, her curiosity was piqued when she saw her boss with a bandage on his face.

"Good morning," I said.

"Are you sure?" She sat in one of the chairs in front of the desk. "What happened?"

"Peeled back a little skin."

I told her about the events of yesterday and she said, "Any other battleground mementos?"

I pointed to the side of my head. "Goose egg." Then did the same to my leg. "And he kicked my knee pretty good."

"But you found your guy."

"I think so, even though he says he's dead."

She got up from her chair and examined the bandage on my cheek. "That looks like it needs changing."

"Yeah, I'll do it in a minute."

"So you're done with this case then?"

"Depends on Carla."

"What more is there? Her brother obviously doesn't want anything to do with her."

"But there's got to be some reason. She may want to know what that is."

"Well, she should start giving you combat pay. Maybe you should see a doctor? You could have a concussion."

"Ah, I'm all right."

She looked at me, her lips pursed, then shook her head and went back into her office.

I finished my coffee and took the cup back to my apartment. Carla could very easily have worked late last night, so I sent her a text, after a couple of botched attempts. Big fingers and small keypads aren't compatible. I told her to call me when she had the chance.

While I ministered to myself in front of the bathroom mirror, I thought about what Mavis had said. What more could Carla want to know if Frankie made it clear he didn't want to be found? However, he'd told her to watch her back. That warning nagged at me. Whatever the hell Frankie was into, how did his sister figure in? Despite the roughing up I got from him yesterday, he needed to do some explaining. That meant another trip to Skid Row. This time I was the one who needed to watch his back. After passing Mavis's medical inspection, I got in my car and once again started threading my way downtown.

I PARKED ON SAN PEDRO IN A two-hour zone. If I couldn't spot Frankie in that period of time, I had an excuse to change locations. I'd brought along my camera and a pair of small Bushnell binoculars. I opened my Thomas Guide map and propped it on the steering wheel, giving the impression I was lost.

The street was quiet. The homeless moved slowly. No need for speed when you've got no place to go. A few delivery trucks lumbered by, and two LAPD black-and-whites glided through the neighborhood. I picked up the camera and started taking pictures. A closer look at them on Mavis's computer might reveal the guy Reggie had described running away.

A young guy sporting a matted, red beard stuck his face into the passenger window. Even from across the front seat of my car, he reeked of cheap wine and the lack of a bar of soap.

"Hey, man, why you takin' pictures?"

"I'm scouting locations for a movie."

"No shit? I wanna be in it."

"You have a SAG card?"

"A what card?"

"You need a SAG card, pal."

"Hell, I'm star material, man. I mean, look at me." He backed up and posed, his arms flung wide, then lost his balance and collapsed on the sidewalk. His pride hurt, he righted himself and stumbled off down the sidewalk. So much for a wannabe movie star.

I changed parking spaces and spent ten minutes watching a turf war unfold. Two black men pushed shopping carts next to a grizzled old guy sitting in a broken-down easy chair. Picking up a wooden cane lying next to him, the old guy started swatting the carts. He connected with a glass jar full of liquid and smashed it. When the two black men didn't move, he struggled to his feet and lit into them. He'd obviously established squatter's rights, because the two men with the carts scooted off. The range war had ended.

My cellphone chirped from the seat next to me. It was Carla.

"Hi Eddie, what's going on?"

"I think I found your brother," I said, and went on to tell her how Frankie had jumped me and what he'd said.

"Are you all right?"

"Yeah, he roughed me up a little, but nothing serious."

"Are you sure it was him?"

"I didn't see his face, but the tattoo looked like the one you described. And I got a sense he recognized your name."

She let out a huge sigh and said, "I can't believe it. Why would he say something like that?"

"I don't know, Carla. How do you want to proceed?"

In the background I heard a car horn. "Oh, shoot. There's Amy. My car's in the garage and I'm riding in to work with her. Can we get together later, Eddie?"

"Sure, no problem. How about if I pick you up when you get off?"

"Would you? You're a sweetheart. I'm done at six. Maybe we could have dinner?"

"Sounds good. See you then."

She hung up and I tossed my cell onto the seat next to me. Dinner with a client. I'd never had that happen, but then, I'd never had a client like Carla Rizzoli.

I continued taking pictures, zooming in on street people, some familiar from yesterday. However, none of them fit Reggie's description. But hell, Frankie—if it was Frankie—could have changed clothes for all I knew. I had a hunch the guy who jumped me yesterday wasn't homeless, but was hiding out from someone. Maybe my dinner conversation with Carla would give credence to my hunch.

A UPS truck double-parked two car lengths ahead of me. The driver darted into a textile shop, two small packages under one arm. A red SUV glided up behind the truck. I glanced at it and went scurrying for my notebook. It was a Toyota RAV4 and the license plate matched the one belonging to James Curran. It edged to the left, the driver no doubt seeing if it was possible to go around the delivery truck. No one was parked behind me, so I started the car and backed up, flipped on my turn signal, and nudged behind the RAV4. Oncoming traffic kept the SUV in place, giving me a chance to verify I had the right license plate.

The UPS driver bounded back into the truck. The hazard lights went off, and it moved down the street. I put two car lengths between me and the SUV and saw it turn left onto Crocker. I waited for an oncoming car and followed. The RAV4 backed into a driveway in front of a windowless concrete building. I glided by and when I came to the next intersection, made a U-turn and parked next to the curb, a half block away from Curran's SUV.

Two men got out of the vehicle and opened the rear door. I trained my camera on them, zoomed in, and began snapping pictures. The driver, who I assumed was James Curran, was black and wore a blue hooded sweatshirt. He had some facial hair and wore a baseball cap on his head. About six feet tall. His passenger was white, slight of build, hatless, with dark hair. His right arm was in a sling. He wore what appeared to be an athletic warm-up jacket.

The men lifted out two wooden boxes on casters. They resembled containers I'd seen on film shoots, ones that carried lighting equipment and electrical cables. The driver slammed the vehicle's rear door shut and they pushed the boxes toward a metal door in the side of the building. Curran pulled out a clump of keys and unlocked it. They pushed the crates inside and closed the door behind them. On the wall above was a number—two sets of three digits separated by a dash—indicating the building occupied a series of addresses. Most likely a warehouse.

After a span of fifteen minutes, the two men emerged from behind the door and climbed back into the Toyota RAV4. They headed west, then picked up Olympic and made their way out of downtown.

I followed, wondering where they were taking me. If they were bound for the house where I first saw the Toyota RAV4, that had to mean the passenger was Phil Scarborough. Phil Scarborough, the victim of a shooting that may or may not have involved Frankie Rizzoli. Pieces of information whirled around in my head as I kept the SUV in sight.

CHAPTER ELEVEN

———◆———

THE TOYOTA RAV4 CONTINUED ON OLYMPIC Boulevard until it picked up the 110 and headed south past the Los Angeles Convention Center and through the Santa Monica Freeway interchange. Curran and Scarborough didn't seem to be in much of a hurry, for which I was glad. My set of wheels wouldn't exactly qualify for the Indy 500. The SUV stayed at a steady sixty and I managed to keep them in sight, even though the freeway exchange provoked white-knuckle driving.

I wasn't sure what I was going to prove by following them. However, as I crossed over Slausen Avenue, which always reminded me of Johnny Carson and his Art Fern freeway directions—"Take the Slausen cutoff, cut off your Slausen"—I recalled that Carla had been tipped fifty bucks by two guys watching her at Feline Follies. One of them was black. The other wore a sling. Here comes that ugly word again: coincidence. But then Junior, the bouncer, had told me they'd asked him my name. Coincidence be damned; I was becoming more and more certain that Curran and Scarborough were part of this puzzle.

THE TOYOTA EXITED ON CENTURY BOULEVARD and headed west. I pulled over to the curb as the vehicle turned into a strip mall. Curran got out and went into a liquor store next door to a Thai restaurant. Ten minutes later he reappeared, carrying a twelve-pack in one hand and cradling a paper bag under the other arm. They got back on Century and continued toward the ocean. La Brea appeared and the RAV4 turned right. When Curran signaled for a right on Hardy, I thought I might be in danger of blowing the tail, so I continued on up to Arbor Vitae, hung a right and another one on Larch, then pulled over to the curb. The house was ahead of me on my side of the street.

By the time I parked, Curran's Toyota had pulled into the driveway behind a black SUV, which I assumed was the Hyundai Veracruz Charlie Rivers had told me was registered to Phil Scarborough. I focused my binoculars on the cars and saw they were empty. After a moment, Scarborough came out of the house, still wearing the sling, but without the athletic jacket. He climbed into the Hyundai, the garage door went up, and he drove inside. After a moment, he reappeared and the garage door came down.

They were both there: prime targets for a visit.

I locked my car and walked down the sidewalk. Across the street in an empty driveway, a young girl jumped rope. Farther up, a little boy pedaled a bike with training wheels. He furiously kept going in circles and shouted at his sister, who paid him no mind.

I came to Scarborough's house and walked up the sidewalk. Next door there was no sign of the old black gardener who'd been tending his rose bushes the last time I was here. Good thing. I wouldn't have to pretend that Phil Scarborough had won the Publishers Clearing House Sweepstakes.

I knocked on the screen door. This time no one peeked through the Venetian blinds. After a moment, the door was jerked open and the black guy loomed behind the mesh. He caught me by surprise and I stepped back. Up close, Curran looked taller than I had guessed. He had a neatly trimmed, salt-and-pepper beard on a long face with sparse freckles on his cheeks. His eyes were heavy-lidded, making him look like he was half asleep. He stepped up to the screen. At this distance, I had the sudden feeling I'd seen him before.

"Help you?" he said.

"Yes, sir. I'm looking for Phil Scarborough." His heavy eyelids raised slightly. I'd caught him by surprise.

"He's not here."

"I see," I said, and turned to look back at the street. "This is where he lives, though, right?"

"He does, but like I said, he's not home."

"Do you know when he'll be back?"

"Soon." He glared at me, blank-faced. I wasn't going to get any more out of him.

"You think you could give him a message?"

"What?"

"Tell him Frankie Rizzoli's looking for him." Again, his eyes told me I'd hit pay dirt. He knew who I was talking about. I was sure of it.

"I'll give him the message."

"Thanks," I said, and turned to go. But then I checked myself before he was able to shut the door. "Oh, by the way, I just flew into LAX. Saw this place called Feline Follies. You ever been in there by any chance?"

"I'm afraid not."

"Thought I might avail myself of a little … you know, entertainment, as it were. Wife's back home. Thought maybe I could get a little wild and crazy. Was wondering if you know anything about the place."

"Can't help you. But knock yourself out." He shut the door and I turned to go. I glanced behind me, and damned if a small gap didn't once again appear in those Venetian blinds.

I walked back to my car. The tot with the training wheels had given up and was watching the girl. He grabbed the jump rope, and she tripped and chased him up the driveway, both of them screaming. I climbed into the car and sat drumming my fingers on the steering wheel, watching the palm trees wave in the wind. I wondered if I had put a target on my back by giving Curran the impression that I knew Frankie Rizzoli. If these two guys were looking for Carla's brother, wouldn't they want to know who I was and what I knew?

Also, the notion that Curran looked familiar wouldn't leave me. I turned on my camera and looked at the images I'd taken earlier. They weren't much help. Too small. I picked up a copy of the photo Carla had given me, the one showing her brother Frankie standing next to a fellow MP somewhere in Iraq. I held it up next to the camera's screen. Maybe. The picture had been taken several years ago. Call me crazy, but I had a hunch. The black soldier in the photo with Rizzoli looked like the same guy I'd just been talking to. James Curran.

Not wanting to risk driving by Scarborough's house, I jockeyed my car around and drove back the way I came. I still had some time before I was due to pick up Carla. Instinct told me I'd caught Curran lying. If I showed her some pictures, maybe she could tell me if these two were the big tippers who'd dropped the fifty bucks on her.

I went back down to Century Boulevard and found a Rite Aid drugstore, then made prints of the pictures I'd taken and found a Starbucks. After an interminable wait behind cappuccinos, Frappuccinos, and double lattes with soy milk and cinnamon, I bought a mundane plain black coffee and found a small table by the window. I pulled the photos out of their envelope and compared them to the image of Rizzoli and the other MP. The years made a difference, but I was further convinced that Frankie Rizzoli's fellow MP was James Curran. Sipping on the cup of coffee, I found myself still shifting around pieces of this puzzle.

But now there was a difference. They'd started to have names.

CHAPTER TWELVE

———◆———

A T TEN MINUTES BEFORE SIX, I pulled into Feline Follies. A couple dozen vehicles were scattered around the parking lot. I sent Carla a text and told her I would meet her in the lobby. As I gathered up the pictures of Curran and Scarborough I'd taken and locked the car door, I congratulated myself for becoming so adept at this texting business. What next, Facebook? I made a mental note not to go there.

I pulled open the door and found an empty lobby. However, the black velvet curtain immediately parted and Junior filled the opening. He and his red blazer lumbered across the room. A look of recognition came across his face and he pointed a finger at me.

"Good evening, Mister ... Collins, isn't it?"

"You got it. And you're Junior, right?"

"Correct." He reached his podium and picked up his cellphone. "You here to see Miss Velvet?"

"Actually, I sent her a message. Told her I'd meet her out here."

"As you wish." He slid the phone into the breast pocket of the blazer.

I reached for the pictures of the two guys I'd photographed down on Crocker and said, "But I'm wondering if I could ask a favor?"

"Depends."

"When I was here before, you said two gentlemen asked you for my name. Remember that?"

"I do."

I handed him the photos. "These the guys?"

Junior looked at them and then pointed to the bandage on my cheek. "Are they responsible for that?"

"No, I had a run-in with a door."

"You should be more careful." He again looked at the photos. "Yeah, these are the same two men."

"You sure?"

"I'm sure," he said, handing me the pictures. "They've been in here several times."

"Carla said they tipped her fifty bucks. Is that normal, in your estimation?"

He leaned on the podium, and in a voice that could shrivel a head of lettuce, said, "In my estimation, tipping one of the ladies that much tells me they might want something from her."

He returned the pictures and I nodded, not needing to ask anything else. Behind me, the employee door opened and Carla came bouncing through. She wore a short black skirt and sandals. A lightweight tan jacket covered a white blouse and she had a sizable tote bag slung over one shoulder. She linked her arm in mine and gave it a squeeze.

"Junior, did you meet Eddie?"

"I did."

"My own private eye. Whoever thought …?" She stopped when she saw my right cheek and the bandage. "Oh, my God, that's more than roughing up."

"Apparently an unfriendly door," Junior said. He looked at me and I actually saw the hint of a smile.

Carla caught the glance between us and gave me a punch on the shoulder. "Well, I don't know what you two boys have been talking about, but I better take care of this guy."

"I never would have thought you'd need the services of a private investigator, Miss Velvet," Junior said.

"Me neither," she replied. "Should I tell him why, Eddie?"

"Better not," I said. "Client confidentiality."

"Oooh, yes, of course. Very mysterious." She pulled me toward the front door. "See you tomorrow, Junior."

"That you will," he said.

We pushed through the door and her eyes widened. "Are you limping? My God, why would Frankie do that?"

"My stomach is growling. Let's try and find an answer over food." She agreed and hugged me as we made our way toward my car.

CARLA SUGGESTED ITALIAN, WHICH DIDN'T SURPRISE me, given the surname Rizzoli. She had a favorite little place close by, and we soon found ourselves tucked away in a corner. The lights were low. A red-checkered cloth covered the table, which had two glasses of red wine and a basket of fresh bread on it.

We toasted each other and I took out the envelope containing the pictures I'd taken. "Take a look at these, will you?" She looked at Curran and Scarborough outside the warehouse on Crocker. "Are those the two guys that have been giving you the big tips?"

"That's them. Who are they?"

The black guy, I think, is a James Curran. The other one is Phil Scarborough."

"Scarborough? The guy who called my folks looking for Frankie?"

"The same." I handed her the picture she'd given me of her brother and the other MP in Iraq. "It's been a few years, but what do you think? Does the guy standing next to your brother look like this James Curran?"

She tilted the pictures to pick up the light from the small lamp at the edge of the table. "Looks like it to me. The beard makes him look different, but I see the resemblance." She handed the pictures back. "What does that mean, Eddie? Are these two guys after Frankie? Is that the trouble he mentioned?"

"I'm not sure. My LAPD source said Scarborough was the victim of a shooting downtown. Then I ran into this homeless guy who told me Frankie may have been there, or even involved. Somewhere there's a connection, but I don't know what it is yet. Maybe that's the reason he jumped me yesterday."

She pressed on the edges of the bandage, but pulled back when I flinched. "Oh, my God, how the heck did he do all this?"

"Caught me by surprise." I dipped a chunk of bread in some olive oil. "I guess he needed to make a point."

"Well, he sure as hell succeeded." She shook her head and sipped from her wine glass. "Why would he tell me he was dead?"

"I don't know. He obviously doesn't want to be found. Do you think he's involved in something illegal?"

"I have no idea."

"What was he doing, job-wise, when you heard from him last?"

"He didn't say."

"Do you have an address for him?"

She nodded. "I think so, someplace in my apartment. I don't know how current it would be, though."

"Give it to me and I'll check it out. Maybe somebody remembers him living there."

A waitress appeared with our orders. I had the gemelli and Carla dug into a plate of shrimp pesto. We were silent as the food disappeared. I refilled her wine glass and mine. The chicken and pasta dish was excellent. By the look on Carla's face, it was ditto for the shrimp. Finally, she pushed her plate aside and dabbed at her mouth with the napkin. She looked at me and smiled.

"It's nice being here with you," she said.

"Even though it's business related?" I replied.

"Yes." We clinked glasses and sipped. She set her glass down and clasped my hand. "Do you remember the first time we went out for dinner together?"

"Oh, boy." I thought for a moment and finally shook my head. "Go on, refresh me."

"It was a little Mexican place on Sunset. We'd finished shooting at Paramount and you asked me if I wanted to get something to eat. They even had these mariachi players come up to the table."

"Yeah, that's right. I remember the guy with the bass stood right next to my ear. Almost gave me a headache."

We both laughed and she sipped from her wine glass and looked at me. "I'm sorry I took a walk, Eddie."

"Hey, don't worry about it. I survived."

"My head wasn't in a very good place then." She paused and sipped from her wine glass. "There was this guy that showed up. We'd gone out a few times. I thought I liked him, but he …. Well, he turned out to be a shit, and …." She set her glass down, and after a moment, her eyes teared up and she dropped her head.

"Hey, hey, what's the matter?"

"I'm sorry, Eddie." She groped inside her tote bag and came up with a pocket-sized package of tissues. She pulled one out and dabbed at her eyes. "I didn't have a lot of self-esteem back then. And now I find out my brother doesn't want anything to do with me. That he wants me to know he's dead. I mean, good grief."

I took one of her hands in mine. "We're going to find him, Carla, and he's going to tell you to your face that he didn't mean it, that it isn't true."

"I hope so." She blotted her mascara and took a long, shaky breath.

I squeezed her hand and ran my thumb along her fingers. "Did you ever play the piano?"

"No, why?"

"You've got such long fingers. Piano-playing fingers."

"Actually, my mother wanted me to take lessons. But I had a macho father and a brother who took after him, so learning to play the piano wouldn't have gone down too well."

She put her other hand on top of mine. "What about you?" she asked. "Did you ever take music lessons?"

"No, 'fraid not. I'm a listener, not a player." We held each other's hands for a moment, which somehow seemed the right thing to do. After exchanging a couple of long looks, we were interrupted by the waitress.

She stacked the plates, tidied up, and asked the inevitable question, "Anything else for you folks?" We shook our heads and she laid the check on the table. Carla made a grab for it, but I beat her to it.

"Let me, Eddie."

"No, ma'am. Legitimate business expense." I got no argument from her, left money on the table, and we made our way out of the restaurant.

"I don't even know where you live," I said.

"Well, get in the car, Mr. Private Eye, and I'll give you directions."

She got no argument from me.

CHAPTER THIRTEEN

———◆———

The directions Carla gave me took us to an address on Jasmine Avenue in Culver City, a stone's throw from the Sony Pictures lot. To me, that real estate remains the home of MGM, but over the years I've had to accept the fact that once again Hollywood tradition has gone the way of Betamax and the manual typewriter. Jasmine was a quaint street, with single-family homes on both sides. Carla pointed to a small bungalow on the right. One small tree stood between the sidewalk and the curb. A light glowed underneath an overhang covering the front stoop.

"You'd better park on the street," she said. "Mrs. Warner, the old biddy living next to me, will get her nose out of joint if she sees a strange car in the driveway."

"No problem."

"Come on in. I'll get you that address I have for Frankie."

We climbed out and I locked the doors. The neighborhood was quiet, something I wasn't used to, living in the middle of Hollywood. For a change, steel bars didn't cover the windows. Instead, birds of paradise reached the bottoms of both sets of them on the front of the house. Farther up the driveway, I could see a canvas-covered carport.

As we climbed up the four bricked steps to the front door, a breeze awoke a wind chime hanging above the stoop. Carla fumbled inside her tote bag, but then threw up her hands. "Oh, shoot. My house key is at the garage."

"Am I going to have to pick the lock?" I said.

"You can do that?"

"I've been known to in the past."

"I swear, you private-eye guys. My neighbors are probably watching." She chuckled and shook her head. "But not to worry. I've got a spare."

She grabbed one of the metal cylinders of the wind chime and pulled out a plug in the end of it. A key dropped into the palm of her hand and she replaced the cap.

"Clever," I said.

"It deadens the sound a little, but I'd rather do that than put it under the mat or in a potted plant." She stuck the key in the doorknob and turned it.

"No dead bolt?" I said.

"Nope."

"Might be a good idea to have one."

"There's a chain inside. This is a pretty safe neighborhood, Eddie."

Famous last words, coming from a woman who carries a piece in her purse. Carla opened the door then replaced the key in the wind chime. She flicked on an entrance light and did the same to a table lamp at the end of a sofa, which faced a television set on the far wall. It was a comfortable house. Soft furniture, lace throws here and there, and pillows everywhere. A coffee table sat in front of the sofa, two easy chairs at either end. Hardwood floors had area rugs strewn over them.

Carla dropped her tote bag on a small table by the door, took off her jacket, and hung it on a hat rack. She pulled off my porkpie and placed it on an adjacent peg.

"I love this hat."

"One of several," I said.

"You want a nightcap?" she asked. "I could use one."

"All right."

"What would you like?"

"You have any beer?"

"You bet. Follow me. I'll give you the cook's tour." She headed down a hallway to a kitchen. A small table sat against one wall. The usual appliances filled the room. The bathroom was at the end of the hall, with bedrooms on either side.

"Nice place. Do you own it?"

"No. Wish I did, though." We went back into the kitchen and she pulled a bottle of beer from the refrigerator, twisted the top off, then fetched a glass from a cupboard shelf. "Go have a seat. I'll be right there."

I took the bottle of beer and glass and walked back into the living room. The *Festival of Death* screenplay lay on the coffee table. I leafed through it and saw that Carla had highlighted her lines in yellow. From what I could tell, her role seemed substantial. The dialogue, however, fell short. But of course, I was reading it out of context. Carla came into the room, kicked off her sandals, and joined me on the sofa, a glass of wine in her hand.

"Have you got your lines learned?" I said.

She waggled her hand and said, "Well, yes and no. Depends on how tired I am."

"You want some help? I can run them with you."

"Really?"

"Yeah. It always works for me." I picked up the script and turned to the first scene with yellow highlighting. "Come on, let's see you do your stuff." The scene involved her character's husband and two cops. We went over it a couple of times and she was, for the most part, letter perfect. "Not bad," I said.

She took the script from me. "That's enough for now."

"I can give you some help over the weekend if you'd like."

"Really? Follies has scheduled me for short shifts tomorrow and Sunday. We'd have to work around them."

"No problem. I can check out that address while you're … ah … doing your thing."

She looked at me over the lip of her wine glass, a twinkle in her eyes. "You mean while I'm taking off my clothes?"

"Now you're putting words in my mouth."

She gave me a Lauren Bacall wink and sipped from her glass. I meant it when I said it always helps me to learn dialogue by having someone feed me cues. But I also wasn't kidding myself. Helping Carla with her lines would give me a chance to spend more time with her. That possibility pleased me. I was opening a door here and wasn't sure what was on the other side. But right now I sure as hell didn't feel like closing it.

Carla slid closer, we clinked glasses, and she leaned over and kissed me on the cheek. "You're a sweetheart, Eddie. I have a confession to make."

"Oh, yeah? What would that be?"

"When I paged through those Yellow Pages looking for a private investigator, I saw your name and went no farther."

"Well, it helps to have a last name beginning with 'C.'"

"True. But knowing you before might have had something to do with it." Setting her glass on the coffee table, she picked up a Rolodex card and handed it to me. "Here's the address I have for Frankie. Like I said, I don't know how much help it's going to be."

The location was in Studio City. The card also listed a phone number. "I assume you tried calling him."

"Yeah. It'd been changed."

"Tell me about Frankie. What was he into? Did you get along with him when you were growing up?"

"For the most part. But he was very competitive, in sports, everything. He always dared me to do things. Climb that tree. Throw the baseball like a guy. I guess he kind of made a tomboy out of me. I always felt the need to keep up, be somebody I wasn't."

"Did you resent it?"

"Once in a while. I even took a poke at him one time." She laughed, picked up her glass, and sipped. "He and some of his buddies were playing touch football. I was watching them with a girlfriend of mine. Frankie dropped a pass and I gave him a raspberry—you know, sort of a Bronx cheer. I looked over at my girlfriend, and he threw the ball at me, hit me in the back of the head. I turned around and punched him in the face."

"What did he do?"

"Nothing. He couldn't believe it. Just stared at me, rubbing his nose. His buddies thought it was hilarious. My girlfriend did too." She set her glass back on the table. "Later that day, he actually apologized. Told me he was just showing off."

I reached for my beer and took a swallow. When I glanced at her, she had a faraway look on her face. After a moment, her eyes filled with tears.

"Sounds like he cares for you, Carla."

"I guess. That's why I can't believe he told you what he did. Maybe the guy who roughed you up wasn't him, Eddie."

"Well, I've thought about that. But he had that tattoo and knew I was looking for Frankie. That's too coincidental. Word somehow got to him and he doesn't want to be located."

"But why?"

I shook my head. "I don't know. That's what we've got to find out. I can't help but think there's some link with those guys Curran and Scarborough. If Scarborough went looking for Frankie when they mustered out of the Army, it could mean he's still at it."

"And so he throws them off by getting word to his sister that he's dead? My God, what is he doing?"

I set my glass down and squeezed the back of her neck. "We'll find out."

"I'm sorry," she said. "I'm being a wuss."

"Nothing wrong with that."

She took a deep breath and looked at me. At that moment, the line between client and private eye vanished and I pulled her toward me. She wrapped her arms around me, and her hands dug into my back, a sense of urgency in them. She leaned back, touched my bandaged cheek, and then kissed me. The kiss was soft, yearning, and I didn't pull away. Lips parted and our tongues explored. After a moment, she broke the kiss and gazed into my eyes.

"What does this do to our professional relationship?" she said, as she ran one finger over the contours of my mouth.

"Beats me. I don't have the PI field manual with me." I kissed her again, and she wrapped her arms around me. When I came up for air, I said, "I suppose I could go get it."

"You stay right here." She put both her hands on my cheeks. "Don't forget, I need a ride to get my car in the morning."

"They don't have a courtesy vehicle?"

"I don't know, and I didn't ask."

"My secretary tells me I'm a very courteous fellow."

"I'll be the judge of that." She picked up her wine glass again, then went to the front door, hooked the chain, and turned off both the entry and exterior lights. She picked up her tote bag and started down the hall, stopped, and turned to me. "Hey, private eye, I've got a clue back here that might interest you."

"Yes, ma'am," I said.

I finished my beer and followed her down the hallway. As if it was a doorbell, I heard the wind chime behind me. I knew the front door was locked. The one I was opening, however, was another matter.

Chapter Fourteen

I HADN'T SHARED A BED WITH A woman in quite some time, and if the old cliché is true, the bicycle was in good working order. Even though the act of undressing was second nature for Carla, I found it endearing how she was somewhat shy in front of me. She wanted all lights off in the bedroom, save for a small nightlight plugged into a socket in the corner. A slight breeze drifted through a partially open window, pushing out a sheer beige curtain. Open about six inches, it was the kind that opened vertically. A shade was pulled down, revealing just a glimpse of the driveway running alongside the house.

I was a different kind of audience in that I did not belong to that crowd of nameless, gaping men. Granted, I could have joined their ranks, but that trim and lithe body in my arms, pressed against me, left no room for awe, just pleasure. And there was plenty of that. She helped me take my clothes off, punctuating her efforts with kisses and small nips here and there. From our time together several years ago, I remembered her as a wonderful lover. Memory served me well. She was intense, vocal, and other adjectives too effusive to mention. When we finished, we lay curled up in each other's arms, both of us expressing amazement that this had happened so quickly.

Carla rolled onto her left side and propped her head up with one hand. She looked at me for a long moment. "This is where we should be smoking, isn't it?"

"Like in the movies?"

"Right," she said. "You'd have the ashtray right here." She poked me in the sternum.

"I sometimes wonder if they ever set fire to the bed when they shoot those scenes."

"Not to mention chest hair," she said, as she ran her fingers over mine.

"That too."

"I never smoked. Did you?"

"Years ago. One of the vices I managed to give up."

"I'm glad," she said, as she slipped her hand under the sheet and began exploring. I unwrapped my right arm from beneath her head and made sure her hand found what it was looking for. She squeezed, then kissed me on the cheek. The hand came out from beneath the sheet and her fingers found the scar on my right arm.

"I know you told me before, but where did this come from again?"

"The Army. Korea."

"What happened?"

"I was an MP, and—"

"Wait a minute. You never told me that. You were an MP … like Frankie?"

"I was."

"That is so weird. Go on. Refresh my memory."

I filled her in on how I was attacked one night by a crazed GI high on all kinds of pharmaceuticals, and how Reggie Benson saved my life by knocking the guy out. I then told her how I found Reggie on the Santa Monica Pier and gave him a leg up.

"So where's this Reggie now?" she said.

"Matter of fact, he was with me when your brother jumped me. My plan is for him to help me when I need him. In the meantime, I got him a job as a night watchman. He's doing well."

"Because of Eddie Collins."

"Well, I don't know. I owed him one."

She leaned in and gave me a kiss, her expression pensive.

"What's the matter?" I said.

"Oh, I was just wondering."

"What?"

"When you watched my set at the Follies yesterday, did it make you feel funny?"

"How do you mean?"

"Well, I don't know. Those guys in there are just faces. I don't relate to them on a personal level. With you, it's different."

"How so?"

"You're in my bed, for one thing," she said, as she poked me in the ribs.

"Carla, look, I know why you're dancing. I'm not going to judge you."

"So you don't regret getting involved with your client?"

"Not as long as she doesn't forget to pay me."

She laughed and began tickling me. When I grabbed both her wrists, she wrestled herself on top of me and leaned down to kiss me. I let go of her hands and wrapped mine around her back as she ground into me. The kiss deepened, but then stopped and we both froze.

Someone was outside the partially open window.

CHAPTER FIFTEEN

———◆———

"Is there a lock on that window?" I whispered.

"Yes."

"That gun of yours still in your tote bag?"

"Yeah. Should I get it?"

"Quietly."

Carla slipped out of bed and picked up the bag lying on the dresser. I stepped into my trousers and loafers and crouched down beside the open window. I could hear the murmur of two voices as footsteps came up the driveway. They approached and I flattened myself against the wall.

"Her car's not here," one of the voices said. "What makes you think she is?"

"I'm not saying she is, but you saw the lights go out, didn't you? Someone's in there."

"That don't mean it's Frankie."

"For crissakes, Phil, I know that. But we're never going to find out for sure if we stand out here arguing. See if you can get that screen off."

Frankie and Phil. No doubt about it. Carla handed me her gun, then wrapped herself in a robe snatched off a hook behind the door and crouched down beside me. I put my finger to my lips and whispered in her ear, "It's Curran and Scarborough. They're looking for your brother." I turned back to the window when I heard the screen come off. Two black-gloved hands reached in, grabbed the sill, and pulled up. The window didn't budge.

"She's got a lock on it," Scarborough said.

"Forget it. Come on."

The two men left the window and started for the rear of the house.

"Do you have a back door?" I said.

"Yes. It's locked."

I stood up and started for the rear of the house. Carla grabbed my arm.

"Should I call the police?"

"The minute they hear a siren they'll run. Let me see if I can surprise them."

I crept toward the rear of the house and saw the back door on the opposite side of a small room. Through the darkness, I could barely make out four panes of glass in the upper half. As my eyes adjusted, I saw the shape of a washer and dryer to my left and a water heater to the right. Storage cabinets were bolted to the walls on either side. I stood in the doorway and listened. Footsteps approached and then I heard the sound of someone bumping into metal. Subdued cursing and mutterings followed. A figure appeared on the other side of the panes of glass. The doorknob jiggled. I started toward the door and my feet got tangled up with something sitting on the floor. I stumbled and crashed into the doorjamb, wrenching my hurt knee and stifling an oath. The knob stopped jiggling. Then a voice shouted from the house on the other side of the driveway. The figure quickly disappeared from view.

I turned the lock in the doorknob and jerked the door open, making a mental note of another absence of a deadbolt. Curran and Scarborough, dressed in black, were disappearing around the corner of the house.

A woman's voice shouted, "What's going on over there?"

It was pitch black outside and I had to brace myself against the side of the house as I made my way down three steps to a concrete sidewalk. I limped toward the corner of the house and ran into an aluminum garbage can, which obviously accounted for the previous cursing. The clanging of the can prompted another outburst from next door.

Feeling my way along the side of the house, I reached the corner and turned to see Curran and Scarborough running down the driveway. Shouts from the neighbor lady accompanied them.

Darkness and unfamiliarity with my surroundings, not to mention my newly painful knee, impeded my progress down the driveway, and by the time I got to the front of the house, the two men had disappeared. I heard a vehicle roar to life around the corner of the next street and then the screech of tires.

A shivering, half-naked man with a gun in his hand is not the best image for any neighborhood, let alone Jasmine Avenue. As I retreated up the driveway, Carla stood at the end with a flashlight in her hand.

"Are you all right, Eddie?"

"Yeah, except I'm freezing my ass off."

A light went on in a window next door and a head of gray hair filled the opening. "Is that you, Carla?"

"Yes, Marge, it's me. The excitement's over."

"Burglars aren't my idea of excitement, my dear." She saw me coming up the driveway. "Who are you?"

"This is a friend of mine," Carla said. "You can go back to bed."

"Well, that's easy for you to say. I won't sleep a wink now."

"Try some hot milk," Carla said. "It works for me."

"Don't get sassy with me, young lady. I've half a mind to call your landlord." The woman muttered something unintelligible before slamming the window shut.

"The old biddy?" I said.

"One and the same. Come on, get inside." She shined the flashlight on the sidewalk and we rounded the corner of the house to see the aluminum trash bin on its side. I righted it and followed Carla up the stairs and inside. Handing her the gun, I went through the door and watched her shut and lock it.

"Maybe you want to give another thought to deadbolts?" I said.

"Message received. You want something hot to drink? Tea? Coffee? You're shivering."

"A warm bed would be nice."

She picked up a black plastic clothes hamper partially full of laundry and set it on the washer.

"That's what I tripped over, I suppose?"

"I forgot it was there."

Once in the bedroom, I slipped out of my shoes and trousers, put on my underwear, and crawled into bed. Carla took off the robe, replaced it with an oversized T-shirt and joined me. Drawing the covers up, she plastered herself against me.

"How the hell do they know where I live?" she said.

"Didn't you tell me they've been at the Follies several times?"

"Two or three, I think."

"Then they must have followed you at some point. They knew your car wasn't here."

"So they've made the connection that Frankie is my brother, right?"

"It would seem so."

"That doesn't explain how they know I work there, does it?"

"No, it does not," I said. We were silent for a moment and Carla snuggled up against me. "But if they're looking for Frankie, it makes sense that they would think he'd hole up with his sister."

"Yeah, I guess," she said. She wrapped one arm around me and ran a bare foot up one of my legs. "Heck of a way to put a damper on a perfect evening, isn't it?"

"The important thing is you're safe. Keep that gun of yours with you, all right? Remember Frankie said to watch your back."

"I will," she said.

"And go to Home Depot. Deadbolts."

"Aye-aye, sir." She turned my face toward her and kissed me. I wasn't sure the perfect evening could be salvaged, but I sensed she was going to make an effort.

CHAPTER SIXTEEN

———◆———

I SAT AT CARLA'S KITCHEN TABLE, SHOELESS, in my trousers and a T-shirt, sipping coffee and watching her talk on the phone. She was barefoot and still wore her oversized tee. She was jotting notes on a pad of paper. The movie company had phoned to give her a call time for Monday morning. We'd already discussed the events of the previous evening and I hoped I'd persuaded her that she would have to be especially careful, given the fact that Curran and Scarborough knew her car and where she lived.

She turned to me and gave me a thumbs-up, then broke the connection. "Eight o'clock. That's not bad, is it?"

"Banker's hours," I replied. "Where do you have to go?"

She glanced at the slip of paper she'd been writing on. "Someplace up behind Magic Mountain. The directions don't seem too complicated."

"When are you supposed to be at the Follies?"

"My shift starts at noon."

"You want to run some more lines before you go in?"

"That would be great." She filled both our coffee cups. "I usually come early to get warmed up, but I think I've already done that, if you get my drift." She bumped her hip against me and then leaned down and kissed me.

"You're warmed up, and I'm worn out," I said, as I pulled her to me and ran a hand up one of those long, gorgeous legs.

She put the coffee pot on the table and plopped herself down on my lap. "Oh, my poor private eye. Did I take advantage of you?"

My hand roamed higher as I said, "I demand a rematch."

"Anytime," she whispered, and brought her mouth to mine.

My hands continued their exploration. After a few minutes, we pulled away from each other and I said, "You know, if we continue this, you're never going to get that dialogue learned."

"You're right." She ran her fingers through my hair. "And we still have to pick up my car." She kissed me again. "Shall we postpone this until after my shift?"

"I reluctantly agree with you."

She gave me a peck on the tip of my nose, squirmed her bottom into my lap, then got up and replaced the coffee pot on its base. "Okay, I'm gonna pop in the shower and we'll run some more lines."

"Sounds like a plan." She picked up her coffee cup and started down the hallway. "The paper should be by the front door."

I buttered a piece of toast and looked around the kitchen, struck by the ease I felt in the face of all this domesticity. It was Saturday morning. I was amazed it had been only Tuesday afternoon when Carla Rizzoli had walked into my office looking for a private eye. This imaginary door I'd been thinking about had swung wide open, and so far I was pleased with what lay behind it.

The shower continued to run as I fetched my shoes, shirt, and jacket from the bedroom. I opened the front door and glanced up and down the street, but didn't see either a red Toyota RAV4 or a black Hyundai. As I walked up the driveway, I still favored one leg, but I didn't think I'd done additional damage to my knee. I replaced the screen over the bedroom window, then turned and saw the neighbor standing behind the window she'd appeared in last night. I gave her a wave, which resulted in a shake of the head and a blind being jerked down. Looked like the old biddy was still on the warpath. Retrieving the paper, I went back in the house and picked up Carla's copy of *Festival of Death*.

In the film, Carla's character is named Diane Carpenter. Her husband is Brad, their two children are Ronnie and Angie. They come to this Renaissance Fair where people start dying. One of the ersatz knights in tarnished armor winds up being stabbed by his opponent's saber. A young man is poisoned by eating a tainted turkey leg. Two ladies-in-waiting are found raped and mutilated in a creek bed. Good, wholesome family entertainment. Actually, given the genre, it read fairly well.

Carla came in with a fresh cup of coffee and sat with her legs tucked beneath her. She took the script from me, opened to a particular page and handed it back. "These are the pages that are up first thing on Monday."

In the scene, she is being interviewed by a police detective. She describes in detail how she and her screen husband came upon the two bodies in the creek bed. We ran it several times, and Carla got better with every repetition. Finally she looked at her watch and indicated it was time to pick up her car.

She gathered her things, and after putting on her jacket, handed me my hat and put her arms around me.

"I'm really glad you were here last night, Eddie. With two against one, I don't know what might have happened."

"Just be alert, okay? Curran drives a red Toyota RAV4 and Scarborough has a black Hyundai. If you see them parked on the street, call me. Or the cops." She nodded and opened the door. "And please get those dead bolts. Both doors. Tell your landlord you need them."

"I will," she said, as she snapped me a salute and shut the door behind her.

"Have you got that handgun of yours?"

She patted her tote bag. "Wouldn't leave home without it."

I didn't think she was taking me seriously about the locks on the doors. But she did ease my mind by saying she was packing heat. In more ways than one.

CHAPTER SEVENTEEN

---◆---

A WISE MAN WHOSE NAME I'VE LONG forgotten once told me the three secrets to peace of mind are a firm mattress, smooth sippin' whiskey at your elbow, and an honest auto mechanic. By the look of Skelly's Service & Repair, Carla had the third part of the formula covered. I counted eleven vehicles parked around the garage, Carla's white Honda Fit among them. The place had three service bays, all of them occupied. While I waited for her to settle up, two more cars drove up and were met by mechanics wiping their hands on shop rags. A busy place.

She came out of the office with a spring in her step that suggested the news about her car was positive.

"Is it done?" I said.

"Ready to go. And it cost less than I thought."

"Can't beat that."

"So, I'm off at four. Shall we run some more dialogue?"

"You bet. I've got to swing by my office and then I'll pop out to Studio City and check that address you gave me."

"Better change clothes too." She pulled me to her and planted a kiss on my lips. "Wouldn't want your secretary to think you stayed out all night."

"I'm safe. Mavis doesn't come in on Saturdays."

"Do you think she'd mind?"

"You kidding? She's in awe that I've got a pistol-packing client."

"A gal after my own heart. I've got to meet this Mavis."

"You will."

We agreed to reconnoiter at her place. She bounced off to her Honda and drove out of the lot, giving me a toot on the horn as she left. As I climbed into my car and headed for the freeway, I kind of wished we didn't have to part. I hadn't felt like that in a while. It was nice.

MAVIS HAD LEFT HER USUAL ASSORTMENT of messages by the telephone. A couple of bills were due. Did I want to renew *The Hollywood Reporter*? I did. The career might be a virtual rumor, but there's no harm in keeping one's finger on the pulse of the biz. In a box on the floor by her desk was evidence that the collectibles trade was flourishing. Bobbleheads of Sonny and Cher stared up at me. She'd never looked so good. I got you, babe.

I stripped and jumped in the shower, then shaved. A scab had started to form over the scrape on my cheek, so I decided to forgo another bandage and let it breathe. Refreshed and wearing a different set of duds, I headed for the front door, but then stopped.

I wrestled a small gym bag from the top shelf of my closet and filled it with a change of clothes. I threw in a stick of deodorant and a toothbrush. If I wasn't asked to spend the night with Carla, I was going to feel awfully foolish. Somehow I didn't think I had to worry.

MACK SENNETT, THE OLD MOVIE PIONEER, gave Studio City its name by building a lot on twenty acres back in 1927. In those days, his Keystone Kops had plenty of room to ramble among the orange groves, unlike today, when over five thousand people occupy a square mile and the only orange you'll find is in a supermarket.

The address Carla had given me was on Acama. Apartment complexes stood on both sides of the narrow street. Tall palm trees swayed in the breeze. I squeezed into a parking place half a block away and walked back. A driveway ran down the side of the building to a parking lot in the rear. A tree in full bloom obscured an unlocked metal gate that led to a courtyard with a small swimming pool coated with leaves. Two boys played in the shallow end, indifferent to the floating foliage.

A barely legible sign on the mailboxes told me the manager was a Floyd McGinty in Unit 101. I knocked on the screen door and turned to my right. An old man limped down the corridor to the rear of the building. He had a small white dog on a leash, and he stopped to look back at me before opening an apartment and shoving the dog through with his foot.

A dry smoker's cough accompanied the opening of Number 101. A small man in khakis and a grimy T-shirt peered out at me. Wisps of gray hair surrounded his head, as though he'd walked through a nest of cobwebs on his way to answer the door. His face resembled a map, with the blue highways covering his nose.

"Mr. McGinty?" I said.

"That's me. But no vacancies now. Sorry," he rasped.

"I'm wondering if you could give me some information about a former tenant of yours."

"You a cop?" he said, taking a pull off an unfiltered cigarette.

"Private investigator," I replied, handing him one of my cards.

He held it up and squinted. "Can't see a damn thing in this light. And I need my glasses. Come on in."

I pulled the screen door open and entered the apartment. A kitchen was on my left, with a counter open to the living room. Dishes were stacked in the sink, and a wastebasket was close to overflowing. A bedroom was at two o'clock, the bed unmade. We hadn't had an earthquake in some time, but you couldn't tell by looking at the interior of the apartment. Keeping a neat abode wasn't part of Floyd's job description. Piles of newspaper sat on piles of magazines, all of them in danger of being toppled by McGinty's coughing. The place smelled of booze, cigarette smoke, onions, and old sweat.

He slipped a pair of readers over his ears and leaned over to hold the card under a gooseneck lamp that had somehow managed to claim space on a cluttered table. Momentarily losing his balance, he steadied himself by reaching out and putting his hand next to a fifth of cheap whiskey and a glass half full of the stuff. It looked like happy hour came early for Floyd.

"Eddie Collins. Hey, used to be a helluva baseball player by that name."

"You got it," I said. "Philadelphia As and Chicago White Sox. In 1912 he stole six bases in one game." It's not the first time my name has been linked to the famous baseball player's. I'd done my research to satisfy the curious.

"So, who're you looking for?" he said, as he tossed the card on the table and puffed on his cigarette.

I handed him the picture of Frankie. "Not exactly *looking* for him, but I'm hoping you can tell me something about him. The guy's name is Frankie Rizzoli. Birth name Francis. That shot of him was taken a few years back. Recognize him?"

The picture went under the gooseneck, aided this time by his hand holding him upright. After a moment, he said, "Oh, yeah, yeah, I remember this guy. Moved out and didn't give notice. I had to keep his deposit." He handed me the picture and stood upright, one hand now clasping the glass of whiskey.

"Any idea why he moved?"

"Well, he might have been in trouble."

"Why do you say that?"

"He left with two cops," he said, gulping a healthy swallow of the whiskey.

"Willingly? I mean, did they have him in cuffs?"

McGinty scratched his head, dislodging a cobweb. "Naw, I don't think so.

Looked to me like Rizzoli knew the two of them. They were real friendly like, it seemed to me."

"So you kept his deposit. He ever come back asking about it?"

"Nope."

"What about his furniture and personal belongings?"

He took a final puff on his cigarette and snuffed it out in an overflowing ashtray. A wisp of smoke drifted up into the light from the gooseneck lamp. "I 'member a couple days later two guys showed up. They had uniforms on, from some moving company. Showed me a piece of paper saying they had permission to take his stuff away. That's the last I saw of him. After a few days, I told the mailman the guy took off."

I handed him the photo of Curran and Scarborough unloading the crates. "Take a look at these two guys in this picture. They look at all familiar?"

Again he steadied himself and stuck the snapshot under the light. After a moment, he shook his head and lit up another cigarette. "Don't recognize either one of them. But tell you the truth, I don't pay much attention to who comes and goes around here. Unless there's somebody complains."

Between the smokes and the whiskey, I didn't think Floyd McGinty paid much attention in general. "Thanks for your time, sir. Give me a call if you happen to remember anything else."

"Yeah, sure. Eddie Collins. Can't forget that name."

I started for the door.

"Luis Aparicio was a damn good shortstop too."

"That he was," I said.

"He and Nellie Fox sure as hell could turn a double play."

I nodded and closed the door behind me before we got into a baseball trivia contest. I didn't think I was a match for McGinty.

The two boys in the pool had a version of Battleship going on. Small plastic action figures sat on the leaves, being bombarded by squirt guns. The metal gate clicked behind me and I headed for my car. Frankie Rizzoli had been taken out of his place by cops. Why? If he really was in trouble, he wouldn't have been acting like he was going out for a beer with the two uniforms. Witness protection? The thought flew into my head, but had no basis for staying. Unless he had something on James Curran and Phil Scarborough. But then why the hell would he be roaming around down on Skid Row?

CHAPTER EIGHTEEN

———— ◆ ————

CARLA'S HONDA WAS TUCKED UNDER THE carport by the time I got to Culver City. I pulled into the driveway and knocked on the front door. She was barefoot and dressed in jeans and a man's blue denim shirt.

"Howdy, Mr. Shamus." She spotted the gym bag. "What's in there? Your PI field manual?"

"Tools. To put in deadbolts."

"Are you serious?"

"Actually, no. Thought I'd bring my toothbrush. You going to invite me in?"

She grabbed my shirt front. "Get in here." I followed directions and accepted the hug and kiss. She hung my hat on a peg, took the gym bag, and headed for the bedroom. "I'm having a glass of wine. Want a beer?"

"Thought you'd never ask." I sat on the sofa and picked up a pretzel from a dish sitting on the coffee table. On the television set, Warren Beatty and Annette Bening were steaming up the screen in the 1991 release *Bugsy*. Carla came in with a bottle of beer and a glass and sat next to me.

"Friend of mine was in that movie," I said.

"Really? What'd he play?"

"I don't know. Some assistant DA. He said Beatty never even acknowledged his presence."

"He probably had someone else on his mind. Isn't that when he and Annette starting fooling around?"

"So they say," I said. She muted the movie and I raised my glass. "Cheers."

We tapped and sipped and she said, "Tomorrow I'm only on from eleven to one."

"On Sunday?"

"Yup."

"What, you pass the collection plate?"

"Right after we hear their confessions."

I raised my glass. "*Touché.* How did it go today? Big tippers?"

"Not really. But you know what? One of those guys was in there again."

"Which one?"

"The white guy. The one that had the sling."

"Phil Scarborough."

"Yeah. I'd forgotten his name. And the other weird thing is, I saw him come out of the back room."

"I thought no customers were allowed back there?"

"So did I. The boss has his office on the second floor."

"Then Scarborough is more than a customer?"

"Beats me. Weird, huh?"

"Yeah." I took a sip of beer. It was strange that Scarborough had been in an area off-limits to customers. Maybe he owned the joint. "Who's your boss?" I said.

"Kenny Mickelson's his name."

"Does he own the place?"

"I don't know. He's the only one we girls deal with."

"These two guys are getting more and more spooky every day."

"I love that word," she said. "Spooky. Sounds like we're in a ghost movie." She leaned in and kissed me, then touched the goose egg on my head. "The bump has gone down. Your cheek still looks like crap, though."

"Thanks. How about the rest of me?"

"Even better than Warren Beatty." She sipped from her wine glass and plucked a pretzel from the dish. On the screen, Bugsy Malone was stomping around the desert, trying to get someone to go along with his idea of building the Flamingo in Las Vegas. "Did you talk to anybody at that address?" she said.

I related my conversation with Floyd McGinty. She listened intently, her eyes widening in surprise.

"My brother is starting to resemble somebody I don't even know anymore, Eddie. Cops? Good grief."

"For a minute I flashed on the idea that maybe witness protection figures in."

"From what? I can't imagine him being involved in anything where he'd have to disappear."

"Maybe he's got something on these guys Curran and Scarborough."

She ran her finger around the edge of her glass, lost in thought for a moment. "Maybe. Where would the cops take him?"

"I don't know, but it sure as hell wouldn't be down on Skid Row, so I think we can throw that theory out the window."

"Done," she said. "What's your next move?"

"Well, I'll make another trip downtown and see if he surfaces again. I can check with the other mission. Maybe they'll recognize him. I'll give Charlie Rivers another call."

"Who's he?"

"My LAPD contact. When two cops escort Frankie out of his apartment, there's got to be some kind of paper trail. If he was arrested, that is."

"What if he wasn't?"

"Good question. Then I don't know." I popped another pretzel into my mouth and we watched Warren and Annette for a moment. "If I put myself out in the open down there on Skid Row, maybe Frankie will reach out again when he realizes his warning didn't take."

"Yeah, maybe." Her reply was muted and full of doubt. She gazed at the television set. I could see the uncertainty on her face. I reached over, grabbed her hand, and gave it a squeeze.

"Don't give up, kiddo. We'll find out what's behind all this."

"I don't know, Eddie. Maybe I should have just ignored that stupid note."

"Frankie reached out to you for a reason, Carla."

"Yeah, to tell me he's dead."

I set my glass on the coffee table and pulled her to me. She wrapped her arms around me and I held her close. After a couple of minutes, she broke the embrace and wiped the trace of a tear from her eye.

"I'm sorry, Eddie."

"Hey, it's okay."

"I'm just worried about him."

"I know. We'll smoke him out somehow." I stroked her cheek and was glad to see a tentative smile break out on her face. "That's better. You've got a big day Monday in front of the camera. Let me worry about this other business. Deal?"

"Deal," she said. Pulling a tissue from the box behind her, she blew her nose, then picked up the script. "You ready for this?"

"I'm Eddie at the ready."

For the next hour or so we ran her lines from *Festival of Death*. Except for a minor correction here and there, she passed with flying colors. After another beer and glass of wine, she thought it would be a good idea to order a pizza. I agreed, and we settled on a pepperoni, ground beef, and mushroom. She put in the call, and as we waited, she scrolled through the TV Guide listings for the evening. I told her to stop when I spotted one I had worked on. She practically squealed with delight.

"You're in that? We've got to watch it."

"Well, I'm not exactly hogging the screen."

"I don't care." She tucked her legs under her and sipped from her wine glass. "I'll even make popcorn. But you've got to promise me something."

"What?" I said and took a swallow of beer.

"We have to mute it when you're not on so we can make out a little."

I almost did the classic "spit take" with my beer and couldn't hold back my laughter. "You mean like in the back row of the balcony?"

"That, or the backseat of a convertible."

The pizza came and we watched some of a Dodgers game as we chomped down. It was good pizza, and we managed to consume it all except for a couple of slices.

"For later," she said, as she closed the box and headed for the kitchen with her empty wine glass. "Another beer?"

"Wouldn't say no."

I felt comfortable enough around Carla to take off my shoes as we snuggled together on the sofa and waited for this Eddie Collins vehicle I'd worked on a few years back. It was a comedy where I played a truck driver who gives a ride to these two young men on their way to the Burning Man thing in Nevada. My character thought the two guys were crazier than loons, and their characters thought pretty much the same of me. I had to confess that, on another viewing, the picture was amusing. That might have had something to do with the company I was keeping. And we did hit the mute button a couple of times to fulfill Carla's wish.

When the picture ended, we started watching another one, but our interest soon flagged. We ended up forgetting about the mute button while we made out. Eventually, we gave up altogether on the movie and made our way to the bedroom.

Our love-making was slow and soft. At one point she cried out and I covered her mouth with mine. Deep kisses, entwined limbs, and various contortions left us sated and breathless, lying on our backs.

"Do you suppose the old biddy heard us?" I said.

"Marge? Wouldn't surprise me if she's sitting at her open window."

"You serious?"

"Yes," she said, then stood up on the bed. "Maybe we should throw up the shade and give her a real show. What do you think?"

"I think we'd better not invite trouble."

"You're right." She lay down on top of me and planted kisses on both my cheeks.

"Speaking of trouble," I said, "Frankie's note said for you to watch your back. You're going to take him at his word, aren't you?"

"I haven't forgotten what that note said, Eddie. I promise I'll smack the first dude who looks cross-eyed at me."

Of course I couldn't resist and crossed my eyes. She bopped me on the forehead and we laughed and picked up where we'd left off.

Chapter Nineteen

———◆———

B IRDSONG WOKE ME UP. I DON'T know how many there were, but they had a nice little concert going. It was not a sound I was accustomed to hearing in the morning. Also, lying next to me was the most unaccustomed part of this picture. Carla slept on her left side, tousled raven hair spilling over the pillow. I watched her sleeping, just the trace of a frown on her forehead. With all the uncertainty surrounding her brother and the visit from Curran and Scarborough, some angst was understandable. As I lay there, watching a ray of sunlight creep across the carpet, I felt frustrated that I hadn't been able to come up with a solution as to the whereabouts of Frankie Rizzoli. A sudden burst of birdsong woke Carla. She scratched her nose and opened her eyes. The first thing she saw was me, and a smile replaced the trace of a frown.

"Morning," she said. "Sorry about the racket."

"What racket?"

"Those damn birds."

"They're better than horns, sirens, and squealing brakes." She sat up and the sheet fell to her waist, adding two more items to my list of unaccustomed morning sights.

"I think there's a nest out there," she said. "How long have you been awake?"

"Not long. The birds didn't wake me."

"Oh, yeah?" She draped herself across my chest. "Not used to sleeping with a woman, is that it?"

"Yeah, sort of. One who snores, anyway."

She raised herself on one elbow and glared down at me. "I do *not* snore."

I rolled my eyes and she swung one leg over, then playfully pounded on me, her breasts bouncing with the rhythm. "I have never snored!"

"Oh, well, then it must have been me." Grabbing her wrists, I pulled her down and kissed her. She responded and started to grind her pelvis. "Is this your warm-up for your shift?" I said.

"Could be," she whispered. "I usually wait until I get to the club, but since you're here, we might as well make the most of it."

And we did, as the birds continued their concert.

The parking lot at Feline Follies was almost devoid of cars. A jet plane, wheels down, loomed over Century Boulevard as it made its final approach to LAX. I pulled up to the front of the building. Carla leaned over and kissed me before opening the car door.

"I'll pick you up at one," I said.

"Let's do something fun today. No more running lines, okay?"

"You got it. What do you have in mind?"

"Surprise me," she said, and got out of the car, blowing me a kiss as she disappeared into the club.

I pulled out on Century and realized I was hungry. Our morning warm-up hadn't left time for even a cup of coffee. I spotted a pair of golden arches and pulled into the parking lot. The coffee was hot and the Egg McMuffin hit the spot. Sitting by the front window, I watched toddlers playing in the fun house area all these fast-food outlets now seem to have.

I'd spent the entire weekend with my client and hadn't regretted one minute of it. I don't know if I was ready to start using that four-letter word that rhymes with dove, but I wanted the relationship to continue; nevertheless, I was frustrated. I'd gotten close to Frankie Rizzoli, and yet I hadn't been able to capitalize on the fact. Instead, I'd allowed myself to be ambushed and banged up.

I sipped my coffee and watched a turf war unfolding in front of me in the play area. A little boy and girl were squabbling over possession of a swing. They reminded me of the two tykes I'd seen across the street from Scarborough's house, where little brother ruined big sister's rope jumping. As the fight over the swing continued, Mom bent down between the two combatants and tried to arbitrate. She didn't have much success and finally gave up. Grabbing the two of them by their chubby little arms, she dragged them off the battlefield. Not even a Happy Meal could resolve this sibling rivalry. My thoughts drifted around to Carla and Frankie. I wondered if something as simple as a spat had precipitated the split between this brother and sister.

A glance at my watch told me I still had well over an hour before I was due to pick up Carla. Enough of this sitting around and musing about what hadn't happened with this case. Time to do some prying. I finished off my coffee, disposed of my trash, and set out for Larch Street, hoping that Phil Scarborough was one of those guys who liked spending Sunday mornings with the paper and televised sports.

SCARBOROUGH'S HYUNDAI VERACRUZ WAS IN THE driveway. No sign of Curran's red Toyota RAV4. I parked and walked up to the front door. As before, the Venetian blinds were closed. I knocked on the screen door and half expected someone to peek out between the slats. Damned if I wasn't disappointed. The blinds parted, I saw an eyeball, and then it disappeared. After a moment, the front door opened and Scarborough stood behind the screen. I was correct on both counts. He had a section of the paper in one hand, and over his right shoulder, I could see a basketball game in progress on a television set. The unmistakable smell of marijuana wafted through the mesh of the screen. He was barefoot, his hair was disheveled, and stubble covered his face. He wore cut-off jeans and a long-sleeved blue denim shirt over a white tee with a breast pocket containing a pack of cigarettes. In his mouth was a wad of chewing gum he worked like it was going to be his only meal of the day.

"Phil Scarborough?"

"Who wants to know?"

I put my license up against the screen so he could see it. "Eddie Collins. I'm a private investigator."

He looked at the ID and said, "You private dicks work on the Sabbath?"

"I'm Seventh-day Adventist."

My response caught him off guard. He folded up the newspaper and tossed it on a sofa behind him. "Sounds like you're also kind of a smart-ass. What do you want?"

I debated whether or not I should tip him off that I knew about his and Curran's visit to Carla's house. I decided against it, figuring that my knowledge might serve to put her in further danger. "I'm trying to find an Army buddy of yours, Frankie Rizzoli."

Mention of the name caused the chewing of the cud to momentarily cease. "Who hired you?"

"That's none of your business." I saw a flash of anger in his eyes, and he stepped a little closer to the screen. "Any idea where this Rizzoli is?" I said.

"I didn't make many friends in the Army."

"I'm told when you mustered out, you called Rizzoli's parents out in Henderson, Nevada, looking for him."

Again, he looked like he'd been caught with his hand in the cookie jar. Then he started to work on the gum again and gazed down at his feet, pretending to be deep in thought. "Henderson ... Henderson. That's by Vegas, right?"

"So I'm told."

"Right, right. Yeah, now that you mention it, I spent a few days hitting the slots. Thought I'd look him up."

"Did you find him?"

"No."

"I'm also told you were involved in a shooting incident down on Crocker."

"Yeah, it was the damnedest thing. I got jumped by a couple of punks." He took off the denim shirt and pointed to the remnant of a bandage sticking out from under the right sleeve of the tee. "Will you look at this, for crissakes?" He seemed to be bragging, as if he'd taken one for the team. "They got me in the shoulder."

I glanced at the bandage, but that wasn't what caught my eye. On his left forearm was a tattoo of a lightning bolt. One I'd seen before. On the same arm of a guy choking me down on Skid Row. Scarborough walked over to the sofa and tossed the denim shirt over it. He ambled back to the door and pulled the pack of cigarettes from his T-shirt and fired up one of them.

"The Lakers and Knicks are in a helluva tussle, Collins. We about done here?"

"Word on the street is that Frankie may have been a witness to that incident down on Crocker. He might even have been involved. Was he?"

"I have no idea."

I pulled one of the pictures out of my shirt pocket and held it up to the screen door. It was the shot of the two MPs. "This is Frankie with a guy by the name of James Curran. He's on the right. You recognize him, don't you?"

"The black guy? Hey, man, you know, put 'em in a dark room and all you'll see is the whites of their eyes."

He uttered a guttural laugh. I watched his jaws working on the wad of gum and had a sudden urge to make him swallow the damn thing.

"His red Toyota RAV4 was parked in your driveway a few days ago. I talked to the man. He stood right where you're standing, while you played peek-a-boo behind those Venetian blinds. So let's quit the tap dancing, pal, what do you say?"

He took a drag off the cigarette and blew it toward me as he worked on the wad of gum. "How come you seem to know so much about me?"

"I'm the smart-ass private dick, remember? The one that works on the Sabbath."

He exhaled a cloud of smoke and leaned against the doorjamb. "Curran and I have business dealings."

"What kind of dealings?"

"That's none of your business."

He had me there. I looked up as another plane zeroed in on LAX. "Those dealings include a guy by the name of Kenny Mickelson?"

"No. I just play golf with Kenny."

"He runs Feline Follies. You ever been in there?"

"Couple of times."

"I hear you're a big tipper."

"Oh, yeah? Who told you that?"

"One of the girls. Velvet La Rose."

"Yeah, I like her. Nice tits."

I prefer to think of myself as a patient man. Right now I had all I could do to restrain myself from yanking open the screen door and reconfiguring this little slimeball's unshaven face.

"So you don't know the whereabouts of Frankie Rizzoli? Is that what you're telling me?"

"That's what I'm telling you."

I stuck one of my cards between the screen door and the jamb. "Give me a call if your amnesia clears up." I started down the sidewalk.

"Hey, Collins."

"What?"

"Did you go to church yesterday?"

"That's also none of your business."

CHAPTER TWENTY

IT WAS A FEW MINUTES BEFORE one o'clock when I drove into the Feline Follies parking lot. I sent Carla a text telling her I was waiting, then listened to Merle Haggard sing "Things Have Gone to Pieces." The ol' Okie from Muskogee's twang brought me around to my own predicament. Who the hell had roughed me up when I was pretending to be homeless down on Skid Row? From the description Carla had given me, the tattoo on the guy's arm had left no doubt in my mind it was her brother. But now I'd just seen the same tattoo on Phil Scarborough's arm. So was it Scarborough or Frankie who'd choked me? The two of them had been in Iraq at the same time. Was this lightning bolt tattoo some sort of a unit patch? A badge of solidarity? To what?

Merle didn't have any answers. I didn't either. But I was sure of one thing: I'd caught Scarborough in a pack of lies. He damn well knew Frankie Rizzoli. Curran, Scarborough, and Carla's brother bounced around in my head. All three were in Iraq, most likely at the same time. They'd all mustered out and now were in the Los Angeles area. Doing what? Frankie had disappeared and reached out to his sister to tell her he was in trouble. What kind of trouble? Did Curran and Scarborough have something to do with that trouble? I had plenty of questions, but no answers yet, and it bugged the hell out of me.

I pushed the questions aside when I saw Carla come out of the club. It was a bright, sunny Sunday afternoon and her appearance made it even better. I gave Merle a break and tapped my horn. She spotted me and started toward the car. A smile broke out on her face, and pure pleasure washed over me. As I watched her, I couldn't fathom how she could be caught up in this intrigue involving these three guys.

She stuck her head through the passenger window. "Are you my stage-door Eddie?" She crawled into the car, then leaned over and kissed me. "Take me someplace."

"How about Venice Beach?"

"Perfect," she said, as she buckled up her seatbelt.

I waited for a stretch limo to glide past and pulled out onto Century Boulevard, headed west. "And how many oglers did you tantalize today?"

"Not many. But there were a couple of business types who started on their happy hour a little early."

"Troublemakers?"

"Not when they kept slipping twenties under my garter."

I laughed and shook my head. "Well, tomorrow you'll start making some real money."

"I know, and I am *so* pumped up. You ever get that way before a job, Eddie?"

"Yeah, when I was young and eager."

"Oh, my poor, decrepit private eye." She poked me in the ribcage and started tickling me.

"Hey, no fooling around with the driver," I said, as I grabbed her hand and tried to put it back in her lap.

"Maybe later?"

"Definitely later," I said.

"Are you telling me you don't feel excited about going in front of the camera?"

"More like terrified."

"Why?"

"That I can't remember the words anymore."

She punched me on the shoulder. "Bull. I don't believe you. What did you do while I was collecting twenty-dollar bills?"

"I went and talked to Phil Scarborough."

"Tell, tell. You find out anything?"

"Not much. He stonewalled me." I related the gist of my conversation with Scarborough as I hung a left on Lincoln Boulevard and began threading my way up into Marina Del Rey. "His lies weren't the big surprise, though."

"Really? What else?"

"He's got a tattoo of a lightning bolt."

"Are you kidding me?"

"Same place. On his left forearm."

"Oh, Eddie, that is too weird."

"Maybe not."

"Why?"

"If he and Frankie were in the same outfit in Iraq, they could have had them put on as some sort of unofficial unit designation, a camaraderie thing." I veered off to the curb as an ambulance barreled toward us. After it passed, I waited for two vehicles behind me before I could edge back into traffic. "But that raises a wrinkle in this whole thing."

"What?"

"Who the hell was it that choked me down on Skid Row?"

"Scarborough's wearing a sling, isn't he? Could he physically do it?"

"His right arm is the one that took the bullet."

"Yeah, right." Carla was silent as we crossed Culver Boulevard and found ourselves behind a muscle pickup looking for someplace to park and having no success. I turned and saw her looking out the window. "You all right?"

"If it was Scarborough who choked you, that means maybe Frankie really is dead."

I reached over and squeezed her hand. "Not necessarily. We can't jump to that conclusion. My Skid Row informant said Frankie may have been involved in that Crocker shooting. If that's true, your brother is out there."

"That's a big 'if.' Just because some derelict says so doesn't make it true."

"We don't know for sure, Carla. Let's not go there, okay?"

"Okay."

The driver of the pickup in front of us saw someone about to pull out. He abruptly stopped and I was ready to hit my horn when he waved me around. Of course I had to wait for the cars behind me. "I found out why Scarborough was probably backstage at Feline Follies, though."

"Why?"

"He said he plays golf with this boss of yours, Kenny Mickelson."

Carla burst into laughter. "That's crazy."

"What's crazy about it?"

"Kenny doesn't play golf."

"How do you know?"

"Because he's only got one arm."

Being rear-ended could not have startled me more. I yanked the car over to the curb into a red zone and jammed it into park. "You have got to be kidding me."

"No. He lost most of it in Iraq." She indicated a spot on her left arm. "This one. From just above the elbow. I've seen the stump. It's creepy. He said it was an IED explosion."

"Then Scarborough's got some other connection to Mickelson."

I drummed my fingers on the steering wheel. Now another Iraq veteran had entered the picture. "Does the club allow just anybody back there where you girls have your dressing room?"

"It's very rare. Junior and Tommy, the other bouncer, are real protective of that area."

"Ah, Christ, this is getting crazier every day. What the hell are these guys trying to cover up?"

"Do you think Frankie knows … or knew Mickelson too?"

"I can't say, Carla. But I do know one thing."

"What?"

"I think better on a full stomach and a cold beer."

CHAPTER TWENTY-ONE

———◆———

VENICE BEACH CAN BE DANGEROUS, IF one has the desire to do some serious thinking, that is. Sensory overload is inescapable. When we finally found a parking space and walked out onto the boardwalk, a virtual smorgasbord of theatricality confronted us. Jugglers juggled everything except chainsaws; even a unicyclist juggled. Acrobats contorted on the sand. A mime made like a statue, defying anyone to break his concentration. The hunks on Muscle Beach grunted, strutted, and preened. I ached just watching them and instead devoted my attention to three bikini-clad rollerbladers, for which I received a poke in the ribs from my companion.

After waiting patiently, Carla and I had secured a table by the front window of a nice Mexican cantina. We'd polished off a basket of chips and salsa, along with two sweating bottles of Dos Equis. The Most Interesting Man in the World didn't appear, so we ordered another round and started to dig into our main courses. She had *arroz con pollo* and I opted for *tacos de pescado*, aka chicken with rice and fish tacos.

Her appetite was something to behold. I'd come to realize that the way she attacked her food was symbolic of how she approached everything. Zest was the word that came to mind. She was passionate. About her upcoming movie, performing at Feline Follies, her brother and his puzzling disappearance, and I hoped, me. I watched her as I sipped on my beer. She looked up and caught my eye.

"So, are you thinking better now?" she said.

"Yup."

"About what?"

"I was wondering if that arm they took off Kenny Mickelson had a tattoo on it."

My remark caught her with a forkful of rice headed for her mouth. She dropped it and burst into what could best be described as a guffaw. "And how were those fish tacos, Mr. Collins?"

"They were fine. Now, come on, confess. Don't you wonder the same thing?"

"Yes," she said, as she refilled the fork. "It seems almost inevitable, doesn't it?"

"You should try to figure out some way to get him to talk about it."

"I guess I can try." She chewed on a mouthful of chicken and rice and gazed out the window. "God, it's beginning to look like Frankie was in some kind of sinister club or something."

"Hey, hey, no past tense. Remember? 'Is, is.' "

"Yeah, okay. But you see what I'm saying?"

"I do. Those tattoos looked too similar to be coincidental. If Curran has the same thing on his arm, there's a bigger link among the three of them."

"I hope it's nothing illegal."

"Frankie ever get into trouble when you were growing up?"

"Oh, no. Our folks wouldn't tolerate anything like that."

"You told me he enlisted after 9/11, right?"

"Yes. And then he re-upped. Made my dad mad all over again."

"So that's six years in uniform." I sipped on my Dos Equis and watched two young black kids set a boombox on the sidewalk and start break dancing. "And you don't know what happened to him after he got out?"

"No. It's like he just disappeared."

"Why did he go into the MPs?"

"What do you mean?"

"There's no draft anymore. Enlistees can choose their MOS."

"MO what?"

"Their Military Occupational Specialty. If he wanted to respond to 9/11, why didn't he choose the infantry?"

She gazed out the window and shook her head. "That's a good question. I don't know."

I vividly remembered the intense fervor on the part of some in the wake of those buildings coming down. Recruiting offices experienced an onrush of enlistees, clamoring for revenge. But if these guys, like Frankie, felt they had an ax to grind, why not put themselves in a situation where they could pick up a rifle and shoot somebody? Military policemen weren't exactly on the front line.

Our waitress came up to the table and asked if we would like anything else.

I raised my bottle of beer, indicating I'd have another, and looked to Carla. She did the same, and pushed her plate to the edge where it was whisked away by the server.

"Do you have any siblings, Eddie?"

"A sister. Deborah. Back in Wichita, Kansas."

"Are you Uncle Eddie?"

"Yeah. She married Walt Griffin. He's an architect. They've got a boy and a girl. Danny is twelve, and Emily is … oh, boy, let me think … seventeen, I guess."

"Are you close?"

"As close as half a continent allows. They've visited a time or two. Done the whole tourist thing. Disneyland, the beach." I finished off my beer and looked at her. Her head was cocked to one side and she had a smile on her face. "What's the matter?" I said. "Didn't I pass muster?"

"With flying colors. The kids think it's cool to have an actor for an uncle?"

"They used to. I think the charm has worn off by now."

"I'll bet it hasn't." She picked up a chip and nibbled on it for a moment. "I never asked you before. Were you ever married?"

I looked at her and grinned. "Are we playing Twenty Questions here?"

"I'm sorry, Eddie. I'm being nosy. You don't have to tell me."

"No, it's okay. I was married once. It was on the rocks by the time I first met you."

"An actress?"

"Yeah."

"Are you still friends?"

"We were. More or less," I said, debating with myself over how much to share. "She died a while back."

"I'm sorry," Carla said and reached over to grab my hand.

"Truth be told, she was murdered."

"Oh, my God. What happened?"

I glanced out the window and saw a guy walking on stilts and dressed up like Abe Lincoln. I cleared my throat and told her of the murder of my ex-wife, Elaine Weddington, and the circumstances surrounding it. After I finished we were silent until the waitress walked up with two fresh bottles of beer. She took our empties and moved off.

Carla took a sip and said, "Did you have any kids?"

I took a swallow of the beer and again had the internal debate about how much I was willing to reveal. I decided to go the distance.

"We had a girl, but she gave her up for adoption. This happened after we split. I've never seen her."

"Do you know where she is?"

"Cincinnati."

"Do you ever want to see her?"

"I go back and forth. Sometimes I think it's none of my business. Other times I'd kind of like for her to get to know who her mother was. The career she had."

We sipped from our beer bottles and looked out the window at the kaleidoscopic scene before us. Our reverie was interrupted by my cellphone. I pulled it out and looked at the screen. The number was unfamiliar. I put it to my ear.

"Hello."

"Mr. Collins?"

"You got him."

"Yeah, this is Floyd McGinty. Over on Acama?"

A burst of coughing filled my ear. I held the phone away from my head and said to Carla, "Frankie's former landlord."

She pointed to the rear of the bar. "I'll be right back." She gathered up her bag and headed for the powder room.

The coughing subsided and McGinty came back on the line. "You there, Collins?"

"Yes, sir. What's up, Mr. McGinty?"

"Hey, I got to thinkin' after I talked to you. I remember a couple of guys come lookin' for Rizzoli one day."

"You recall what they looked like?"

"One for sure. A black guy. Not many of those around this place. Now you didn't hear it from me, y'understand, but I don't think the owner rents to them. The other guy was white. But here's the thing ...." Whatever the "thing" was had to wait for another round of coughing. "The thing is, they were both in uniform. Army uniforms. Those camouflage jobbies, y'know, like they wear in the desert?"

"I gotcha," I said, as I pulled out my notebook. "Can you tell me when that would have been, Mr. McGinty?" The answer had to wait for another burst of coughing.

"I'd have to guess," he said. "But I went lookin' through my books here. Rizzoli's apartment was cleaned out in June of 2012. Couldn't a been more than a week after those cops took him away. So I'm thinkin' those two Army guys showed up a couple years earlier. Summer of 2010, maybe? Understand I'm only guessin', though, y'know?" I held the phone away from my ear again while the sounds of more phlegm on the rise filled the airwaves.

"I understand. I appreciate the information."

"Yeah, well, you told me to call."

"And I'm glad you did, sir. Take care of that cough." After I broke the connection, I jotted the dates in the notebook. Carla returned and scrunched her chair up to the table.

"What did he have to say?"

"We've got a little better idea where your brother might have been in the last few years." I shared the dates McGinty had given me. "Two GIs, one black, one white, showing up at Frankie's apartment tells me they were Curran and Scarborough."

"Then what about the cops, Eddie? Doesn't that tell us that he was," I opened my mouth to interrupt, "sorry, *is* involved in something illegal?"

"I honestly don't know, Carla. The only way to find out is to smoke him out. Wherever the hell he is."

I paid the check and we walked along the boardwalk for an hour or so until the sun started to paint sheets of glass on the ocean. I drove to her place and parked in the driveway behind her Honda Fit.

"What time's your call again?" I asked.

"Eight."

"That means you've gotta get up at the crack of dawn."

"At least." She unbuckled her seatbelt and leaned over to me, her face inches from mine. "Will you be my alarm o'clock?"

"If the birds don't beat me to it," I said.

Chapter Twenty-Two

———— ◆ ————

THERE WAS NO NEED FOR AN avian alarm clock; the buzzer went off while it was still dark. Carla punched the infernal thing into silence, rolled over, and slid one arm over my chest.

"Are you ready for your close-up, Miss Rizzoli?" I said.

"I'm ready for coffee." Her hand started making circles and then began drifting downward. "Damn, I'm ready for this too, but I better not, right?"

"You're asking me? I'm the out-of-work actor. But I think that's probably a good idea. How does your coffee pot work? I'll brew, you get yourself ready."

"I suppose." She sat up on the edge of the bed and I ran my fingers up her back. "Don't use the electric coffee pot. I've got one of those Keurigs. Great for individual cups. You know how to use it?"

"I'll figure it out."

She switched on a bedside lamp and padded off to the bathroom, once again providing a morning sight I hadn't enjoyed in some time. I got dressed, carried my overnight bag into the kitchen, and brushed my teeth over the sink. I'd seen one of these Keurig coffee makers in action before. *Might be a good thing to have in the office*, I thought, as I poked through the assortment of little packets. The contraption brewed a cup and I pushed open the bathroom door. Steam swirled and Carla was doing vocal warm-ups under the shower.

"Your coffee awaits, madam."

"Thank you, kind sir." She opened the shower curtain and peered around the edge. "They'll have breakfast there, right?"

"More breakfast than you could ever wish for." Which was true. Movie locations are famous for the quality and quantity of chow. Well-fed crews make for efficient film shoots.

Carla opened the shower curtain a little farther, put one foot on the edge of the tub, and swayed her glistening leg back and forth. "Too bad you got dressed, mister. You could have washed my back." I didn't think it possible anything could be so alluring this early in the morning. I was wrong.

"You better give me a rain check," I said.

She flicked some water at me and slid the curtain shut. I brewed myself a cup of French Roast, carried my bag into the living room, and turned on the TV set. Monday morning reality filled the airwaves. Bombings, shootings, and mayhem everywhere. If it bleeds, it leads, as the adage goes. I did some channel surfing and settled on an old movie with Burt Lancaster playing an Indian, obviously before politically correct casting became the norm.

I switched it off when Carla came in, coffee cup in hand. She wore a UCLA sweatshirt, jeans, and sneakers. She set her coffee cup on a table and rummaged through her tote bag.

"What do you think, Eddie? Should I take this with me?"

I turned and saw her holding up her handgun. "Probably not. You don't want to shoot your director, at least not on your first day. Besides, you never know who goes through those honey wagons." I was referring to the mobile dressing rooms used on movie sets. "I'd lock it in your car."

"Good idea." She stuffed her script into her tote bag, then grabbed a baseball cap off a peg, popped it on her head, and handed my hat and jacket to me. When I had them on, she wrapped her arms around me and tilted her face up to mine. "I really enjoyed being with you this weekend, my own private eye."

I leaned down and kissed her. We held it for a long moment and then broke apart. "Me too," I said. "What say we find your brother so we can take this private-eye business out of the equation?"

"I couldn't agree with you more." She kissed me again. Keys and coffee in hand, she doused the lights and we stepped out into the morning darkness. It was a tad chilly. A soft breeze stirred the wind chime and brought the aroma of night-blooming jasmine. Made sense. After all, we were on Jasmine Avenue. Carla set her coffee cup on top of her car, unlocked the hatchback, and stuffed her handgun under the mat.

"Do you have a jacket?" I said. "Might be a little cool up there before midday."

"Got one in the backseat."

"Directions?"

She pulled a sheet of paper from the tote bag. "Aye-aye, sir. Do you think the 405 will be crowded?"

"Who knows? But you're leaving early enough. Should be okay. Send me a text later on if you're free. I'll be anxious to hear how it's going."

"I will. And I'll call you tonight, okay?"

"Sounds good." I climbed into my car and backed out of the driveway. She followed me as I turned left on Culver, then right on Overland, past Sony, and up to Venice. I sat in the right-hand lane and waited for the light. Carla pulled up next to me, intending to turn left for the freeway. She slid her window down and blew me a kiss.

"Have a good day, Mr. PI."

"You too," I said. "Knock 'em dead."

We got a green and turned in different directions, she to a movie shoot, me to my little cubicle of an office where a puzzle still waited to be solved. I was envious of her being on a film location; at the same time, I was anxious to find the elusive Frankie Rizzoli.

Thankfully it was early enough for me to get back into Hollywood before Mavis arrived. The sight of her boss coming home with an overnight bag would no doubt prompt endless questions. I won't say Mavis pries, but she is definitely curious about what her employer is up to. And I can't really complain. Over the years, she's become a solid partner and a sounding board for the cases I've handled.

If traffic conditions allow, Venice Boulevard can become a mini-freeway. And so it was as I headed east, mulling over a wonderful weekend with Carla and the progress of my search for her brother. Even though I was reluctant, another trip to Skid Row and both the Union Rescue and Midnight Missions was necessary. It could be Frankie knew or had been seen by someone hanging around these two institutions. The attachment I was starting to feel for Carla also put to rest my reluctance to go back downtown. I was still of the opinion that Frankie had choked me, regardless of how many of these damn lightning-bolt tattoos surfaced.

I crossed over Redondo Boulevard and spied what could be the dissipation of the mini-freeway. Flashing lights caused traffic in front of me to slow, and then stop. The trouble appeared to be at the intersection of Venice and La Brea, which was, of course, where I wanted to turn left and head north into Hollywood.

I inched along, trying to find some report on the radio about the accident. Nothing. The sun started to peek over the horizon and into my eyes. *Terrific.* Now I was sitting and just waiting for someone to rear-end me. Driving in La La Land. What an adventure.

The vehicle queue finally approached the intersection and I looked at the damage. A Mercedes trying to make a left-hand turn apparently had been T-boned by an SUV headed west, which then caromed into another SUV going south. La Brea was closed and cops were routing northbound traffic onto Highland, which therefore became a bottleneck.

After nearly forty-five minutes, congestion eased and I glided through Hancock Park and into Hollywood. I glanced at my watch. It looked like I'd beaten the arrival of my inquisitor. Or so I thought.

When I tried the key in my office door, it was already unlocked. Mavis sat behind her desk, eyes fixed on her computer screen. She wore a pale-yellow blouse and a light-green scarf around her neck, which was cinched up with a gold ring.

"Morning," I said.

"Good morning."

I sat down in the chair in front of her desk. "What are you doing here so early?"

"I had to get an order shipped. I left you a message on Saturday telling you that. Didn't you get it?"

"No."

She picked up her coffee cup and sipped, then pointed to the overnight bag in my lap. "What's with the bag? Don't tell me you've been to a gym?"

"I was visiting a friend."

The look on her face told me I wasn't going to crawl out of this hole easily.

"This better be good. Sit right there. I need a another cup."

She went into her little private cubicle and returned with a refill. *Here it comes*, I thought. She sat down and looked at me for a moment, a very long moment.

"Well, am I going to have to pry it out of you?" she said.

"I guess not. I spent the weekend with Carla."

"Carla. As in your client?"

"Right."

"Do you think that was a good idea?"

"Turned out to be a wonderful idea."

"She came in here only a week ago, Eddie."

"Yeah. But I knew her prior to that. Before I opened up the business."

She eyed me over the rim of her coffee cup, a look I'd seen before, one that required me to give her more information without her having to ask.

"Is that it?" she said.

"What can I tell you, kiddo? I find her very attractive."

"I see. Did you work on the case?"

"I did."

"Any progress? On the case, that is."

"I don't know yet. Tell you what. Let me get showered and shaved and I'll bring you up to speed. I've also got some computer searches that need your magic." I stood up and headed for my office. "You ever use one of those Keurig coffee makers?"

"Fritz and I have one at home."

"Really? We should get one for the office."

"Not a bad idea. Then you won't have to keep nuking stuff that should go into the La Brea Tar Pits."

I must admit, she does have a way with words. I glanced through the mail on my desk and pawed through the beaded curtain into my apartment. Shower, shave, and change of clothes accomplished, I nuked a cup of tar and found a bagel ready to apply for fossilhood. I started gnawing it into submission and went back to the front office.

Mavis was weighing a small box. She took her seat and folded her hands in anticipation. "Okay, Romeo, fill me in."

I did so. She asked some pertinent questions and expressed genuine surprise at the revelation of yet another lightning-bolt tattoo.

"Isn't there an Army unit with that kind of patch?"

"Yeah, the 25th Infantry. But the tattoo on Scarborough's and Frankie's arms is a little different."

"Sounds to me like your client's—"

"You can call her Carla."

Her lips actually formed a little grin as she continued, "Sounds to me like Carla's brother may be involved with some shady characters."

"Could be, but I hope not." I broke off a chunk of the bagel and dipped it into my coffee cup. It didn't help much.

"So, what do you want done on the computer?"

"Can you expand on that search you did on Enigma Productions?"

"No problem. What am I looking for?"

"I want to see if there's any connection between it and Feline Follies. Ownership, financial dealings, management, things like that."

"Are you suggesting money laundering?"

"You took the words out of my mouth."

"Okay." She made some notes on a pad of paper and watched as I dunked the bagel in my coffee. "What are you going to do today? After ruining your dental work, that is."

"The only possible location I've got for Frankie is down on Skid Row. I don't think he's moved to Brentwood. So I'm going to do some more snooping. I need to check with the people at both the Union Rescue Mission and the Midnight Mission. Maybe it'll turn up something."

"You're going to have to get a room down there," she said.

I started back to my apartment with the cup of tar and the partially eaten fossil. "Tonight I stay home," I said, then stuck my head back through the door. "In case you were wondering."

CHAPTER TWENTY-THREE

———— ◆ ————

B OTH THE UNION RESCUE AND MIDNIGHT Missions are on San Pedro, so a single parking space allowed me to walk between the two. Nothing had changed since I'd been down here before. That's not surprising, I suppose. To those whose existence has been narrowed down to a cardboard box, a shopping cart, and two or three square blocks, life isn't exactly a day at the beach.

On the way to the front door of the Union Mission, someone had constructed a virtual cave using a tarp and an inverted bed frame. The inventiveness of the homeless is awe-inspiring. A young man sat on a bicycle at the curb. He wore a tattered raincoat and stared off into the distance, as if trying to remember where his wheels were supposed to take him.

I walked inside and up to the counter. Mounted on the wall behind was the logo of the organization, a stylized rendering of someone holding out their arms under a couple of lines representing a roof. A burly black man with salt-and-pepper hair leaned over a computer. He was dressed in khakis and a white shirt and red-striped tie. A nameplate on his shirt pocket identified him as Thomas. He looked up as I approached.

"Good morning, sir. How can I help you?"

"My name is Eddie Collins. I'm a private investigator." I showed him my license and then pulled out the picture of Frankie and showed it to him. "I'm trying to locate this gentleman. His name is Frankie Rizzoli, also known as Francis. The photo was taken when he was in the army. It's a few years old by now. Does the name ring a bell? Or the face happen to look familiar?"

Thomas looked closely at the picture, finally putting on a pair of reading glasses. "The eyes aren't what they used to be."

"Yeah, I know what you mean," I said.

He sat at the computer and held the picture closer to the light coming from the screen. "The name doesn't ring a bell, but then, that's not unusual. We get an awful lot of guys coming through here."

"How about the face? He could have a beard."

Thomas picked up an index card and covered the bottom part of Frankie's face. "I usually remember the eyes. When they walk in here, that's the first thing I notice. They're as good as any means of identification." He continued to look at the photo and said, "Like I mentioned, his name doesn't ring a bell, but his face looks familiar."

"Does the Mission house people?" I said. "Would he be listed on some sort of roster you keep?"

"That's a possibility," he said, as he handed the photo back to me. "Let me check."

He started clicking on his keyboard and I watched the different light patterns from the screen bounce across his face. He paused and leaned in for a closer look. "Well, now, let's see. Back in August of 2013 we had a Francis Rizzoli in our shelter for a few days."

"Could you tell me how long he was here?"

Thomas pointed to a section of the screen. "Looks like it was only from the sixth through the tenth of August." I jotted the dates in my notebook. "As you can imagine, our turnover is considerable."

"Thank you very much for your time," I said as I handed him one of my cards. "If you happen to think of anything else regarding Mr. Rizzoli, I'd appreciate hearing from you."

"You bet," he said, and stood up to shake my hand. "I hope when you find him, he's doing well."

I nodded and walked back out to San Pedro. The young man on the bicycle must have remembered where he was going, because he was gone. I started walking toward the Midnight Mission, somewhat heartened by the knowledge that the phantom known as Frankie or maybe Francis Rizzoli had surfaced after being evicted from his apartment on Acama Street. The question was, where the hell was he now?

THE MAN BEHIND THE RECEPTION COUNTER inside the Midnight Mission reminded me of the Hispanic actor René Enríquez, who played Lt. Ray Calletano on the television series *Hill Street Blues*. His name was Carlos. He was short and had a bit of a paunch. Jet-black hair surrounded a bald dome. He wiped a sheen of perspiration off it with a handkerchief. I showed him the picture, and while he said Frankie looked familiar, he wasn't sure. I thanked him and gave him the obligatory card with the request to give me a call if he remembered anything. As I left, he was being hassled by two women quarreling over a newspaper. I wasn't hopeful of getting a call anytime in the future.

The area between the front door and the iron gate leading to the street was called the Wallis Annenberg Courtyard. Concrete benches provided a place for the wayfarers to take a load off their feet. A kiosk next to a couple of payphones overflowed with offers of employment and pictures of homeless being sought with numbers to call. Blood plasma donations were needed. Alcoholics Anonymous meetings were listed.

I leaned against a light post and took in the scene. An elderly gent wearing a dented white hard hat, a plaid shirt, and soiled jeans expounded on something having to do with the government. I'm not sure what it was exactly since his speech was garbled. He was getting attention, however—not because of his diatribe, but because his pants kept falling down. He repeatedly had to grab them before they hit the concrete. His performance got jeers and catcalls from those within hearing distance.

I made the rounds with my photo and my questions, but got nothing in return except requests for money and cigarettes. One guy said he was starting school at UCLA and needed help with his tuition. I had to admire his chutzpah. After ten minutes or so I took a seat on one of the benches next to an elderly black woman wrapped in two ragged shawls and wearing a scarf on her head. Her face was wrinkled. She was munching a donut with what appeared to be only a few teeth. Sneakers that had seen better days were on her feet and she wore a pair of faded khaki trousers. She watched me jotting down some notes.

"Ain't havin' much luck, are ya?" she said.

"Excuse me?"

"I been watchin' you axin' your questions. You wearin' that nice uptown hat and all, but you still comin' up empty."

I chuckled and said, "Yeah, looks that way."

"You ain't axed me."

I glanced at her. *Okay*, I thought, and showed her the photo. "All right. Have you seen a guy that looks like him? His name's Frankie."

"That's what I hear."

"You know this guy?"

"No suh. But my friend Willie do."

"Where's Willie?"

She put two fingers in her mouth and let out a whistle heard throughout the courtyard. A few crumbs flew out with the whistle and she brushed them off her chin. She gestured to a black man sitting against the wall of the Mission.

"Hey, Willie. Come here, man."

Willie climbed to his feet and shuffled across the courtyard in our direction. Somewhere in his thirties, he wore a black watch cap, a faded army fatigue jacket over a green sweatshirt and cargo pants, and scuffed desert combat boots.

"Wassup, Babs?"

"Sit your black ass down here and talk to this man."

Willie eyed me, not sure he wanted anything to do with this dude wearing an uptown porkpie hat. He pulled a rumpled pack of cigarettes from a pocket and lit one.

"What you want?"

"You know a guy by the name of Frankie? Frankie Rizzoli?" I handed him the photo and he cocked his head as he looked at it and blew smoke out of the side of his mouth.

"I seen him around."

"Can you tell me when? Where?"

"Nah, I ain't seen him in a week or so."

Babs reached across me and whacked Willie on the leg. "Fool, tell him 'bout that thing went down on Crocker."

"What about Crocker?" I said. "There was a shooting there a while back, right?"

"Thass right," Willie said.

"Was Frankie involved?"

"Could be."

"Tell me what you know, Willie. I'll make it worth your while."

"How you gonn' do that?"

"I'll lay some money on you," I said, as I reached into my pocket. "But I don't want you telling anyone. All right? I don't want somebody jumping my ass when I walk out of here."

"Nah, man, I be cool."

I separated four twenties and gave two to Willie and two to Babs.

"Sweet Baby Jesus," she said. "Thank you, Mr. Uptown Hat."

"Come on, Willie," I said. "What went down?"

Willie stuffed the money in his fatigue jacket before anyone could notice, took a puff off his cigarette, then squeezed the hot end off and put what was left back in the pack.

"There's this warehouse on Crocker between Seventh and Eighth. Across the street's a Dumpster in front of a paper company. They have a truck come by in the afternoon and empty it. There's this fence, see, and I sometimes climb over and crawl into the Dumpster. I can get me some shuteye for a few hours, nobody hasslin' me. So I'm there, see, and all of a sudden there's guns goin' off, man. I peek my head out and see cops drawin' down on this black SUV. Then I see Frankie crawlin' outta the back of the damn thing."

"How did you know it was Frankie?" I said.

" 'Cuz he was wearing this crazy-ass jungle hat, man. And he had a brown leather jacket, looked like shit. We'd shared a joint that afternoon, and that's what he was wearin.'"

"What happened to him?"

"He starts barrelin' down the street. All of a sudden this cop car comes around the corner. Not a squad car. One of those plain ones."

"How'd you know it was a cop car?"

"Had one of those bubble lights on the dashboard. You know? Besides, you can spot something like that right away, man. Ugly brown thing, plain black tires."

"All right, so what happened?"

"One of the cops jumped out, grabbed Frankie's ass, and threw him in the backseat."

"And that's it?"

He nodded and fired up another cigarette. The orator with the falling-down pants had ended his spiel and walked past us, mumbling to himself, in search of another audience or some way to hold up his pants. Babs whacked Willie again.

"Go on, tell him what happened later. What you tol' me, Willie."

"Yeah," he said. He relished the cigarette for a couple of puffs, then continued, "So I watched an ambulance come and haul off this one dude who'd been shot and was lyin' in the street. The SUV peeled out, but there was only one police car and they didn't chase it; they was on their radios and shit. After the ambulance hauled the guy off, the police car left and things was quiet, you know? I had me a taste off a bottle I scored earlier, and was gettin' ready to crawl back into my crib when the goddamn plain cop car came around the corner and slammed to a stop. The back door opens, a cop drags Frankie out, and starts beatin' on him, man. Then the fucker jumps back in the car and they drive off."

"What did you do?" I said.

"Well, shit, I drag my ass outta the Dumpster and go to Frankie. He lyin' on the street, moanin' and groanin', man. I axed him if he all right, and he say, yeah, he's okay. I tell him he better come in here, to the Mission, you know. Get some help. He shake his head, get up, and stumble off down the street. I figure he know what he doin', so I crawl back in my crib and forget about it."

"Have you seen him since then, Willie?"

"Naw, man, I ain't seen him around. I hope he's okay. I mean, he's straight, man. Solid."

"Can you describe him for me?" I said. "Does he have a beard or anything?"

"Naw, man, he ain't got no beard. But he's got these long sideburns and one of those cookie dusters that droops down, you know. Real bushy."

"You mean a mustache?"

"Yeah, yeah, that's what they call it."

"How about his hair? Long? Short?"

"Long, man. Way down over his ears."

"Do you know if he's got a tattoo of any kind?"

"A tat?" He thought for a moment, then said, "I ain't ever seen no tats."

I made some notes for myself and put the notebook back in my pocket. "Thank you, guys. You've been a big help."

"Why you wanna find him, man?" Willie said.

"Somebody in his family is looking for him."

Willie nodded and I stood up and offered my hand to both of them. Willie's handshake was surprisingly firm, and he turned it into a fist bump. Babs stuffed the rest of her donut into her bag and squeezed my fingers.

"You take care, young man. Maybe one of these days I come uptown and get me one a them hats."

"I hope so, Babs. I do indeed."

CHAPTER TWENTY-FOUR

———◆———

I WALKED OUT OF THE WALLIS ANNENBERG Courtyard into sunshine that poked through the customary haze of the Los Angeles Basin. The glare bounced off panes of glass in the windows of a two-story building across the street. Above a door was a sign that said "Hot l." A hotel without the "e." An elderly black man leaned on the sill of an open window on the second floor, puffing on a cigarette. Eyeing me, he pointed to the top of his head and gave me a thumbs-up. My porkpie was getting rave reviews.

As I turned to go, another figure appeared in a window two openings to the right of the old black guy. It was a man, and he wore a jungle hat. His long sideburns and mustache were just like those Willie had described on Frankie. I stepped into the street and started to make my way toward the building when the guy turned and spotted me. He ducked back into the opening.

I walked up to the side of building and shouted up to the old black guy, "Somebody just popped his head out of a window over there." I pointed to his right. "The guy's got sideburns and a mustache. You know who he is?"

The black guy put his hand to his ear and shook his head. "Can't hear what you sayin', man."

"Two windows over to your right. A guy wearing one of those jungle hats. Can you tell me who he is?"

He cupped his hand to his ear again and said, "Yeah, man, I like that hat of yours. Where'd you git it?"

This conversation wasn't getting me anywhere. I walked over to the door below the sign and pulled it open. To the right was a directory above six mailboxes. One of them was without a door and a couple others had severe dents in them. The directory had intercom buttons next to each name slot, but there were no names listed. I had a strong suspicion the place was either a flophouse or a shooting gallery. The steel door leading to the inside of the building was locked. I went outside and walked back to the old black man's window. He was gone, and the window was shut. So was the one where the guy in the jungle hat had appeared. I stood beneath it and shouted out Frankie's name for a couple of minutes, but stopped when somebody across the street told me to quit acting like a fool and shut up.

I took his advice and started to walk away, convinced I had just seen where Frankie Rizzoli might be lying low. It made sense. The hotel without an "e" was a stone's throw from one of the missions, on whose letterhead his note to his sister had been written. Frankie knew what I looked like, which was reason enough for him to duck out of sight when he saw me.

I pulled the door open again and pressed the intercom button next to each of the tenants with a name. No one answered. I pushed the rest of them and got the same result. I knew at least two occupants were home, so it was apparent the intercom system wasn't working. I pushed the door open and jotted down the address, then looked up at the windows. Both of them were still shut.

The donut Babs had been gumming wasn't exactly appetizing, but it had nevertheless stirred a pang of hunger. It had been a while since I'd gnawed on my fossilized bagel. On the way back to my car, I spied a corner convenience store. A bell jangled as I pushed open the door. The clerk sat behind a wire-mesh cage reading a Korean-language newspaper. As I entered, he looked up, and I felt his eyes follow me as I plucked a can of beer out of a glass case. The pre-packaged sandwiches looked a bit dodgy, but I threw caution to the wind and grabbed a roast beef, along with a bag of chips.

"You want mayo?" the Korean clerk said.

"Yeah. Mustard too."

"Sure, you bet." He reached to his left and dropped a couple of packets of each into the bag. "I keep back here. All time they steal. No good." He forced a smile and nodded a few times as he took my money.

A young kid clutching a skateboard under one arm held the door open for me. I unlocked my car, crawled into the front seat, cracked the windows, and set about eating lunch. The mayo and mustard made valiant efforts, but as I mulled over my interview with the two homeless people, I felt like Charlie Chaplin eating his own shoe in *The Gold Rush*.

Willie's depiction of Frankie's presence at the police action on Crocker proved that he was alive. That was good news. But then, why was he pretending to be dead? And why the hell did the cops pick him up, beat the crap out of him, and then let him go? Carla's brother was becoming more of an enigma the deeper I dug into this investigation.

I gave up on the bogus sandwich, finished the chips and the beer, and pulled out my cellphone. My call to Charlie Rivers went to voicemail. I said I'd call him back later and shut off the phone. I was in a two-hour parking zone, so I fired up the car and moved it to 8th, in front of a boarded-up barbershop. I reached into the glove compartment and pulled out a small flashlight and a thin leather case containing my lock picks. I locked the front door, flipped up the lid of the trunk, and punched in a four-digit code on a small metal lockbox. Inside was my Beretta Bobcat 21. I wasn't sure I needed it, but I figured if I was going to snoop, it might come in handy. I checked the action, glanced around to make sure nobody was watching, and stuffed the handgun into the waistband at the small of my back.

Crocker was the next block up. I took the sidewalk across the street from the warehouse where I'd seen Scarborough and Curran unloading those wooden crates. Willie's Dumpster appeared on my left as a pickup came toward me. I stopped, leaned down, and tied my shoelace, all the while looking across the street. The building appeared to be half a football field in length. The sidewalk running along it was wider than normal. A slanted ramp interrupted the curb in front of a roll-up metal door that had a combination padlock on a hasp on one side. I didn't know if Frankie had access to the place, but he'd been seen in front of it. Either he was in cahoots with these guys, or they were chasing him. Seeing what was inside might give me an answer.

There was a gap between the building and a chain-link fence, on the other side of which sat another concrete building. The pickup passed, and I straightened up and walked across the street, trying to look inconspicuous.

When I came to the gap between the buildings, I glanced up and down the street. It was empty. I ducked into the passage and started for the back of the building, approximately a hundred feet away. I didn't know for certain if there was a rear exit, but I had to assume that fire regulations would require one. Of course, with these old buildings in this part of town, it was possible nobody heeded the fire department.

Tufts of dry grass sprouted from cracks in the pavement. Bits of paper and clothing littered the ground. Chunks of the concrete blocks were scattered under my feet. A tattered sleeping bag lay against the wall. Whoever used it last had evidently left it behind. The only windows were a couple of feet above me. They were those glass-block ones that let light through but don't allow anyone to see inside. The building on the other side of the chain-link fence was completely windowless. No activity anywhere around it. Another shell waiting for urban renewal.

I got to the end of the warehouse and peered around the corner. Nobody camping out. Running along the side of the building was a five-foot high wooden fence badly in need of repair. On the other side, stacks of wooden pallets were scattered over a small lot that looked to be the back end of a shipping company. Again, no activity.

I ducked below the fence and came up on a door. There were two locks on it—one in the knob, similar to the lock on Carla's front door, and another one above it. I turned the knob. Locked. This one shouldn't be a problem. I wasn't sure about the dead bolt, but nothing ventured, nothing gained, as the saying goes. I pulled out the leather case containing the picks and squatted on my haunches. I hadn't picked a lock in some time, and didn't profess to be an expert, but I kept at it for seven or eight minutes and finally was able to turn the knob. I pushed, but no dice. The dead bolt was locked also. Another few minutes and I heard the click and turned the knob. Bingo. As I put the picks back in my pocket, I mentally crossed my fingers and hoped I wouldn't encounter another hurdle—an alarm. Lady luck was on my side as I slowly pushed the door open and was met with no obstacles or warning sounds.

I shut the door behind me and stood for a moment, getting my bearings. The place smelled musty. I turned on my flashlight. To my immediate right was a makeshift hallway, flanked on one side by the exterior wall and on the other by a series of wide wooden shelves, much like stacks in a library. I could see spools of electric cable and piles of cords filling them. On the nearest shelves sat lights of various sizes.

To my left was another hallway, again flanked by the exterior wall, and yet another four feet away. At the end of this corridor sat a small water heater. Above it was an electric fuse box. In front of the heater, two wooden ladders were stacked against each other and leaning against the wall.

I took a few steps into the room and shined my light around the interior. The metal front door was at two o'clock. A refrigerator sat along the wall to my left. I pulled the door open. Two six packs of beer sat on one shelf. A single can had been pulled from one of the plastic yokes. A Styrofoam container sat on the top shelf. I opened it and quickly closed it again. Whatever the hell was in there was now a science project. The freezer compartment was empty.

Next to the refrigerator was a cot covered with a shabby blanket and a single pillow. In the corner was a small bathroom, the door open and revealing only a commode and a sink. To the right of the bathroom stood a three-foot square safe. I walked over to it and squatted down. It was sturdy, looked heavy, and had a combination lock beyond my expertise. A collapsible table with four chairs scattered around it sat in the open space. A light suspended from the ceiling hovered over a table where an ashtray, a deck of cards, and a Cribbage board were at the ready. The end of a joint and cigarette butts filled the ashtray.

In the far corner beyond the safe and table was what appeared to be another small room. Sheets of plywood were nailed to 2x4 uprights, making partitions that served as walls. I poked my flashlight inside and found more shelves with all sorts of paraphernalia. Glassware, picture frames, dusty books, table lamps, telephones, holsters, and fake guns filled the room. The enclosure was obviously a theatrical prop room.

I walked to the other side of the warehouse, my flashlight beam preceding me. Several bays, or stalls, occupied the far wall. Stage flats filled them. I pawed through a few and saw that they were fake walls. Next to the bays stood six upright metal stands, similar to those weight lifters use. Spanning them were metal pipes hung with lighting fixtures. Spotlights of varying sizes stood next to the rear wall, along with wooden crates on casters like the ones I'd seen Scarborough and Curran unloading. They were three feet square and about four feet off the floor. I lifted the lid on one of them. Empty.

I stood in the middle of the enclosure and looked around at what had to be a storage unit for some television or movie enterprise. Enigma Productions had a very successful cable television show called *Flashpoint*. Was the equipment in this room for that show? I pulled my notebook out of my pocket and flipped it open to the notes I'd taken. My light picked out the name Fred Curran, one of the principals of the company. And now a James Curran had been seen loading equipment into what appeared to be a theatrical warehouse. Was James Curran, and by extension Phil Scarborough, involved with *Flashpoint*? How did Frankie Rizzoli fit in, if indeed he did? More questions that needed answering.

But right now I had something else to deal with.

I heard the slam of a car door and turned to my left. After a moment, a metal chain started to crank and the roll-up door slowly began to rise.

CHAPTER TWENTY-FIVE

———◆———

I PULLED THE BERETTA OUT OF MY waistband and ran for the back of the warehouse, then ducked into the corridor to the right of the back door and hugged the interior wall. Common sense should have told me to get the hell out of there, but I acted on instinct. Whoever was outside that roll-up door would see me trying to haul ass away from the building.

When my heart stopped pounding, I looked to my right and scooted down to the water heater to see if there was room to hide behind it. The only thing it was hiding was a nest of cobwebs. As I crept back along the interior wall, I spied a chunk of wood missing. When I peered through the hole, I had a good look at the front door that was still grinding its way open.

A set of legs appeared at the bottom edge. When the door was about a yard off the ground, Phil Scarborough ducked underneath and helped it along by pulling on a chain. He wore sneakers, jeans, and a gray hooded sweatshirt. The door finally stopped and he reached up and hit a switch. The light hanging over the table came on, as did several others throughout the warehouse.

The back end of a white delivery truck filled the opening. Scarborough opened one of the doors and the truck's engine stopped. A front door slammed shut and James Curran appeared and swung open the other door. He had on a dark-blue warm-up suit and a black leather flat cap tilted to one side of his head. Scarborough pulled out a metal ramp from under the truck's bed and attached one end of it to slots above the bumper.

"Six out and six in?" he said.

"Like always," Curran replied.

He stepped up into the truck and began pulling out a wheeled crate. It was a carbon copy of the empty ones I'd seen in the far corner. Scarborough yanked on it until a set of casters sat on the ramp and then began pulling it down with his left hand. Curran helped the crate along and lifted his section onto the ramp. Scarborough guided it to the floor and pushed it toward the far corner of the warehouse, then helped Curran push another one down the ramp. The two men had started rolling the crates when Scarborough stopped, sat down, and grabbed his right shoulder.

"Hang on a minute, Jimmy."

Curran looked behind him. "Now what the hell's the matter?"

"My shoulder, man."

"Why the fuck don't you keep that sling on?"

"Then how am I supposed to lift these goddamn things?" He stood up and kicked the crate he'd been sitting on. It skidded toward the stalls holding the flats. He grabbed it with his left arm and again plopped down on it. "We should get some Mexicans to do this grunt work." Scarborough's voice had an irritating whine to it, far different from when I'd caught him at home and he couldn't resist showing off his gunshot wound.

"Come on, man," Curran said. "Use your head. You want a bunch of wetbacks poking around these things?" He sat down on the crate he'd been pushing and lit up a cigarette. "All right, look. I'll wrestle them off the truck. Can you at least push with one arm?"

"Yeah."

"Go get your damn sling."

Scarborough started for the front of the delivery truck as Curran shook his head and puffed on his cigarette. He pulled a cellphone from a pocket. I could hear him muttering to himself as he punched keys, but couldn't make out what he was saying.

A new development. Something more valuable than theatrical lighting equipment was in those crates. I started to think about what it could be, but stopped and focused my attention on the door I'd come through. The damn thing was slightly ajar. About two inches. I thought I'd shut it behind me, but obviously I hadn't. The angle between it and the roll-up front door didn't allow Scarborough and Curran to see it hanging open, provided they stayed away from the table and the refrigerator. I didn't want to risk any movement, even though I couldn't be seen.

I returned to the peephole. Scarborough came back from the front of the truck wearing a sling on his right arm. He had a joint in his mouth and sat down on the crate and fired it up with a Bic lighter. Curran glared at him for a long moment, then put the cellphone back in his pocket.

"How many of those things you do a day?"

Scarborough looked at the joint in his fingers. "Medicinal purposes, Jimmy."

Curran scoffed and shook his head. "Yeah, right. You carryin' that when we're coming through San Ysidro, man, we're in a world of hurt."

"Nah, nothin' to worry about."

Curran puffed on his cigarette and stared at him. "That's your own damn fault, you know."

"What?" Scarborough said, as he expelled a cloud of smoke.

"Your shoulder."

"My fault? How you figure that? You're the one that shot me, amigo."

"You shouldn't have been in the way."

"And you should have had somebody driving besides that asshole Ernie. Bouncin' off curbs and shit? The guy's a retard, man."

"I had a clear shot at Rizzoli."

"Bullshit. He had the back door open before you fired. He was gone, Jimmy."

Taking a final pull off his cigarette, Curran dropped it on the floor and stepped on it. "Yeah, well, I'll be sure and get his opinion when we catch up to him. If he hasn't gone to ground. Come on, let's get this done. I gotta get back to Chula Vista. Fill the empties with as many lights and cords as you can find." He stood up and started walking back to the truck's ramp.

Scarborough pinched the end of his joint and stuck it in a cigarette pack, which he stuffed in the pouch of his hoodie. Using his left arm, he pushed his crate into the far corner of the warehouse. The sound of the casters rolling across the concrete was deafening.

For several minutes I watched the men busy themselves with the crates. Curran pushed them down the ramp, then Scarborough rolled them into the corner and returned with an empty. I could hear him banging around at the end of the line of shelves on the opposite side of the back door, but he didn't stick his head out, and therefore didn't see me.

Curran rolled another box off the truck and shoved it to the side.

"This is the last one," Scarborough said, as he pushed another crate to the foot of the ramp.

"Shove it into the prop room and fill it up."

"With what?"

"Anything that'll fit."

"Right."

Scarborough started rolling the crate toward the prop room, which meant he was going to cross in front of my peep hole and the partially open door.

Only now it wasn't partially open.

The gap was widening, helped along by the furry paw of an animal. When the door was about a foot open, the paw gave way to the striped head of a feral cat. I have nothing against the creatures. In fact, I rather like them.

But not now, not here.

I glanced through the peep hole to see where Scarborough was. He hadn't yet crossed the room. I lunged at the opened door and shoved my foot in the cat's direction. It let out a yowl and jumped back. I shut the door, locked the locks, and ducked back to the hole in the wall.

"What the hell was that?" I could hear Curran say.

"A cat," Scarborough replied, as he shoved the crate toward the door of the prop room. "Those fuckin' homeless guys sleep back there. Sometimes they leave food, and then the rats come, and then the cats. I've seen two or three of them back there. Big suckers."

"That one sounded like it was indoors. Take a look."

Scarborough shook his head, grumbled, and started for the back door. If he saw me, I was going to need to do some fast explaining. I scooted down the corridor and squeezed myself behind the two ladders leaning against the wall. I wasn't completely out of sight, but hopefully Scarborough wouldn't look in my direction. I held my gun next to my head and listened to him muttering as he made his way to the back door. He bent down to look at the two locks, then tried to twist the knob. It wouldn't open.

"The door's locked, Jimmy. There ain't no cat back here."

"You sure?"

"Yeah. Here, kitty, kitty." He stood still for a moment and listened, then threw up his hands. "There, you see? No cat."

He walked back to the front of the warehouse and I crept back to my peephole. Scarborough finished pushing his crate to the door of the prop room. Now Curran crossed my line of vision, pushing the crate he had set to the side of the ramp. He stopped in front of the safe, pulled over a chair, sat, and began twirling the dial. After a moment, the heavy door creaked open. He separated a key from a ring he took out of his pocket, stuck it into a lock on the crate, and flipped open the lid. He started transferring something into the safe. I couldn't see what it was because of the open lid.

Scarborough was in the prop room, tossing various items into the empty crate. He stuck his head around the corner of the wall. "When are we supposed to be in Valencia tomorrow?"

"Late afternoon. They said to be out there by the time they wrap."

"You know anything about that film?"

"Just what I heard from the old man. Low-budget stuff. Probably go straight to video."

I took my eyes from the peep hole, leaned against the wall and digested what Curran and Scarborough had been talking about. I assumed that since they'd taken a shot at Frankie, he wasn't in league with them. He'd also been beaten up by some plainclothes cops, so it didn't look like he was running with them either. So what the hell was my client's brother up to? And what the hell was Curran putting in that safe?

Whatever it was had been transferred, because I heard the creak of the heavy safe door. Eyes again to my surreptitious hole in the wall, I saw Curran slam down the lid of the crate and begin wheeling it toward the far corner of the warehouse. Scarborough finished rummaging around in the prop room and pushed his crate to the foot of the ramp.

"You gotta push this one up, Jimmy."

"Yeah, yeah, hang on." I heard the sound of two crates colliding and Curran call out from the far corner of the room.

"You sure there ain't a goddamn cat roaming around in here?"

"I'm sure."

"Then let's split."

He pushed the crate up the ramp into the truck, jumped down, and shoved the metal ramp into its place under the bed. Scarborough hit the light switch and the room plunged into darkness. Curran swung shut the doors of the truck, locked them, and started for the driver's side. Scarborough yanked on the chain with his left arm, but stopped after only one pull.

"You gotta help me with the door, man."

Curran returned, reached up and pulled the door down. "Sometimes you're about as worthless as tits on a boar. You know that?"

I couldn't hear Scarborough's reply as the door descended and clunked into the concrete floor. The combination padlock was replaced, two car doors slammed shut, and the engine started. Finally the delivery truck drove off, leaving me with a headful of questions.

CHAPTER TWENTY-SIX

———◆———

I STAYED PRESSED TO THE WALL FOR a few minutes in case Curran and Scarborough had forgotten something. They hadn't. I turned on my flashlight and walked to the safe. Wishful thinking, I suppose, but I grabbed the handle on the door and gave it a yank. Locked. I'd heard the two men imply that they'd come through San Ysidro, the border crossing north of Tijuana. They hadn't brought refried beans; something valuable had to have been in those boxes.

I headed back to the corner of the warehouse where I'd seen the wooden crates. Padlocks hung from the hasps, and when I pulled on them, they stayed locked. I pushed aside the last one as I started toward the back door and yanked on the lock.

This one was loose.

I removed the lock from the hasp and opened the crate. Empty. I'd started to close the lid when I noticed one corner of the bottom seemed to be uneven. I flipped the lid all the way open and stuck my flashlight into the box. In each corner, holes the size of a finger had been drilled into the bottom. Holding the flashlight in my mouth, I stuck two middle fingers into two of the holes and lifted. The box had a false bottom, made of half-inch plywood.

Underneath was a cavity a foot deep, and it too was empty. I looked around at each of the locked crates and wondered what the hell had been inside. Money? Drugs? Or both? I put the lid back on, replaced the lock the way I'd found it, then walked past the shelves to the rear door and unlocked it. The dead bolt was going to have to stay that way, but I turned the lock in the doorknob and pulled the door closed behind me.

As I turned to retrace my steps to the street, the cat I had almost kicked hissed at me from a perch on top of the wooden fence. It didn't move, and looked at me like it was hungry and I was a can of tuna. I took a step forward and it let loose with a low, throaty growl. Now, this was ridiculous. I pounded the top of the fence and the cat jumped off and scampered away, ending our *High Noon* moment.

The only movement on Crocker was a garbage truck across the street, emptying Willie's hideout. A guy wearing a yellow hard hat and vest held the gate open while his partner wrestled the Dumpster from the truck to the rear of the building.

I walked down the block to 8th and turned left toward my car. A young kid wearing a down vest, jeans, and white tennis shoes sat on the hood, facing the street. He had a baseball cap backwards on his head, a fashion statement I've never understood. A skateboard was clutched between his legs, and headphones covered his ears, pounding out his own private symphony. Since he didn't see me approach, he jumped when I slapped my hand on the car. Pulling the headphones off, he turned to me.

"These your wheels, man?"

"You got it. And why the hell do you think you can sit your ass down on them?"

"I'm just chillin'."

"Well, chill someplace else." I unlocked the door and started to climb in.

He slid off the hood. "Where you headed, man?"

"Home."

"If that's the west side, can I hitch a ride?"

"Sorry, wrong direction."

"Then where you goin'? I gotta get outta downtown."

"Try the bus. Better yet, why don't you use that thing?" I pointed to the board that had to be at least a yard long and was smeared with psychedelic paint.

"Shit, man, you nuts? That'd take all day." Shaking his head in disbelief, he replaced the headphones, dropped the board on its wheels, and pushed himself toward San Pedro Street.

I got in the car, opened the windows, and turned on my cellphone. No message from Charlie Rivers, but there was a text from Carla. *Hey, PI man. Shoot's going well. Having fun. Call you later.* The news I had for her reinforced the fact that her brother wasn't dead, which was good. The fact that I wasn't any closer to finding him wasn't.

I called Charlie's phone and still got voicemail. This time I left a message for him to call me. I fired up the car and started making my way up into Hollywood.

*

THE ELEVATOR LUMBERED TO MY FLOOR and the door shuddered as it opened, ending yet another miraculous ascent. I've often thought I should stock up on donuts before getting in the damn thing in case it stops and I'm stranded. As I headed for my office, the door to *Pecs 'n Abs* opened and the magazine's editor, Lenny Daye, stepped into the hall. Flamboyant as always, Lenny was decked out in skintight black jeans and a silver, sparkly shirt open to the navel. Gold chains hung around his neck and a fire-engine red derby sat on his head.

"Lenny, you look like something out of a psychedelic film."

"I know, honey. It's the derby, isn't it? Malcolm McDowell in *A Clockwork Orange*, right?"

"Yeah, I can see that."

"I know where you can find a porkpie in this color, Eddie. Put a little spice in your life."

"I've got enough spice. Thanks, anyway."

"Later, gator." He punched the down button on the elevator and the door creaked open and swallowed him.

Mavis looked up as I entered the office. "Hey, boss man, how'd it go downtown?"

"Well, Frankie Rizzoli is still on the loose. But I had a conversation with a homeless guy that led to some interesting stuff." I plopped down in a chair in front of her desk and filled her in on the events at the Mission and the warehouse.

"Smuggling?" she said.

"Kinda looks like it, doesn't it?"

"This is getting more serious than finding someone's brother, Eddie."

"Yeah, I know."

She picked up a sheaf of papers and handed them to me. "You've got some interesting reading here."

"Oh, yeah? What'd you find out?"

"This Enigma Productions has its fingers in a lot of pies."

I got up and carried the papers into my office. "Any mail of interest?"

"Your SAG dues statement. Are you still an actor?"

"I'm thought to be so in some quarters."

"Then you better pay them."

"Noted." I hung up my porkpie and sat down at the desk. "Any calls? Lieutenant Rivers, for instance?"

"Nope. Just telemarketers. I assume you aren't interested in a time share in Palm Springs?"

"I hate the desert."

"That's what I figured." She appeared in the doorway as I scanned the papers she'd given me. "I'm gonna split. Fritz is taking me to the Hollywood Bowl tonight."

"Great. Who's on the bill?"

"Some dime-store cowboy I've never heard of."

"Wear your spurs."

"Yeah, right," she said. "See you in the morning."

I flipped through a few more pages and decided I needed company. With a cold beer and a shot of Mr. Beam at my elbow, I tilted the chair back and propped my feet up on the corner of my desk. Mavis had indeed done some digging. Enigma Productions, in addition to being the producers of that television series *Flashpoint*, had done several made-for-TV movies. I recognized a couple of the titles.

A Los Angeles County business license revealed Enigma Productions to be a subsidiary of Foxtrot Enterprises. I continued reading and discovered Feline Follies under the company's banner. Two other properties that appeared to be gentlemen's clubs were listed: Foxy Alley in Orange County and Fun 'n Fantasy in Pacoima. Also listed as being a branch of Foxtrot were Xerxes Press, a periodical distribution outlet, and Four Star Amusements. Mavis had placed a Post-it next to that name with an arrow and the words "see over." I had a taste of Mr. Beam, followed it with a swallow of beer, and flipped to the next page.

Four Star Amusements owned four adult entertainment outlets in Calabasas, Chatsworth, Sylmar, and Torrance. I reached for my drink and gazed across the office as I sipped. Three gentlemen's clubs, a magazine distribution company, and adult entertainment stores? Foxtrot Enterprises didn't seem to be a candidate for the Good Housekeeping seal of approval. Carla was a part of these endeavors. I couldn't help but wonder if dancers at the Follies knew about, or had anything to do with the other parts of the parent company. That thought left a sour taste in my mouth that even good sippin' whiskey couldn't dispel. The ringing of the cellphone interrupted my train of thought. The display said the call was from Charlie Rivers. I pushed a key and put the phone to my ear.

"Hey, Charlie."

"Generally speaking, if someone leaves a message they get a response much quicker," he said.

"So I've heard. Thanks for getting back to me."

"You find your guy yet?"

"Working on it. That's why I wanted to talk to you."

Charlie let out a huge sigh. "You know, Collins, maybe you should try to get into the Police Academy. You could be your own source."

"Yeah, but where would you get your free lunches, Charlie?"

After a moment and a slight chuckle, he said, "Always got an angle, don't you? All right, what now?"

"This Frankie Rizzoli's real name is Francis. He used to live on Acama in Studio City. According to his former landlord, two uniformed cops came and escorted him out of the place back in the summer of 2012."

"I already told you there's no arrest record on the guy, Eddie."

"I know. But maybe he wasn't arrested."

"What do you mean?"

"The landlord said Rizzoli acted like he knew the two cops."

"So?"

"So, when that shooting went down on Crocker, Rizzoli got picked up by an unmarked unit. Or so says my witness."

"How the hell does he know that?"

"It had a light on the dash."

"Who's the witness?"

"A homeless guy. He was in a Dumpster across the street."

"Wait a minute. You're listening to some fuckin' guy who sleeps in a garbage bin?"

"My witness knows Rizzoli, Charlie. He said the unit brought him back a few minutes later. They dragged him out of the car, beat the shit out of him, and then took off, leaving him in the street."

There was a pause on the other end of the line and I heard him slurping some sort of liquid. "Okay, so what do you want from me?"

"Somebody in the department knows this guy, Charlie. I've got a client who hired me to find out where the hell he is. If any cops have rubbed elbows with Rizzoli, maybe they'd know where to find him."

Another long pause and then, "I'll make some calls."

"Appreciate it."

"Can you wait until tomorrow morning?"

"No problem."

"I mean, I've only got a homicide and two B&Es staring me in the face."

"I owe you, Charlie."

"Big time," he replied, and ended the call.

I refreshed my liquid companions, tilted the chair back and resumed my reading. I'm not sure I made sense of what was in front of me, except to conclude that Foxtrot Enterprises was a successful endeavor. That wasn't surprising. The male side of the public has never been shy when it comes to patronizing adult entertainment. Not that the ladies are excluded, but I don't think the clientele of Feline Follies and Four Star Amusements go out of their way to appeal to the fairer sex. I sipped on my Jim Beam when the cellphone chirped again. Speaking of the fairer sex, the display read Carla.

"Hey, how's the working actress?"

"On my way home. If I ever get through the Sepulveda Pass, that is."

I could hear the hum of traffic in the background. "Better not let any of LA's finest see you on your cell."

"I've got a Bluetooth. That way I can flip the bird with both fingers."

"Good thinking," I said. "How did your day go?"

"Great. Three scenes. Complicated, though. Lots of extras. The guy who's playing my husband is real nice. Don Atkinson. Do you know him?"

"No, don't think so."

"You'd probably recognize the face." All at once the sound of a loud exhaust filled my ear. "Good grief. These bikers, man! A guy dressed like Santa Claus just blew past me." She burst into laughter. "And he had a Nazi helmet on."

The image didn't surprise me. LA freeways never disappoint. "Maybe he's late for an audition," I said.

"The question is, as what?" She broke into laughter at her own joke, and I joined in. "Did you find that elusive brother of mine?"

"I got close. He may be staying in a broken-down hotel across the street from one of the missions. I also found a guy who knows him. In fact he shared a joint with Frankie the day of the shooting on Crocker."

"That's weird," she said. "I never knew Frankie to have anything to do with drugs."

"Maybe he started when he was in the army."

"Yeah, could be. You find out anything else?"

I then filled her in on what I'd discovered in the warehouse and the information Mavis had compiled for me. There was silence on the other end of the line.

"Are you there?"

"Yeah, I was just thinking about what you said. I had no idea the Follies was part of anything bigger."

"I don't know what help that is in trying to find your brother though."

"I don't either," she said. "Look, Eddie, I really want to see you tonight and hash over this stuff, but I've got another early call in the morning."

"I understand."

"Besides, this freeway is kicking my ass."

"Give me a call tomorrow when you can."

"Will do. I miss you."

"Same here," I said, a bit surprised that the words came to me so easily. "Get some rest."

"You too," she said. "Bye for now."

She broke the connection and I put the cell back on the desk. A brief wave of melancholy came over me as I realized I wouldn't be seeing her tonight. Carla Rizzoli was beginning to work her way into my life. I liked the development. What I didn't like was that I still couldn't get a bead on the whereabouts of her brother.

CHAPTER TWENTY-SEVEN

———◆———

GRAY CLOUDS HUNG OVER THE BOULEVARD. We Angelinos refer to it as the June Gloom. The only problem is that this was February. As I sipped on my morning coffee, I watched a young woman with blue hair jaywalk across the street. She held a yipping toy dog in her arms and was met by a guy dressed completely in black. Black and blue. Hmm … could be a new rap duo.

I set the cup on a small circular table in the corner of my mini-balcony. It once held a plant Mavis had bestowed upon me that had given up the ghost shortly after arrival. The closest I've ever come to having a green thumb is one night a few years back at a wrap party in Chasen's when I attempted to fill a tortilla chip with guacamole and the thing snapped in two, sending my thumb in up to the knuckle.

I hadn't slept well last night. After talking to Carla, I'd gone out for Chinese food, then sat and tried to concentrate on a Gene Hackman film, but it didn't work. I kept trying to insert Frankie Rizzoli into this Foxtrot Enterprises maze with no success. I'd finally turned off the film and pored over the sheaf of papers Mavis had provided. Still nothing, so I'd given up.

I heard Mavis stirring in the front of the office. She called out, "Eddie, are you up?"

"Yeah, be right there." I finished my coffee, shut the window, and poured another cup. Mavis was at her desk. I slumped down in a chair in front of her. "How was the dime-store cowboy?"

"Tiny, from our seats. The speakers were huge, so at least we could hear him. Waylon or Willie he ain't, but he wasn't bad." Mavis and I share the same tastes in country music. She gestured to the sheaf of papers in my hand. "Did you go through that stuff?"

"I did."

"And?"

"All very interesting, but I'm stumped."

"How so?"

"I can't figure out how Carla's brother fits in."

"Does she have any ideas?"

"I don't think so, but I'm going to see her when she's done shooting today. See what she thinks."

"And what are you going to do in the meantime?"

"Well, the only place Frankie's been seen is on Skid Row. I don't know where else to look."

"I can start checking for rentals there if you'd like."

I glanced at her and saw her grinning like the Cheshire Cat.

"You want me to write these gems down?" I said.

"Just trying to lighten your load, boss," she replied.

"Yeah, right. But as long as you've got rentals on your mind, can you check this out for me?" I gave her the address of the hotel with the "e" missing. "See if you can find an owner or a manager. I saw Frankie there, and need to know if it's a legitimate hotel. I have my doubts."

I swallowed the last of my coffee and took the cup back to the sink in my apartment. On my way back to the front door, I grabbed my porkpie. Mavis had her eyes glued on her computer screen. "If Lieutenant Rivers should call," I said, "tell him I'm on my cell."

"Okay."

I popped the hat on my head and opened the door.

"You know, Eddie, that thing you've got on your head doesn't exactly blend into the background. If this Rizzoli character is trying to avoid you, maybe you shouldn't be drawing attention to yourself."

"Good idea, kiddo." I closed the door behind me and headed for the elevator. Besides sharing my tastes in country music, my secretary sometimes has instincts that leave mine in the dust.

ON THE WAY DOWNTOWN I POPPED into a Denny's and had me some Moons Over My Hammy. I sat at the counter with the *Times* and was forced to listen to a guy two stools over audibly assessing the day's Santa Anita odds from the *Daily Racing Form.* When it looked like he was going to ask my opinion, I paid the bill and crawled into the front seat of my car. I no sooner pulled out of the lot when my cell rang. I glided over to the curb and took the call.

"Good morning, Lieutenant."

A grunt on the other end of the line, then, "Your formality is overwhelming,

Shamus." He took the phone away from his ear and I could hear chatter in the background. Finally he said, "I made some calls."

"Turn up anything?"

"Bupkis. There's no Francis Rizzoli in the system, anywhere. Hollenbeck busted an R. Frank Rizzoli two years ago. He died in custody. I had my girl run 'Frankie Rizzoli' through the system again, and she got no hits, nowhere. If your guy knows any cops, Eddie, it's not on an official basis."

"Yeah, sounds like it. Thanks, Charlie."

"You can return the favor by keeping me in the loop, you know. If he was, in fact, roughed up by some cops, the department needs to know. Understand?"

"I'll be in touch."

I broke the connection and slipped the cell into my shirt pocket. So, Francis Rizzoli did not have a run-in with the LAPD. But his former landlord McGinty said the two uniforms escorting him out of his apartment seemed like buddies. If they weren't cops, what were they? Actors? Rent-a-cops? Considering the permanent haze of cigarette smoke in McGinty's eyes and the taste of rot-gut whiskey in his mouth, maybe he was mistaken. A uniform doesn't necessarily mean law enforcement. I put the car in gear and got back into the flow of traffic down Western, more questions swirling around in my head.

There was only one person who could answer them, and he wasn't talking. Not yet, anyway.

CHAPTER TWENTY-EIGHT

---◆---

I PARKED THE CAR NEAR ONE OF the missions and rummaged around in the trunk, where I keep a battered box full of various hats and articles of clothing. Some of them I use for auditions, and others when I want to gain the confidence of a person I'm interviewing. Following Mavis's suggestion, I decided on a black watch cap and a tattered Army fatigue jacket. With the cap pulled over my ears, I set off on foot.

For an hour and a half I strolled past the two missions and around the neighborhood, shuffling through the conclaves of homeless scattered over the streets. Many of them I recognized from my previous visits, but no one fit the description of Frankie that Willie had given me. Nor was I remembered as the guy with the porkpie hat. Instead, I was asked for cigarettes and money. One enterprising guy wearing a long leather overcoat tried to sell me a couple of joints.

I ducked into the convenience store where I'd bought the cardboard sandwich and found a tall bottle of Colt .45 that fit nicely into a paper sack. *Might as well walk the walk,* I thought, as I screwed the top off, had a swallow, then stuck the bottle into a pocket of the field jacket. I leaned against a light post and gazed up and down the street. An elderly black man shuffled up to me on my right side.

"Hey, man," he said. "I's wantin' to buy me a taste of what you got in your pocket. But I'm a buck and a half short. Help me out, brother?"

I stuck a hand in my pocket and pulled out some change. "This is all I got, pardner, but you're welcome to it." He held out his hands and I dumped the coins into them. Doffing his cap, he walked into the store. I took another pull from the bottle and ambled down the street.

A garbage truck rumbled past as I sat down and leaned back against a wall. The chill of the concrete seeped through the field jacket into my back and my rear end. I watched the parade of hopelessness in front of me as the street people huddled in their cardboard boxes and makeshift shelters. Here and there I saw a fist-bump of recognition, heard a raised voice warding off an interloper. I couldn't help but wonder how they managed to stave off the uncertainty, the utter futility of their mere existence. It seemed to me that there was a certain amount of courage displayed on that street. A person had to have fortitude and sheer guts to deal with the ordeal on a daily basis.

I was about to hoist the beer bottle out of my pocket when I spied Willie crossing the street in my direction. He was dressed as before and stopped to talk to a couple of black guys leaning against a metal fence. I hunkered down as he approached. Without recognizing me, he walked past and went into the convenience store. A few minutes later, he came back out, stood on the curb, and tore the wrapping off a pack of cigarettes. He lit one, flipped the match into the gutter, and headed back across the street.

Instinct told me to get up and follow him. If he'd been hanging out with Frankie the day before, what's to say that it wouldn't happen again? I crossed the street and stayed back about thirty yards. He strolled along San Pedro, stopping now and then to shake a hand, carry on a brief conversation.

When he turned onto Crocker, I waited a few beats to give him a chance to get farther around the corner. I sidled up to the intersection and peered from behind a building to see where he was, and then quickly ducked back out of sight.

Another truck was backed up to the door where Curran and Scarborough had been unloading those wooden crates. I estimated Crocker to be the length of a football field. The truck was at the fifty-yard line across the street. I took another look and saw Willie step into a recessed doorway twenty-five yards down the block. He looked like he was watching the truck. The metal sliding door was up, but there was no movement. A black paneled van was parked along the curb in front of me. I darted to the rear of it, edged to the street side and peered around the van toward the delivery truck. After a moment, I heard the sound of voices and two men appeared at the rear of the truck. I didn't recognize either of them. They were talking to each other, but I couldn't understand what they were saying. They ended their conversation and one of them pulled down the door. The other got behind the wheel. Roaring to life, the truck rolled to the far end of the street, then turned right and disappeared.

I went back to the street side of the panel truck and watched Willie in the doorway. He crouched on his haunches, puffing on a cigarette. After a moment, he caught sight of something and stood up. I looked down the street.

A figure appeared from around the corner, talking on a cellphone. As the guy approached, Willie stepped out onto the sidewalk and started toward him. The guy took the phone away from his ear and held it in his hands as if he were sending a text or checking email. As he got nearer, his appearance struck a chord in my memory.

"Hey, Frankie, wassup?" Willie called out. "I been lookin' for you, man."

The guy with the phone raised his head and I could see that the description fit. It was Frankie Rizzoli. My search was over. He and Willie greeted each other and I saw Frankie put the cellphone in a pocket. I started walking toward the two men. They talked with their backs to me, so I couldn't hear what they were saying.

When I got within twenty yards of them, I called out, "Frankie!"

The two men whirled around at the sound of my voice. When Frankie spotted me, he took off running down the street. I started after him and Willie grabbed at me, trying to get in my way.

"Hey, man, what the hell you doin'?"

"Get out of the way, Willie." He kept grabbing at my jacket. Every time I got loose he latched onto me again. "Goddammit, Willie, let go of me!"

"Aw, c'mon, dude, Frankie ain't done nuthin'."

Realizing he wasn't going to let go of me, I thought I could maybe divert his attention. I pulled the bottle of beer out of my pocket and thrust it into his hand. "Stay here," I said, "and take this. I'm the guy who gave you the money. Remember?"

"Yeah, you the dude with the hat."

"That's right. Now stay put. I need to talk to you."

Willie grabbed the bottle and nodded as I took off running. Track was never my sport in school, and it sure as hell wasn't now. Besides being out of shape, I was hampered by the roughing up Frankie had given me earlier. I was about twenty yards from the building at the intersection. I turned the corner and saw him crawling into a rusted-out gray pickup truck halfway down the block.

"Frankie, hold up!" I shouted, but he didn't stop. The truck turned over and burned rubber. I tried to get a tag, but I was too far away and the license plate was too corroded for me to make out anything. The truck barreled down the street and squealed around another corner out of sight.

I stopped running and bent over, trying to catch my breath and thinking that a membership in a gym might be a good idea. I straightened up and limped back to Crocker. Willie was sitting on the curb, paper sack tilted up. I walked up to him and leaned against the wall of the building.

"That was Frankie Rizzoli, right?" I said.

"Yeah, man. Why the fuck you chasin' him?"

"He's the guy I've been looking for. What were the two of you talking about?"

"I scored a coupla doobies. Offered him a toke or two." He drank from the bottle. "Thanks for the beer, man. Why'd Frankie take off like that?"

"He doesn't want to be found."

"How come?"

"I don't know, Willie. Yesterday I saw him in that hotel across from the mission. That one that's got the 'e' missing from the sign? You know what I'm talking about?"

"Yeah, I know the place."

"Does he live there?"

"Shit, man, I hope not."

"Why?"

"That damn place is foul."

"How do you mean?"

"People shootin' up and shit."

"Frankie too?"

"Nah, man, I don't think so. He has him a toke or two, but that's it. I dunno know where he lives. I only seen him on the streets."

I finally caught my breath and pushed myself off the wall. "Do me a favor, would you?" I leaned over and handed him one of my cards. "You got a phone?"

"Shit yeah, man, my cousin got me one of them pre-paid jobbies."

"You ever call Frankie on that phone he had?"

"I don't even know the fuckin' number."

"You sure?"

"Damn straight."

"He ever call you?"

"No, man. Why you axin' me that?"

"All right. Well, listen, if you see Frankie again, tell him his sister wants to see him. And then you call me. You got it?"

"I got it."

"Okay. Don't forget."

I straightened up and started walking back to my car. I'd almost had my man, but was left with only the burning question as to why the hell he was so skittish.

From behind me, Willie said, "Hey, Collins."

"Yeah?" I turned and watched him walk up to me.

"Frankie done something wrong?"

"I don't know, Willie. I hope not. And so does his sister."

CHAPTER TWENTY-NINE

———◆———

CLOSE, BUT NO CIGAR. THAT SAYING bounced around in my head while I slowly drove through the Skid Row neighborhood, trying to spot a rusty gray pickup. No luck. Frankie Rizzoli had disappeared. Again. I eventually gave up, stowed my fatigue jacket and black watch cap in the trunk of my car, and made my way back to my office.

I couldn't figure out why Frankie had taken off when he saw me. I sure as hell wasn't a threat to him, since he didn't even know my name. Unless he was into something he shouldn't be doing and didn't want his identity known. What that something was eluded me. However, I couldn't help but think it somehow involved Phil Scarborough and James Curran. And wooden crates with false bottoms. Hopefully Carla could provide some insight. I was anxious to hear from her. Not only for professional reasons, but—I was pleased to realize—personal as well.

I pushed open the door to Collins Investigations and was greeted by the sight of the Three Stooges sitting on my secretary's desk. In the form of bobbleheads. Mavis was standing behind a small cardboard box, studying an invoice. She looked up as I entered.

"Hi, Eddie. How did it go?"

"Carla's brother is definitely alive and well. But he sure as hell doesn't want to talk to me."

"You actually saw him?"

"I did. And then he took off like he'd been caught with the crown jewels." I plopped myself down in a chair in front of her desk and pointed to the three bobbleheads. "Moe, Larry, and Curly going into Fritz's den or something?"

"He should be so lucky. Some collector out in Reseda is dying for these little guys." She sat down and noticed me staring at my lap. "You look like somebody died. What's the matter?"

"This guy is driving me nuts. I can't figure out what the hell he's up to."

"Did you talk to him?"

"Didn't get a chance. He split." Mavis set the cardboard box on the floor and crossed into her little alcove, then came back with a small roll of bubble wrap. "We've used a cellphone directory before, haven't we?" I said.

"Sure. Why?"

"He had a cellphone on him."

"That's kind of unusual for someone who's trying to be homeless, isn't it?"

"Not unless he's got one of those pre-paid ones."

"True."

"Punch his name in and see what you can find."

"If he's got a pre-paid, chances are it can't be traced."

"Yeah, I know, but when I spotted him, he looked like he was texting or something, so maybe he's got a smartphone too. Give it a try."

"You got it." She pushed the Stooges onto the corner of her desk, where they glared at me with scorn. Mavis tapped some keys on her computer and said, "How do you want to enter his name? Frankie? Francis?"

"Try Francis."

She clicked and paused to look at the screen. "We're in luck. There's a listing for a Francis Rizzoli. On Acama. Where's that?"

"Studio City, but he doesn't live there anymore. His former landlord told me he cleaned out the place and left."

"But he could still have the same phone."

"He could. What is it?" She rattled off the number and I wrote it down in my notebook, then pulled out my cellphone. "Here goes nothing." I dialed and after a few rings, a robotic voice came on the line and told me the number was currently unavailable and to leave a message at the sound of the tone. I nodded to Mavis and she gave me a thumbs-up. After the beep I said, "Frankie, this is Eddie Collins. I'm a private investigator. Your sister Carla hired me to find you. She got your note and she's worried about you. That's all. Call me, so I can tell her you're all right. No hassles, no trouble." I broke the connection and slid the phone into my shirt pocket.

"Was it him or an automated voice?"

"Automated. I suppose that means it's not necessarily his phone."

"Yeah, it could have been lost or stolen. You'll never know if he doesn't call you back."

I got up from my chair and went into my office. I hung my hat on its hook, looked at the mail Mavis had deposited on my desk, then pawed through the hanging beads into my apartment. Some leftover coffee had all the appeal of a cup of pine tar, but I took the bite out of it with milk and set it on the desk. My SAG dues paid, I stared at the cellphone sitting in front of me, as if willing the damn thing to ring. It didn't cooperate. I paid more bills and leaned back in my chair. A feeling of restlessness came over me, sitting there waiting for an inanimate object to talk to me. I picked it up and dialed Reggie's number. He answered after two rings.

"Hey, Eddie, how ya doin'?"

"Good. What are you up to?"

"I'm on my way to get some batteries."

"Where are you?"

"Down on Hollywood Boulevard someplace."

"Got time for a cup of coffee?"

"You bet."

"There's a Starbucks on Hollywood at Mccadden. How 'bout I meet you there in ten minutes or so?"

"Sure thing."

I slid the phone back in my shirt pocket, retrieved my hat, and went into the outer office. Mavis had finished wrapping Moe, Larry, and Curly and was sealing up the box.

"Was that Reggie?"

"Yeah, we're going to grab a coffee. Maybe he's got an idea or two."

"Say hello for me."

"Will do," I said as I shut the door behind me.

As I WALKED UP, REGGIE WAS bent over, looking at one of the stars on the Hollywood Walk of Fame in front of the coffee shop. The slab of marble belonged to Betty White.

"You know who that is?" I asked.

"Yeah, wasn't she one of those golden girls?"

"You got it. And she's still going strong."

"Where's yours, Eddie?"

"My what?"

"Your star."

"I've got my people working on it." He laughed and adjusted his baseball cap. "What do you need batteries for?" I said.

"Bought myself a little kitchen timer."

"You telling me you're turning into a cook?"

"Yup, yup, I'm trying."

"Well, you're one up on me, Reggie." We went inside. I pointed to a small vacant table in the corner and said, "Grab that. I'll get us some coffee. What do you want?"

"Just regular."

He started to reach into his pocket for money. "It's on me. Cream or sugar?"

"Little cream would be good."

I got in line behind two young girls who couldn't decide what they wanted. When the barista rolled his eyes a second time, they finally opted for something with enough ingredients to bake a batch of cookies. I got us two regular coffees, added some cream to both and scrunched down at the table across from Reggie.

"Thanks, Eddie."

"You're welcome."

"How's your case comin'? You find that Frankie guy?"

"Got close," I said as I took the lid off the cup to let the coffee cool. Then I reached into my shirt pocket and laid the cellphone on the table, making sure I wasn't going to miss any calls from either Carla or her brother. I gave Reggie the rundown on where I stood in my investigation.

"Wow, this guy looks like he's got somethin' to hide."

"That's what I'm thinking too, but I can't for the life of me figure out what it might be."

We sipped our coffees and watched the parade of tourists on the Boulevard. Reggie uncrossed his legs and leaned over the table.

"What did that note say? The one Carla said she got from her brother?"

I pulled out my notebook and retrieved the slip of paper I'd folded and stuck between a couple of pages. I held it up and read, " 'I'm in trouble. Watch your back.' "

"What if he thinks *you're* the trouble?" Reggie said. "That's why he doesn't want anything to do with you."

"He doesn't know who the hell I am."

"Then why did he jump you the other day?"

"Somebody tipped him off about me."

"So he tried to scare you off. When it didn't work, he figured he had to keep away from you. To him, you're why he's in trouble."

"From who?"

"I don't know, but those two guys, Scarborough and Curran, sound like they're after him. Maybe he thinks you're in cahoots with them."

I sipped from my coffee cup and thought about what he'd said. "Well, in any case, I left a message and told him who I was."

"Yup, that's good. Hope it's his phone."

He turned to watch two young men sit down at the table next to ours. They had mugs of some sort of concoction with dollops of whipped cream on top and small pieces of pastry. Reggie sipped and set his cup down.

"But you know, Eddie, what kinda makes me wonder?"

"What?"

"Why would he tell Carla to watch her back when he thinks *he's* the one in trouble?"

"Good question," I said.

"Maybe she knows what he's up to. Did you ever think about that?"

His words caught me by surprise. "No, I haven't." I drank some coffee and looked at him for a long moment. "So, you're saying she knows where he is?"

He shrugged his shoulders. "Somethin' to think about."

It was. And I didn't like what it implied.

We finished our coffees, threw the cups in the trash, and stepped back onto the street and Betty White's chunk of fame.

Reggie stuck out his hand. "Hope I didn't throw a curve at you, Eddie."

"You didn't. That's partly why I called you. See if you had a different slant on things. Thanks for your input."

"Anything else I can do, you let me know."

"Maybe you can have me over for dinner sometime."

"Hey, yeah, that'd be a kick. I'll see ya."

He turned and walked down the Boulevard, pausing to look at the pentagrams on the sidewalk. I headed back to my office, pondering what Reggie had suggested. Was I being set up? I found that hard to believe, but if Frankie was indeed in trouble, why would he bother to tell Carla? And why would he then think his sister should watch her back? I needed to talk to her. The sooner the better.

When I got behind my desk, the first thing I did was send her a text, asking her to either text me back or call me. Then I followed up the text with a phone call, which went to voicemail. I relayed the fact that I thought I had a phone number for her brother and for her to call me asap. Another call to the number I had for Frankie also went to voicemail.

Mavis stuck her head into my office. "How's Reggie?"

"Great. He's teaching himself to cook."

"Really? That's terrific."

"Sit down for a minute, will you?"

"What's up, boss man?" She took a chair in front of my desk.

I pulled Frankie's message out of my notebook and handed it to her. "Read this and tell me what you think."

She did and then laid it back on the desk. "Sounds to me like this guy is concerned about his sister. "

"But he says *he's* the one in trouble. Why should Carla watch her back?"

She looked at the note again, and after a moment said, "Maybe he's saying whoever's after him is after her too."

"That's my gut reaction. But Reggie brought up another point."

"What?"

"That maybe she knows what he's up to."

Mavis picked up the note again. "That implies she would know where he is."

"Exactly."

"Then why the heck would she hire you to find him?"

"Why indeed?"

She looked at me for a long moment as her brow furrowed. "Are you trying to tell me you're being set up?"

"I don't know. After Reggie raised the possibility, it's been going through my head."

"Why would she do that?"

"I don't have a clue."

"You told me that after you worked together, the two of you dated for a while, right?"

"Right."

"What happened? Why'd you break up?"

"She told me another guy came back into her life. Apparently it was a mistake. The guy turned out to be a schmuck."

"Well, that certainly wasn't your fault. You didn't do anything to tick her off, did you?"

"Not to my knowledge." I leaned back in my chair and tapped a pencil on the inkpad of my desk. Mavis got up and leaned across.

"Listen, Eddie, I know you like Reggie's instincts, but if you ask me, I think it's a stretch to conclude Carla's setting you up. For what? Don't let paranoia into your head. You're supposed to get together with her later today, right?"

"That's the plan."

"Well, ask her."

I leaned forward, stuck the pencil back in a plastic cup full of pens, then picked up the cellphone. "I'm beginning to run out of versions of texts and messages." I started pushing keys to send her another one.

"I'm going to split. I'll be anxious to hear what she says." She went back into her office and after a moment she called out, "See you in the morning, Eddie."

"Roger," I said, as I finished the text and again dialed Carla's number. She still didn't pick up, even after I called both her cell and her landline. I put the phone in my shirt pocket and went back into my apartment for a beer. I punched the remote on the TV and aimlessly turned to ESPN and watched the last quarter of the Lakers trying to beat the Celtics. They weren't successful.

I knew how they felt.

Chapter Thirty

———————•———————

After watching the Lakers collapse, I'd had a taste for Thai food. There's a cozy place on Hollywood Boulevard that has always been pleasing to the palate.

Tonight had been a bit of a letdown. I'd failed to detect one of those little peppers in a forkful of some kind of noodle dish. For the next ten minutes I silently cried out for mercy, leaving the clientele wondering if they should call the paramedics for this poor unfortunate man who looked like he was having an epileptic fit.

The only solution was a cold beer, which I found in a little hole-in-the-wall tavern. On a TV hanging from the ceiling, another basketball game was in progress, this one between the Blazers and the Warriors. I started on the second cold draft and pulled my cellphone out of my shirt pocket. Still no message. With the freeways in LA being the jungle they are, an accident is always possible. However, in this 24/7 cellphone era with texting such a prevalent means of communication, I began to worry as to why Carla was not answering my messages.

I finished the beer and went back to my office, thinking maybe she'd called there. The answering machine wasn't blinking. After a brief pit stop, I locked up and headed for my car. I didn't think I'd need it, but I took my handgun from its box in the trunk and clipped the holster on my belt.

There was clear sailing down La Brea and then right on Venice out to Culver City. By the time I got to Jasmine Avenue, the streetlights were on, throwing patches of light at hundred-foot intervals. Carla's house was dark. I parked at the curb and saw that her Honda Fit wasn't under the carport at the end of the driveway. As I walked up to the front door, I looked around the neighborhood. Across the street, a front window was open, and I could see a television set flickering. Closed curtains filled the windows of the houses on both sides of Carla's.

A rolled-up newspaper lay on the front stoop. It was today's edition. Looking over my shoulder, I removed the plug from the wind chime and the key dropped into my hand. I tried the door, which was locked. I slid the key in, turned the knob and entered the darkened house. Laying the key on a table next to the door, I turned on a small lamp and stepped into the living room. There was no sound from anywhere in the house. I turned on another table lamp at the end of the sofa. Yesterday's edition of the *Los Angeles Times* was spread out on the coffee table.

Her telephone sat in a little recessed niche in the far wall. A light on top of the handset was blinking. There were three messages. I pushed the play button and the voice of someone by the name of Janice from Morton and Hayes gave Carla her call time for tomorrow's shoot. That would be her agent. I replayed the message and jotted down the agency's name and telephone number. On a film or TV shoot, an assistant director would normally give an actor a call time for the next day's shooting before they left the location. To cover themselves, the production would also inform the actor's agent. Apparently Carla hadn't yet picked up this message. The other two messages were from me, telling her to call me.

I walked into the kitchen and flicked on the light. A coffee cup and a cereal bowl and spoon sat in a white plastic dish rack. Her Keurig coffeemaker was turned off. Nothing seemed out of place. I poked my head into her bedroom and flicked on the light. The bed was made up without a trace of anyone having sat or lain down on the quilt. The bathroom was also undisturbed. I felt the towels and washcloth. Dry. Same with the inside of the shower curtain and the floor of the tub.

I'd started walking toward the rear of the hallway but froze when the front doorbell rang.

Lights were on so I couldn't very well pretend there was no one here. I walked down the hallway and peered through the peephole in the front door at two LA cops. I picked up the key from the table and dropped it into my pocket, then pulled the door open and turned on the porch light. One of the cops was black, the other Hispanic.

The black cop had a shaved head, and if Los Angeles ever got another NFL franchise, he'd be a candidate for the defensive line. He said, "Good evening, sir. Do you mind stepping outside?"

"Not at all," I replied as I pulled the door closed behind me and stood under the light. "What's the problem, officer?" His nametag identified him as Williams. The other cop was smaller and had a mustache. His name was Duran. He stood to the left of his partner.

"Could I see some ID, sir?" Williams said.

"Sure thing," I replied. I reached for my wallet in my hip pocket. The movement revealed the holstered gun on my belt. Duran immediately stepped back, pulled out his weapon, and dropped into the classic policeman's stance we've all seen a hundred times.

"He's armed, Stan," Duran said.

Williams also drew his gun and held it next to his head. "Turn around, sir, and spread your hands on the door! Do it now!"

He got no argument. Williams kicked my legs apart, pulled my gun from its holster, and then frisked me.

"Do you have a permit for this weapon, sir?" he said.

"I'm a private investigator. The permit's with my license."

"Sir, I want you to very slowly turn around and produce some identification."

Both cops had backed up and their weapons were trained on me. I cautiously reached for my wallet, then handed Williams my driver's license, PI license, and the permit for the gun. He replaced his weapon in its holster and held up the documents to the light.

"This is not your address, Mr. Collins," he said.

"No, this house belongs to a friend of mine. Carla Rizzoli."

Duran relaxed his stance and pointed to my car parked at the curb. "Is that your vehicle, sir?"

"Yes, it is. I'll be happy to get the registration."

"Not necessary," he said. Of course it wasn't. They'd no doubt run the plates the minute they pulled up.

"How did you gain entry to the house, Mr. Collins?" Williams said.

"I have a key," I replied. "It's in my front pocket. Do you want to see it?" Williams nodded his permission and I pulled out the key and held it up.

He looked at the doorknob. "Would you use it to lock the door, sir?"

I stuck the key in the knob and showed him it was locked.

"And now unlock it, please?"

I unlocked the door and pushed it open a couple of inches.

"What's your relationship to Miss Rizzoli?"

"She's a friend," I said, deliberately not telling him she was my client. "She gave me a key to the house. We were supposed to meet here. I arrived first." Williams handed my documents back to me. "I didn't break in, officers. Who called you?"

"A neighbor," Duran said. "Reported seeing an unfamiliar vehicle and a person entering the residence."

"Well, I haven't been here that often. I can understand that."

Williams handed my gun back. "Appreciate your cooperation, sir. Have a good evening." Duran nodded. He holstered his weapon and the two cops walked to their squad car parked behind mine.

I stepped back inside and peeked out through the front curtains. Duran stayed by the black-and-white while his partner walked across the street to the house where I'd seen the flickering television. My guess was that whoever lived there had phoned in my appearance at Carla's door. I walked back through the hallway to the rear entrance. It was locked, and I couldn't identify anything out of the ordinary in the second bedroom and the laundry room. It didn't look like Carla had been here today, and that thought weighed on me as I sat on the sofa, waiting for the cops to drive off. She wasn't here, but somehow I felt like she was. I entertained the thought of waiting for her, but then rejected the idea. She was a grown woman, but I was still worried. Better to wait and see what tomorrow would bring.

I checked the front of the house to see if the cops were gone. They were. The house across the street now had its curtains closed. I turned off the lights, locked the front door, and kept the key. If someone had seen me fiddling with the wind chime, I didn't want them to get the idea to do the same.

I crawled into my car, fired it up, and sat for a moment, looking at Carla's house. I'd never had a client disappear before I'd completed a case. It didn't sit well with me.

A chirp from my cell indicated a text. I pulled the phone from my pocket and looked at the display.

It wasn't Carla. It was from Frankie Rizzoli's phone.

The text read, *Tell her I'm OK.*

CHAPTER THIRTY-ONE

———◆———

YOU'D THINK I'D HAVE THE NUMBER memorized by now, but I didn't. I poked around the display on the phone and finally found the number for Frankie. Again, the call went straight to voicemail. Resisting the urge to throw the damn thing into the street, I sent him a text that read, *When I find her, I will.*

I started the car and headed for Century Boulevard. The parking lot of Feline Follies was almost full. I parked under one of the light poles. As I locked the car door, I glanced above the entrance at the neon cat wearing the top hat and bustier. Several light bulbs were burned out, making it look like something had taken a bite out of the animal's flicking tail. But when I got closer, I saw that they weren't burned out. They'd been smashed.

At the front door, four young men were jostling one another. One of them twirled a garter around his hand, trying to keep it away from his companions. I pulled the door open. Junior stood behind his podium, checking the IDs of two young men. They passed muster and walked through the black curtains leading to the main room.

"Hey, Junior," I said, "I'd be flattered if you carded me."

He looked up and flashed a huge grin. "What would you hand me? A Medicare card?"

I laughed and said, "Not yet, my friend. I'll have one soon enough, though."

"I'm just foolin' with you." He uttered a deep rumble of a chuckle and stuck out one of his meat-hook paws. I grabbed it and watched my hand disappear in its grasp. "Good to see you, Mr. Collins," he said. "Are you looking for Carla?"

"Yeah. I haven't been able to locate her. She's not answering her cell or responding to texts. Has she called in?"

He glanced at some papers in front of him. "She hasn't been scheduled for a couple of days, so I don't imagine she has. Something about landing a movie?"

"Right. You think any of the other girls have heard from her? Someone named Amy, maybe? Cocktail waitress?"

"That's right. Amy Corrigan."

"Is she working right now?"

"Let me check." He pulled a cellphone from the breast pocket of his blazer and punched in a number. "Ralph, it's Junior. Is Amy working the bar tonight?" He listened and took the phone from his ear. "She's on. Did you wish to talk with her?"

"Yeah. Just for a couple of minutes. If it's all right."

He put the phone back to his ear. "Can you spare her for a few? There's a gentleman out here who'd like to talk to her. About Carla." After a pause he said, "Thanks," and broke the connection.

"She'll be right out," he said. "You think something's happened to Carla, Mr. Collins?"

"I don't know. We were supposed to get together last evening. So, yeah, I'm a little worried."

Junior again looked at the sheaf of papers. "According to this, she's due for a late shift tomorrow. She might have made arrangements to switch with someone, but if so, nobody has told me."

Amy came through the curtains and walked up to us. She was definitely the girl who'd waited on Carla and me the other night. As before, she wore shorts so tight they looked like she'd been poured into them. A scanty red top completed the outfit. I stuck out my hand and introduced myself.

"Yeah, hi," she said. "I remember you. You're a friend of Carla's."

"That's right."

Behind us the front door opened, admitting a man and a woman. Amy gestured across the lobby to a bench covered with red satin and we sat down.

"Has something happened to Carla?" she said.

"I don't know. Has she called you?"

"No. I've sent her a few texts, but she hasn't responded."

"Same here," I said. "You know that she booked a part in that movie, right?"

"Yeah, and she was real gassed about it. I wanted her to tell me how it went. I'm kinda thinking about trying to get an agent myself."

"Would it be normal for her to be unresponsive like this?"

"No way. Carla is on that phone of hers constantly."

We glanced up as the couple crossed in front of us. "Amy, can you think of anywhere she might be? Friends? What she does when she's not here?"

She crossed one bare leg over the other and thought for a moment. "I know she goes to an acting workshop every once in a while. I don't know when, though."

"Do you know where it's held?"

She shook her head. "I'm not sure. One of the other girls might."

I fished out one of my business cards and handed it to her. "Could you ask around and let me know?"

"Sure." She looked at the card and said, "Eddie Collins, Private Investigator? Like in PI?"

"That's right," I replied.

"You looking for her brother?"

I nodded. "Did Carla tell you about him?"

"Yeah, she showed me the letter she got."

"When I was here the other day with Carla, you handed her a fifty-dollar tip. You said it was from two guys, one of them wearing a sling. Remember?"

"Sure do. We don't get tips like that around here very much."

"Had you seen those guys before?"

"A few times."

"Did they ever talk to Carla? Have anything to do with her?"

"No, I don't think so. They usually just sit and watch."

The curtains parted and a bartender stuck his head through. "Amy, we're getting behind in here."

"Okay, Ralph, be right there."

We stood up and shook hands. "Thanks for your time, Amy. Give me a call if you hear from Carla, would you?"

"Sure thing. And if you talk to her, tell her to call me."

"Will do," I said, and started for the front door as Amy walked through the curtains.

Junior sat on a stool, intent on his cellphone clutched in his massive hands. He looked up and said, "Any help from Amy?"

"No, she hasn't heard from Carla either."

He put the cell in his pocket and shook his head. "Damn, she's a real sweetheart. I hope nothing's happened to her."

I handed him one of my cards. "Give me a call if you hear from her."

"You got it, Mr. Collins." He stuck the card in his shirt pocket, and I walked to the front door.

"Oh, by the way, you're missing some bulbs in your sign."

"I know. A couple of gents got a little frisky last night."

"What happened?"

"One of them had a concealed weapons permit. I made him check his gun. On his way out I guess he decided he was going to 'get a little tail.' "

"Boys will be boys."

"Maybe so, but he's eighty-sixed from this playground."

I opened the door and headed toward my car. With this kind of workplace, I was glad Carla was carrying a gun.

I only hoped she hadn't been forced to use it.

Chapter Thirty-Two

I'M CONSTANTLY AMAZED WHENEVER I SEE people, young people in particular, glued to cellphones as if the contraptions were sources of energy, like batteries. In coffee shops, cars, at bus stops, everywhere, lives in jeopardy unless oblong chunks of plastic are clutched in both hands, thumbs flying. All in the name of communication. Or so I'm told.

And yet, there I was, sitting on the edge of my bed, running in the middle of the herd. My cell had not rung, even though I had kept it plugged in overnight. And now, as I clutched the phone in my hands, my thumbs sent yet another text, followed up by a call that again went to voicemail. No communication from Carla. *Nada.*

I stood in the shower and mulled over the idea of filing a missing person's report but decided it was probably inappropriate, if not premature. I was not an immediate family member, and Carla had not been incommunicado for that long. Besides, she was a grown woman. Packing a handgun, able to take care of herself, right? And yet concern gnawed at me.

I decided to make another visit to her house to see if she had shown up. After completing my ablutions, I filled a go-cup with zapped coffee and left a note for Mavis telling her my whereabouts. Traffic on surface streets was light and I got to Jasmine Avenue a little before eight thirty. Her Honda Fit wasn't in the driveway, nor under the carport. I pulled in, picked up the newspaper, and opened the front door. The phone was blinking. I pushed the playback button and listened to the first message.

"Carla, honey," a male voice said. "This is Patrick from Morton and Hayes. We need to know where you are, darlin'. You're in danger of having this job taken away from you. Give us a ring asap." Another call from her agent. I wasn't the only one looking for her. The next two messages were from me. I fast-forwarded through them and a woman's voice came on. "Carla, this is Amy. Call me when you get this. That PI Mr. Collins came by the Follies looking for you. Are you okay? Call me, please."

The messages stopped and I looked around the living room. Nothing had changed since last night. Same with the kitchen. And her bedroom. The bathroom was also undisturbed. I pulled the front door open and locked it behind me.

As I started for my car, I noticed an elderly woman in the front yard of the house across the street. She wore a brown sweater, jeans, and black, high-top tennis shoes. In her right hand she held a garden hose with one of those squeezable nozzles. She was spraying a bed of flowers. An adjustable dog leash was clutched in her other hand. On the end of it, digging up the grass next to the curb, was one of those dogs I've often heard people compare to Winston Churchill. Without the cigar, of course. This one was brown and white and looked like he'd met up with a brick wall and the wall won. He had stubby legs and froth around his mouth that flew in all directions whenever he moved his head. She called out to me as I opened the car door.

"Excuse me, sir?" She dropped the hose and reeled in her flat-faced pet. "Could I talk to you for a minute?"

"Yes, ma'am. Can I help you?" I walked across the street. The dog looked up and grunted.

"I'm sorry for siccing the cops on you last night."

"Oh, no problem."

"I didn't recognize your car and thought I should call them."

"I understand."

"Are you a friend of Carla's?"

"I'm a private investigator," I said as I gave her one of my cards and offered my hand. "What is your name, ma'am?"

"Audrey Westbrook," she said as she offered a damp handshake.

"Have you seen Carla lately, Audrey?"

"I'm afraid I haven't. What does she need a private investigator for? Do you think something's happened to her?"

"I don't know. Should I be worried?"

She looked at my card and tugged on the leash as the dog made a move toward me. "Well, I'm not sure. There's been another unfamiliar car parked in her driveway."

"When was that?"

"Day before yesterday. I had just gotten back from Ralph's. They had a sale on artichokes. When I walked into the front room, I saw it pull into her driveway."

"Could you describe the car for me?"

"It was one of those Toyotas. I think they call them Raves, or something like that."

"A Toyota RAV4. Is that what you mean?"

"Yes, that's it. My nephew has one and I couldn't remember what he calls it."

"Did you happen to catch the license plate?"

"It was too far away. I couldn't see. Cataracts, y'know?"

"Could you tell what color it was?"

"Oh, yes. No mistake about that. It was bright red."

Bright red. Just like the vehicle belonging to James Curran. "Did you see who was driving it?"

"Well, after a few minutes, the driver's door opened and a black man got out. He walked down the driveway, looked around, and then came back and knocked on the front door."

"Hang on a minute, will you, Audrey? I want you to look at a couple of pictures." I walked back to my car and picked up the photos of Frankie and Curran that Mavis had made for me. When I walked back, the dog snuffled at me and got a yank on his leash for his efforts. I handed Audrey the picture of Curran in his MP uniform.

"Did the driver resemble this guy in any way? The picture was taken a few years ago, so he may look a little different now."

She looked at the photo for a long moment and handed it back to me. "I couldn't say for sure but I can see a resemblance."

"How about this man?" I handed her the picture of Frankie in his desert fatigues. "Have you ever seen him visiting Carla?"

She shook her head and gave me the picture. "No, I've never seen this guy."

"Thanks, Audrey. I appreciate the help."

"Is she in trouble?"

"No, I don't think so, but I'd like you to call me if you see anyone coming or going over there. Or if you see her."

"Yes, yes, I sure will," she said. The Sir Winston lookalike sniffed at my shoes and the leg of my trousers. She gave the leash a yank. "Buster, come here!"

"That's a nice dog," I said. "A bulldog, right?"

"Yes. He's supposed to be a guard dog, but I sometimes think he's too friendly."

"Thanks for your help, Audrey," I said. "You have a good day." She nodded and picked up the hose as I walked across the street and crawled into my car. As I pulled away from the curb, I gave a wave to Audrey and Buster.

There are a hell of a lot of red Toyota RAV4s in Southern California. James

Curran owned one. No big deal, right? Except for the fact that he'd showed up at the home of my client.

I stopped at an Arco and gassed up, then parked next to the air pump and called Mavis. "Hey, kiddo. Any calls? From a missing client, by any chance?"

"Nothing, Eddie. You have any luck?"

"Not much."

"Hey, I got to thinking. Maybe we should check with the ERs. She could have had an accident."

"That's not a bad idea. Could you do that for me? I'm on my way back to the office."

"I'll get right on it," she said, and hung up.

I hoped Carla hadn't crashed her car, but as any Angelino knows, the possibility rides shotgun with every driver on these freeways.

I swung by Larch street and Scarborough's address to see if there was a red RAV4 or a black Hyundai on the premises. I was out of luck.

Chapter Thirty-Three

---◆---

W HEN I WALKED IN THE DOOR, Mavis was on the phone. She listened for a moment while I sat down in the chair in front of her desk. She hung up and said, "No luck, Eddie. Nobody by the name of Carla Rizzoli was admitted to a hospital. Anywhere."

"Well, that's some comfort, I guess."

"She still hasn't shown up at home?"

"No. And it's bugging the hell out of me."

"Oh, and I got some info on that downtown address you gave me. It's due for demolition. The management company says they've given front-door keys to only three tenants. But the lady went on to say that she knows for a fact that copies have probably been made. Sounds like people come and go all the time."

"That's what I figured," I said. "Thanks."

Her phone rang and she picked it up. I went back to my apartment for a pit stop, made up my bed, and was suddenly struck with an idea. When I came back to her office, Mavis was on the phone with a bill collector. She hung up, a scowl on her face.

"I'm going over to Morrie's office," I said.

"You owe him commission?"

"No. I'm going to ask him to put me to work."

My comment wiped the scowl off her face and replaced it with something far more pleasant. Puzzlement.

MORRIE HOWARD'S OFFICE WAS IN AN old brick building a block and a half south of Hollywood Boulevard. He'd been there for years, waiting for the inevitable wrecking ball. So far he'd managed to escape. There was no elevator, so I climbed a set of stairs that creaked with every move. The middle of each wooden tread on the steps was worn down, probably from years of actors trudging up to Morrie's door, hoping for a sliver of fame and fortune in the celluloid circus.

I pushed open the door and immediately smelled cat urine. I'd never detected this odor in my previous visits to his office. His assistant, Kevin Reynolds, a young man on the forefront of mod fashion, sprawled behind a desk. His black hair stood straight up like he'd stuck his finger in a light socket. He wore a black T-shirt with snarling, drooling dragons on the front. The piercings in his ears and nose would give a TSA agent nightmares.

"Hey, Kevin. What's with the cat piss?"

He rolled his eyes and pointed behind me. Curled up in a threadbare easy chair was a huge black tabby. The animal looked up at me, yawned, and assumed its original position, obviously put out by the interruption.

"Why?" I said.

"Mice. Or so the boss says."

"What's its name?"

"Hitchcock."

"Catchy."

"Not my choice. I lobbied for Elvis."

I chuckled and walked into Morrie's office. He was behind his desk, leaning back in his chair, his feet propped up on an open drawer. The sole of one of his shoes had a small hole in it. Morrie was nearly bald, and what strands of gray hair that remained were combed over the top of his head, so that the part in his hair ran right above his left ear. Rimless John Lennon glasses were perched on his nose and he was reading what looked like a script. He glanced up at me and tossed it on a shelf behind him, sending dust motes into a beam of sunlight filtering through a grimy window.

"Eddie Collins. Be still my heart. Are you lost?"

"Since when did you get mice?"

"I wish I knew."

I pointed to a birdcage in one corner of the room. Sitting on a perch were two yellow parakeets. "What about those guys? They're lunch for Hitch in there."

"Who, Thelma and Louise? Nah, not a chance. That cat's got more arthritis than me. He'll never get up there." He took his feet off the drawer, slammed it shut, and leaned on his desk. "Are you a client of mine today, or are you here with gum on your shoe?"

"A little of both. There's a film called *Festival of Death* shooting up in Valencia. Can you tell me who's casting the extras?"

He peered over his glasses. "Why?"

"I want you to get me on it tomorrow."

"You want to do extra work?"

"You heard me right."

He took off his glasses and rubbed his eyes. "Oh, boy. I suppose there's a reason for this?"

"A client of mine was booked on it and she's disappeared. I need to find out what the hell happened to her."

He gave me a long look, then shook his head and hit the space bar on his computer. The screen came alive. "Let's see what the Breakdowns say."

The Breakdown Service provides agents and managers with information on who is casting what. An agent subscribes to the service, sees something that is right for his client, and submits the actor's picture and résumé to the casting director. If they like what they see, they call the agent and set the actor up with an audition. With extras, or background performers, it's a little different and not quite as specific. The background casting director may want thirty men, twenty women, housewives, and dads. You get booked, stuff part of your closet into a garment bag, and then show up and sit around, reading and working crossword puzzles and trying not to look bored. It's never been my cup of tea, but I figured if I could get on the set, maybe I could find out from somebody what may have happened to my client.

Hitchcock the Cat wandered into the office, gave the obligatory sniff to my trousers, and limped to a bowl of dry food in the corner.

Morrie leaned back from looking at his computer. "Pinnacle Players."

"Terrific. I know Judy Meeks over there. She owes me a favor."

"They need forty middle-aged men. Are you middle-aged?"

"I've always been middle-aged, Morrie. Get her on the horn."

Judy Meeks used to be an actress. We shot a television commercial together a few years back before she gave up the business to hold sway over other actors' lives. We'd remained friends over the years and the favor she owed me involved a former boyfriend of hers. The guy was fooling around on her, a fact I had discovered quite by accident. I took a few pictures, and the guy ultimately had a change of heart.

Morrie cleared his throat and spoke into the phone. "Judy Meeks, please. This is Morrie Howard." He handed the phone to me. "Here, gumshoe, work your magic."

I put the phone to my ear and after a moment heard, "This is Judy."

"Hi darlin'. It's Eddie Collins."

"Oh, my God, I haven't heard from you in donkey's years. What's up?"

"I see you're casting *Festival of Death.*

"Yeah. This one might go straight to video."

"I need a favor."

"Sure thing. Name it."

"Can you get me on it for a couple of days?"

"You mean background?"

"That's right."

"What, no more principal work?"

"I need a few extra bucks, Judy."

"Can you work tomorrow?"

"Absolutely."

"Okay. Dad. Casual. Bring a couple of changes. Sweaters and stuff."

"You're a peach."

"I'll fax Morrie the directions."

"Great. How's that boyfriend working out?"

"Pretty good. I married him three years ago."

"Terrific. Hey, thanks for the help, Judy."

"Anytime, Eddie."

She hung up and I handed the phone back to Morrie. He replaced the receiver and pulled a bottle of Mountain Dew from a mini-fridge next to the cat dish. Hitchcock had retreated to his chair in the other room.

"You know you run the risk of them thinking you're only an extra now, right?"

"Yeah, I hear you. But this is a one-time deal."

"From your lips to my ears, bubbeleh."

Bubbeleh was a nickname Morrie loved, a Yiddish term of endearment. I wondered if he'd considered it for Hitchcock. The fax machine starting squirting out directions to the shoot. He scribbled the call-time on the top of the page and handed it to me. Six a.m. at the Magic Mountain parking lot. An early night for the gumshoe.

CHAPTER THIRTY-FOUR

———◆———

I ONLY GET UP BEFORE THE CRACK of dawn for early call times on a film or TV project. Rising early is not my strong suit. I suppose that comes from closing up as many bars as I have over the years. As I sat on the edge of the bed letting the cobwebs dissipate, I checked my cellphone. Still nothing from Carla.

One benefit of being an early bird in Los Angeles is less traffic. It was smooth sailing through the Cahuenga Pass and up into the Antelope Valley. Of course everyone was going to work. So was I, but in the opposite direction.

I have many actor friends who started out in the business doing extra work. Even now, some of them rely on the gigs to make ends meet. Auditioning is not a factor. If you've got the right look, you're golden. There used to be a Screen Extras Guild, but in what was considered by some to be an unpopular move, SAG absorbed the extras, and now the more politically correct term is "background performers."

I knew I was facing a bit of a demotion, in the sense that an actor on a "principal" contract gets a few more perks, having lines and getting your name in the credits among them. A principal also merits a dressing room, for instance, which usually comes in the form of a honeywagon, a cubicle that can make even changing your mind a challenge. Background performers usually are last in the chow line. Never offer free food to an actor; they can be voracious, which many extras are. They're also notorious for looking into the camera when they're not supposed to. Many of them want their fifteen minutes of fame and will do any outrageous piece of business to get it. So the challenge for me was going to be staving off boredom. Hopefully, being in the background would give me opportunities to inquire about a cast member missing in action.

The morning was chilly; I had to turn the car's heater on, something I was unaccustomed to. Given the considerable difference in elevation between the Los Angeles Basin and the Antelope Valley, the heat felt good. The Hollywood Freeway merged with the I-5 coming in from my left. Traffic continued to be light as I snaked up through the Valley into Valencia. The directions said to get off on Magic Mountain Parkway and follow the signs. They were impossible to miss. "Base Camp," as it's called, occupied one corner of the amusement park's vast parking lot. Yellow plastic stanchions with rope connecting them outlined the perimeters of cast and crew parking. Twisted Colossus, Apocalypse, and Goliath—three of the amusement park's rides—loomed in the pre-dawn gloom. Traces of daylight caressed the tops of the mammoth skeletons, making them look even more intimidating and further confirming that no way in hell would I ever get on any of them.

The production's security crew waved my car into a row already taking shape. I shut off the engine, opened the trunk and hustled myself into my down vest. I was going to need it. I grabbed my garment bag and followed directions to three white vans parked near the entrance, exhaust plumes floating upward in the morning cold.

I piled into the first vehicle and sandwiched myself into the rear seat. Three other men and two women joined me, all with garment and shoulder bags. We exchanged good mornings and waited while the van filled up. Finally, a production assistant gave the Teamster an okay and we pulled out and headed for the location.

From their conversation, I could tell my fellow background performers knew each other. They chatted about yesterday's work and one woman expressed the hope that they would wrap a little earlier today.

The man sitting next to me sipped on a cardboard coffee cup and stuck out his hand. "Mornin'. I'm Darryl Jackson."

"Eddie Collins."

"First day?"

"Yeah. How's the shoot going?"

"Well, they ran into a little hiccup. One of the leads didn't show up yesterday."

"Really? How come?"

"They don't know."

"Who was it?"

One of the women in front of me turned in her seat. "Her name is Carla Rizzoli. I heard somebody say she wasn't cutting the mustard."

"Really?" I said. "So they replaced her?"

"That's what I heard," the woman said.

Her seat mate chimed in, "I don't know if that's true. She finished the day. If they were going to fire her, seems to me they wouldn't continue to shoot."

The van pulled onto a frontage road running alongside the freeway. It was gravel and full of bumps. The coffee drinkers held their cups out in front of them to prevent any spillage. A small arc of the sun peeked over the hills to the east. I somehow couldn't agree with my van mates about Carla's ability to cut the mustard. Based on the one time I had worked with her in the past, she didn't strike me as being mediocre. Something else had caused her to be replaced.

We meandered over hills, traveling into the boondocks behind the amusement park. After swinging around a bend, we had a view of the location. A Renaissance Fair lay spread out in front of us. Several tents with Medieval-looking banners on top dotted the landscape. I could see grips moving lights and camera equipment into what could pass for a village square. Trucks, honeywagons, and production trailers were lined up on both sides of the entrance to the fair.

The van pulled up next to a tarp covering collapsible tables and plastic chairs. On the far side were long tables stocked with food. As we sidled out of the van, I saw people lined up in front of a roach coach, plates at the ready. They looked like crew, tool belts strapped around waists.

Another PA came up to us and began giving directions. She pointed to the other side of the tables and chairs where breakfast was available. We were to hang on to our bags, and a wardrobe person would soon tell us where to go. It didn't take long for me to start feeling like a member of a herd. I followed Darryl, and we draped our bags over a table and headed for craft services, which is the designation for food and snacks.

There was ample fruit, pastries, and cold cereal. Also coffee, which I eagerly sought out. Next to the big stainless-steel urn lay an 8½-by-11-inch call sheet. I picked it up and stuck it in a pocket of my vest. Filling a paper plate with a banana, a yogurt, and a couple of muffins, I went back to where Darryl and I had placed our garment bags.

I set my breakfast on the table and settled into the plastic chair. It sunk into the wet turf under my weight and I grabbed the table to steady myself. Darryl saw my predicament and laughed.

"Those damn things aren't made for us big boys, are they?"

"I guess not," I replied. The coffee was hot and felt good against the chill. I unfolded the call sheet and smoothed it out next to my paper plate.

"Where'd you find that?"

"Somebody left it lying next to the coffee," I said.

"That's a find. They don't give us those things."

"I know."

"You do much extra work, Eddie?" Darryl said, as he dug into a bowl of Cheerios.

"Haven't for a while. I needed a few extra bucks."

"I hear you."

We sipped our coffee and munched on our food as I scanned the call sheet. On one side was a list of the characters needed for today's shoot. I remembered Carla telling me her character's name was Diane Carpenter. The role was now assigned to one Claudia Burns. Right above her name was Brad Carpenter, played by Don Atkinson.

I looked farther down the list and saw the name of an actor I knew. In the role of Detective Draper was Arnold Glover. Arnie and I had played two corporate executives on a made-for-television movie. The rest of the page listed the number of people needed for the different departments. Electric, construction, Teamsters, etcetera. Also listed were above-the-line personnel, the director, assistant directors, and production people. My eye landed on a producer whose name was Fred Curran. Brother of James? Father? If possible, I intended to find out.

I peeled my banana and asked Darryl, "Were you anywhere near this Carla Rizzoli?"

"Yeah, I was part of a crowd watching these two cops interviewing her and her husband about a murder." He swiveled on his chair and pointed into the set. "There's a small creek running next to that big yellow tent. A body is discovered and the cops are interrogating people at the fair. I was only in the background for one shot, then they moved the camera to another angle."

"Did she look like she was messing up?"

"Not to my eyes," he said as he pried off the rind of an orange. "Do you know her?"

"I do, as a matter of fact."

"Any idea why they would replace her?"

"Can't think of one," I said.

He shook his head and pulled apart a sliver of the orange. "Aw, man, who the hell knows? Maybe a producer's girlfriend needed a job. So kick someone off a payroll. Happens all the time, doesn't it?"

"Yeah, I guess," I said. Stuff like that frequently does happen in this damn business. But that doesn't mean you all of a sudden stop communicating with someone who's looking for you. There was another reason, and I had a feeling it had something to do with two ex-MPs.

I was on my second cup of coffee when a wardrobe lady carrying a clipboard walked into the background staging area. She began calling out names, mine being one of them, and we picked up our bags and followed her to the wardrobe truck. We were individually summoned inside for wardrobe inspection. For me, they settled on a pair of tan Dockers, brown cardigan sweater, and a dark-blue shirt, along with a tweed newsboy hat. In front of the wardrobe truck was an enclosed tent where male background could get dressed. I changed clothes, making sure to keep my valuables with me. Then it was into makeup.

I was directed to an empty chair and a slim black lady wearing a white smock.

"Good morning," she said. "My name's Wanda. How're you doin'?"

"Trying to wake up."

"Yeah, ain't that the truth." She looked me over and fluffed the edges of my hair. "They give you a hat to wear?" I held up the newsboy cap. "You look ruddy enough, young man. You're good to go."

Crawling out of the chair, I headed back to the staging area, had another cup of coffee, and awaited my call to background performer.

Chapter Thirty-Five

---◆---

Two more vans drove onto the location as Darryl and I stood in a patch of sunlight, which didn't as yet provide a lot of warmth. Hot cups of coffee clasped in our hands helped. As soon as the vans emptied, an assistant director shouted out last names and instructions. People began to shuffle off to their various assignments, some to wardrobe, others to hair and makeup. Those who didn't hear their name drifted to the craft services tables. Several of the passengers without garment bags started walking toward trailers. I assumed these were principal performers who had their own dressing rooms. From a distance I recognized my friend Arnie Glover, but before I could call out to him, he disappeared into one half of a trailer that was divided into two separate cubicles.

I looked at the call sheet I'd picked up earlier, showed it to Darryl, and pointed to the first scene on the schedule. "Is this what they were shooting yesterday?"

"Looks like it," he said. "They ran out of light before they could get it."

"Do you know this Don Atkinson? The guy playing the husband?"

"I've seen him around at auditions and stuff. Never really met him though."

The same AD who earlier had been giving directions, a stocky young woman bundled up in a ski jacket and stocking cap, walked into the staging area and began calling out more last names. Both Darryl's and mine were among them. She told us to leave our garment bags draped over a table in the corner. Security would look after them. We did as she asked and then followed her through the entrance of the fair.

I was among a group of twenty—ten men and ten women. As we walked we had to shield our eyes from the sun that had by now cleared the ridges to the east. On our left was a booth with a sign above it advertising turkey legs, which I guess is a staple at these Renaissance Fairs. A booth to our right was dubbed Ye Olde Grog Shoppe. Pewter mugs hung from hooks on a weather-beaten piece of lumber. Set decorators fussed over several other booths that sold wreaths made of flowers, Medieval costume pieces, and other paraphernalia, all meant to thrust the fair-goer back to the age of jousts, damsels in distress, and knights in shining armor.

The AD led us to the edge of a small creek—one that was real, not manufactured by movie magic. Grips adjusted lights and a small clump of technicians huddled around a man I assumed was the director, Lester Wells. He peered through a lens dangling from a cord around his neck, moved slightly and framed a shot with his hands. His crew focused on him, hanging on his every word.

Our AD summoned us, and we clustered around her. "Listen up, folks. My name's Beth. I'm a second AD and you're my platoon today. I want all cells powered down. Not in vibrating mode. Off completely."

Hands went into pockets, cellphones came out, and fingers flew. Before shutting mine off, I checked for messages. Nothing.

"I'm going to pair you up," Beth continued. "For this scene, you and your partner will essentially be married. We'll put some kids in later."

She started her matchmaking. I got hooked up with an attractive, slender brunette by the name of Sasha Evans. After we introduced ourselves, we both admitted that we hoped to wind up childless. We shared a good laugh as we recalled W.C. Fields' admonition to never work with children or animals. She was a pleasant lady, which was going to make the day's tedium much easier to deal with.

Beth began explaining what the scene was about. Two detectives—one played by Arnie Glover, the other by a black actor named Phil Prescott— were going to be interviewing Don Atkinson and his on-screen wife, Claudia Burns, formerly played by Carla Rizzoli.

A technician unspooled a roll of yellow police tape in front of us. Our directions were to stand behind the tape and whisper among ourselves and act horrified by what had just happened. The focus of our attention was a young man who walked to the edge of the creek, lay down, and slid into the water, leaving head and shoulders on the grass. A crew member sprayed his upper body with water, giving the impression he'd tried to crawl up the bank. I hoped to hell the guy was getting paid more than scale, because that water was going to get damn cold real fast.

After more adjustments and consultations, the first AD told Beth to bring in the first team. These were the four principals, the two detectives, and Atkinson and Burns. The four of them walked into the scene and exchanged greetings with the director and his camera crew. Four children—three girls and a boy—were brought onto the set and Sasha and I gave each other high fives for remaining childless.

Quiet was called for, the AD yelled, "background," and we started dredging up horrified expressions. We whispered amongst ourselves, and the women clasped hands to their shocked faces. I put my arm around Sasha and with no reservations she buried her face in my chest, dabbing a handkerchief to her eyes. This girl was committed; I had to give her that. We watched as Glover and Prescott talked to the other principals, taking notes and periodically pointing to the young man halfway submerged in the creek.

After a few minutes, the director called "Cut" and conferred with Atkinson and Burns. They listened intently and nodded their heads. He then spoke to the first AD, who shouted "Back to number one," which meant another take was coming. The director did three more, again called "Cut," and followed it with "Check the gate." This prompted a camera assistant to examine the slot through which the film is fed to ensure the camera is free from lint or other substances that would show up on the processed film. He gave his okay, and the AD announced that they were moving on to the next set-up, the next camera angle.

Beth told us to relax for a bit, but to stay close. She pointed out a honey wagon back by the hair and makeup trailers, which is where restrooms were located. Crew members had carted in plastic chairs for us to sit on. They'd also trucked in a coffee urn and fixings. As I siphoned out a cup, I spotted Arnie Glover. Whoever had cast the principals was spot-on with him playing a police detective. He stood about five feet eight, and wore a trench coat and a rumpled suit with tie askew. His face was craggy and dominated by a cleft in his chin deep enough to rival Kirk Douglas'. Salt and pepper hair was fashioned into a crew cut. When he saw me, his face broke into a huge grin and we shook hands.

"Hey, Eddie, what the hell are you doing here?"

"Trying not to steal the scene from you."

He filled a Styrofoam cup with coffee. "You working background?"

"Yup. Somebody's got to keep you honest. And I can use the dough."

"What about that private eye business of yours? You still trying to be Sam Spade?" He chuckled and sipped on his coffee.

"Yeah, I'm also working a case. Carla Rizzoli is a client. I need to find out why the hell she's not on the picture anymore."

"Man, I don't know, that was the damnedest thing. I got here and—"

He was interrupted by the AD shouting, "First team in, please." That was Arnie's cue and he dumped his coffee on the ground and threw the cup into the trash.

"I gotta go, Eddie. But hey, listen, let's hook up at lunch and I'll fill you in."

"I'd appreciate it," I said.

Arnie moved off. I finished my coffee and looked around for my mate for the day, Sasha Evans. We found chairs and made small talk about the business and the pursuit of fame and fortune until our platoon sergeant Beth found us and herded us off to another part of the location. We were told to hover around one of the booths as the two cops walked along the fair's street, dogged by a court jester juggling three colored balls. Since our faces were recognizable in the scene down by the creek, we were now told to have our backs to the camera. The term "background" was apt. For the next couple of hours, Sasha and I found ourselves in different locales with different costume pieces added and subtracted.

At one point we were told to relax while they shot a close-up of two of the street performers in the fair. I took advantage of the break and went in search of the men's restroom in the large honey wagon. The trailer was in two sections and had stair units leading up to the cubicles, making it look like a caterpillar on wheels.

A dressing trailer with "Star Waggons" emblazoned on the side sat next to it. Lyle Waggoner, an actor who spent seven seasons as the resident hunk on the old Carol Burnett show, founded the company in 1979. Since then it has grown into one of the largest suppliers of movie trailers in the industry.

I completed my business and decided to amble around the location a bit. It had gotten considerably warmer and a slight breeze floated through the oak trees surrounding the site. I wasn't looking for anything specific, but I thought maybe I could pick up some clue as to why Carla was no longer on this shoot.

As I walked around the corner of the production trailer, I found it.

James Curran stepped out of the trailer and caught sight of me. I could have turned and walked the other way, but it was too late. Even though the previous conversation I'd had with him through the screen door at Scarborough's house had been brief, he definitely recognized me. He wore dark aviator sunglasses under a black baseball cap. He walked up to me and stood, glaring, giving no indication as to what he was going to do.

"You ever find Phil Scarborough?" he said.

"Matter of fact, I did."

"So what the hell are you doing here?"

"Plying my trade."

"Really?"

"You want to see my SAG card?"

"Humor me."

I reached into my hip pocket, pulled out my wallet, and showed him the card in its plastic sleeve. After taking a quick look, he handed the wallet back.

I put it in my pocket and took out the call sheet. "Now why don't you humor me? What the hell are you doing here?"

"I'm involved in the production."

I looked at the sheet and said, "Fred Curran? That you?"

"How do you know my name's Curran?"

"I had the plate run on that little red RAV4 of yours."

"Nosy son of a bitch, aren't you?"

"Curious, is all."

He pulled out a pack of cigarettes and lit one up. "Fred Curran is my old man. I'm an associate producer on this movie."

"Well, then, maybe you can answer my question. Why isn't Carla Rizzoli still in the picture?"

"I don't know. You'd have to ask the director. I don't concern myself with artistic decisions."

"Was she fired?"

"Beats me. You also shouldn't concern yourself with artistic decisions."

"What about her brother, Frankie?"

"Don't know the man."

I pulled out the picture of Frankie and his fellow MP in Iraq and showed it to him. "That's you, isn't it?"

"Hard to say. We brothers all tend to look alike. Don't you know that, Collins?" He took a deep puff off the cigarette, exhaled, and watched the smoke drift away in the breeze. "You better fade off into the background before someone fires you."

I looked at him for a long moment and walked off, but stopped when he said, "I'll see if I can find out what happened with the Rizzoli girl."

Right, I thought. I'd have a better chance of finding a snowman at the corner of Hollywood and Vine.

CHAPTER THIRTY-SIX

———— ◆ ————

L UNCH WAS CALLED AT TWELVE THIRTY, whereupon the class divide on this movie set quickly became evident. Only crew members and principal performers were served from the roach coach. We backgrounders were relegated to steam trays set out under the tarp. I filled a paper plate with a chicken concoction of dubious origins. Brown rice, a dollop of green beans, and a couple of brownies completed the midday meal. I sat at one of the long tables, twisted off the top of a bottle of Snapple, and dug in. Surprisingly, the chicken was quite palatable. The way my colleagues shoveled it in showed that they agreed.

From the information Mavis had dug up for me the other day, I wasn't surprised to see Fred Curran involved with *Festival of Death*. But James Curran's presence was a curve ball. Did that mean Phil Scarborough was also lurking around somewhere? The coincidence of these two guys circling Carla and her disappearance kind of spoiled my lunch.

I looked up to see Arnie Glover headed my way. Behind him was Don Atkinson. They straddled chairs across from me and I saw further evidence of the movie's class divide. Arnie had a small rib eye in front of him, and filling Atkinson's plate was a fine looking chunk of salmon.

"Eddie, this is Don Atkinson," Arnie said. "Thought maybe he could give you some help."

"Eddie Collins," I said as I stuck out my hand, careful not to drag my cuff across his fish. He looked to be in his thirties, had sandy blond hair, and a face fair enough that he could have started out as a model. Both he and Arnie had white bibs around their necks to prevent any traces of lunch from winding up on costumes.

"How are you, sir?" Atkinson said. "Arnie tells me you're a private investigator."

"That's right. I'm also an actor."

"Damn good one, too," Arnie chimed in. "He's aced me out of a couple of jobs."

"Flattery will get you everywhere, Arnie," I said.

The two men laughed and Atkinson forked a bite of salmon into his mouth. After a moment he said, "So, what brings you to our little film here, Eddie?"

"Carla Rizzoli is a client of mine, and she's disappeared. Thought maybe I could get some sort of hint as to why she isn't on this shoot anymore."

Arnie sliced off a chunk of his steak and dipped it in a little plastic cup of sauce. "Well, as I started to tell you earlier, it was the damnedest thing. We showed up yesterday morning and she'd been replaced by this Burns gal."

"Any explanation for why?" I said.

"Some family problem," Atkinson said. "At least that's what the first AD told me." He lifted a piece of salmon into his mouth and chewed with undisguised appreciation, as if unconsciously mocking my meager chicken concoction.

"Did the AD give any more specifics?" I said.

"That's what I was told too, Eddie," Arnie said. "What did she hire you to do? Or is that none of my business?"

Client confidentiality should have persuaded me to evade his question, but I didn't think this was the time to worry about it. "Normally, it would be, Arnie," I said, "but if I can't find my client, it seems like it's a moot point. She hired me to locate her brother. So that's why I'm wondering if your AD mentioned a specific family problem."

Arnie looked at Atkinson as the actor sipped on a glass of milk. "Nope. He didn't say anything more to me."

"Same here," Atkinson said.

"What about Monday?" I asked. "Was that the first day both you guys were called?"

They looked at each other and Arnie said, "Yeah, it was mine." Atkinson nodded in agreement.

"Did she seem bothered by anything?" I asked.

"Not that I noticed," Arnie said. "But I didn't say much to her between takes. Don here would be more help to you on that score."

I turned to Atkinson and watched him fill a fork with salad. "Did she seem all right to you?" I said.

He chewed for a moment. "Absolutely. She was funny and upbeat. I happened to mention that I was involved in this acting workshop. She'd been working with another guy, so we got to comparing notes. It looked to me like she was really pumped up about being in front of the camera."

I took a swallow of my Snapple and watched a couple of crew members tossing a football. The information Atkinson gave me coincided with the feeling I'd gotten from Carla when we'd parted on Monday morning. She was enthusiastic and gave me the impression she was going to do her best. I had no indication anything had been bothering her.

"Don, let me ask you this," I said. "Since Carla was playing your wife, I imagine you stuck close to each other on Monday, right?"

"Yeah, pretty much. About ten thirty or so, we had a little break. They'd turned the camera around and we weren't needed, so we were told to relax for a while."

"So you went back to your trailers?" I said as I finished off my chicken whatchamacallit.

"Right. We were in one of those dual trailers. She had one half, I had the other."

"Same thing with me, Eddie," Arnie said. "Prescott and I share a trailer. I suppose the company saves a little dough. Two for one, you know."

I nodded. On a previous occasion, I'd been assigned half a trailer alongside a giggly young starlet. She'd had more clout, or looked better in a miniskirt, because at one point a Teamster came by and confiscated my cable-TV hookup and gave it to her. He'd promised to replace it. I'm still waiting.

"Don, could you tell if anyone else was in Carla's trailer?" I said. "You hear voices?"

"After a couple of minutes I could hear music, but that's all."

"How long was your break?"

"A PA knocked on my door after, oh, I don't know, forty-five minutes?"

"And then did the same to Carla's?"

"Yeah, I told him to leave my door open, so I heard him knock on hers. Her door slammed and she poked her head in my room. Then we walked back to the set together."

"Any change in her mood?"

"Nope. We got back to talking about the business. That's when she told me she worked at that club."

"Feline Follies?"

"Yeah."

"That place on Olympic?" Arnie said. "By the airport?"

"That's the one," I replied. "You a regular, Arnie?"

"Nah. I popped in one day a few years ago. Just curious, you know? My cell died. I had to use the payphone."

"Yeah, right." I chuckled and caught his wink over the bottle of iced tea he'd raised to his mouth. "When did you wrap on Monday?"

"The light started to fade," Arnie said. "I guess it was four thirty or so. Right, Don?"

"Sounds about right," Atkinson said.

That corresponded with the time Carla had called me from the 405 Freeway, when she was flipping off drivers through the Sepulveda Pass. "And you guys didn't see her until Tuesday morning?"

"Actually, the three of us rode back to base camp in the same van," Arnie said.

"Then we parted ways," Atkinson added. "I remember telling her I'd bring her some literature on that workshop I'm taking."

I munched on a brownie and watched a football toss miss its mark and crash into some light stands. That ended the lunchtime recreation. "What about Tuesday? She called me from the 405 on Monday and said she had an early call. The same for you guys?"

Arnie pushed his tray to the side and sipped on his iced tea. "Yeah, Christ, five a.m. at Magic Mountain."

"All three of you?" I said.

"Actually the four of us," Atkinson replied. "The first setup was Arnie and his partner interviewing Carla and me in the back of an unmarked police car."

"Damn good thing, too," Arnie said. "Colder than hell when we got to the set."

"Any change in Carla's mood from the day before?" Both men shook their heads. "What was the rest of the day like?"

"Carla and I had most of the morning off," Atkinson said. "The sequence they shot was the discovery of the body and a lot of extras milling around. After lunch they brought us in for a quick scene, but that was it."

"What do you mean?"

Arnie set his empty iced tea bottle on his tray and wiped his mouth with a napkin. "They spent the rest of the day with me and Prescott poring over where the body was found. I thought that poor fuckin' kid lying in the water was going to sprout gills and swim away, he was in the water so much."

"So, Don, what time were you and Carla wrapped?" I said.

"I think it was two o'clock."

"And nothing seemed to be bothering her during the time you were together?"

"No," he said, as he dipped a spoon into a dish of ice cream that was slowly becoming liquid. "She was psyched about the workshop stuff I gave her, and she said she might give it a try at some point."

My interview with Atkinson and Glover ended when a PA walked up. "Don and Arnie, we need you back in makeup for touch-ups," he said.

"Right," Arnie said. He and Atkinson got up and shoved their chairs under the table. "I hope nothing's happened to her, Eddie. She's a real sweet kid."

"Thanks, you guys," I said, as we shook hands. I handed my card to each of them. "Let me know if you can think of anything else, okay?"

They told me they would, bused their trays, and headed for the makeup trailer. After a couple of steps, Atkinson stopped and turned back to me.

"Hey, I just remembered something, Eddie," he said.

"Save it for later, Don," the PA said. "You guys are first up. Let's go."

"Okay. I'll catch up with you, Eddie," Atkinson said.

"I'll wait for you at base camp," I replied.

"You got it." He followed the PA.

I found the appropriate bins for paper plates and silverware, then laid eyes on Sasha, my on-screen wife, sitting at one end of a table. She was on her cellphone. I sat next to her and 'fessed up as to my real reason for being on this shoot. Like me, she was on her first day, and so couldn't shed any light on the events of the last couple of days. We swapped stories about the biz for a few minutes until Beth, our platoon sergeant, announced we were back on the clock.

For the next two hours, Sasha and I were part of a group of Renaissance enthusiasts milling around the various booths and concession stands set up inside the fair. Camera angles changed and more costume pieces disappeared and reappeared until it got to the point where we tried our damnedest to stick to the fringes of the camera's frame. At one point Beth shoved two little boys in front of us, as if they were supposed to be our children. After a quick consultation with another PA, Beth reassigned them, provoking a silent sigh of relief from both Sasha and me.

I didn't see Curran again, nor Phil Scarborough. It looked like my efforts to find out anything about Carla's disappearance had come up short, unless whatever it was that Atkinson had forgotten would prove me wrong. Four o'clock came and the light started to fade as the sun began to sink toward the tops of the hills to the west of the location. Shadows lengthened, and tempers flared between the director and his crew. Finally, at four thirty, Beth announced that we backgrounders were wrapped and to check with our agents about tomorrow. I didn't see the need for me to show up again, so I shook hands with Darryl Jackson as we rescued our garment bags, then made our way to the vans waiting to transport us back to base camp.

When we arrived back at Magic Mountain, I crawled out from the backseat and assisted an elderly lady behind me, all the while thinking that she could have found more fulfilling ways to spend her retirement than standing around trying to be seen on camera. The lure of fame and fortune knows no age limit, I guess.

I hung out by my car and watched another van arrive from the location. When I saw Atkinson step out, I waved my hand and he came over to me.

"I think that Teamster hit every pothole he could."

"Yeah, I know. What was it you forgot to tell me earlier?" We stepped aside to let an SUV pull out of the parking lot.

"After we wrapped, Carla and I had just started for the vans when she got stopped by a guy."

"Another actor?"

"No, I hadn't seen him in any of the scenes during the day's shooting."

"What did he look like?"

"He was a black guy, wearing sunglasses and a leather cap."

"Did it look like she knew him?"

"Yeah, she seemed to recognize him."

"Where did he take her?"

"He grabbed her by the arm and sort of pulled her toward the production trailer. She told me she'd see me the next day, and then she disappeared with the guy behind the office."

"Did she come back?"

"No. I missed the last van and had to wait for the next one. After a couple of minutes, a car pulled out from behind the production trailer and took off. I could see her through the windshield in the front seat. The black guy was driving."

"What kind of car was it?"

"One of those Toyota RAV4s. Bright red."

CHAPTER THIRTY-SEVEN

———— ◆ ————

I NOW KNEW WHAT HAD HAPPENED TO Carla, but I didn't know why. Nor did I know where she was, and it weighed on me. A lot. She had mentioned last week that both Curran and Scarborough were familiar because of the tips she'd received from them at Feline Follies. Those tips had been intended to gain her trust. Now that trust had blown up in her face. She'd put her handgun in her Honda, so Curran wouldn't have had any problem taking her at gunpoint.

As I started for my car, I turned on my cellphone to check for messages. None from either Carla or Frankie, but Morrie Howard had called. "Bubbeleh, I know you're probably standing around watching people make more money than you are, but call me when you can. I need to know if you're backgrounding tomorrow."

I wasn't planning on it, but he needed to know that. Kevin answered the phone.

"Boss man in?" I said.

"He's feeding Thelma and Louise. Hold on."

After a moment Morrie came on the line. "So you're now a professional extra? How did it go?"

"It was thrilling."

"And under the gumshoe hat? Did you find what you were looking for?"

"Pretty much."

"Now I suppose you're going to tell me you're done?"

"I'm done," I said. There was an audible sigh on the other end of the line. "Call Judy Meeks and tell her I'm unavailable."

"Eddie, this does not make my job easy. Clients backing out of bookings?"

"She'll understand, Morrie. Trust me. She's an old friend."

"Yeah, right. One of those old friends left standing on a burning bridge? You better give her a call and explain yourself."

"I will," I said, and hung up. Since my car had been in the sun all day, I cracked the windows to give the inside a chance to cool off. I caught sight of a security guard sitting on a plastic chair by the cordoned-off entrance to the production's parking area. I walked over and saw that the golf umbrella giving him shade was stuck in a bucket of sand. The thirtyish young man wore a baseball cap and shirt stitched with "CYA Security" and had a wad of chewing tobacco in his mouth. As I approached, he picked up a Styrofoam cup and spit.

"Yes, sir, can I help you?" he asked. He wiped the juice from his chin on the leg of his jeans.

"Were you here on Tuesday?"

"Yeah, I come on at three."

"Do you happen to remember seeing one of those Honda Fits, white, leaving about four, four thirty?"

"Ah, man, I don't know. Lot of cars, you know?"

"All right. Let me try this. You know what those Toyota RAV4s look like?"

"Yeah. My uncle, he got one of them. Nice ride."

"Do you remember a bright red one coming in here? Black guy driving? Girl in the front seat?"

He thought for a moment and then unloaded another mouthful of tobacco juice into the cup. "Hey, yeah, now you mention it, dude, I did see one. Came from the location. The windows were tinted, though, so I couldn't see who was driving."

"But it drove into the lot here?"

"Okay, yeah, now I remember. It came in and cruised around a little bit, you know?" He chewed on his wad, nodded, and then pointed to a far corner of the lot. "A black guy got out from the driver's side, and then another guy got out from the backseat. The black guy got back in and pretty soon he drove out of here."

"Headed where?"

"Toward the freeway."

"What about the other guy?"

"I saw him get into another car, and pretty soon he came driving out too." He pounded his knee and stood up. "Damn, man, you're right. The car was white. I don't know if it was a Honda, though. I don't know what those Fits look like."

"Thanks for your help," I said, as I turned to go and watched him deposit another mouthful in his cup. "Your wife like you chewing that stuff?"

"Ah, she don't mind. But my girlfriend gives me shit about it."

As I walked back to my car, I had to chuckle.

Before hitting the freeway, I called Judy Meeks to give her the bad news that I wouldn't be returning to the set tomorrow. She wasn't happy, but she understood. I promised I'd make it up to her with dinner at a restaurant of her choice. The more expensive the better. She said she'd hold me to it.

I glided out of the parking area and returned the guard's salute as I passed him. The I-5 south was still crowded, the rush hour beginning in earnest. I sandwiched my car in behind a semi and headed back to Hollywood.

I now had a client who had been kidnapped. The questions why and where plagued me as I drove. When I merged to the right and picked up the Hollywood Freeway, an idea struck me. I knew a location frequented by both Curran and Scarborough, someplace that might provide an answer. It had a cot, a bathroom, and a refrigerator. Perfect for stashing someone.

It also had some wooden crates with false bottoms.

As I began to warm to the idea of heading downtown again, my cellphone went off. It was Mavis.

"Hey, kiddo."

"Are you still working?"

"No, I'm heading downtown."

"Why?"

I filled her in on what I'd learned and my plan to visit the warehouse on Crocker.

"Well, for Pete's sake, be careful," she said.

"Will do."

STREETLIGHTS FLICKED ON AS I DROVE through Skid Row and parked on San Pedro, around the corner from Crocker. I took my gun out of its box in the trunk, along with a flashlight, then replaced my porkpie with a ball cap and walked to the intersection. The street was deserted. I leaned against a building for a few minutes to make sure, then strolled down the street on the same side as the warehouse. I didn't see any movement or hear any noise coming from the Dumpster across the street. Willie was either asleep or still prowling the neighborhood.

I came up on the gap between the warehouse and the fence, looked around to see if anyone was watching, and made my way down the walk.

The flashlight revealed the remains of a KFC dinner and a rat picking at the leftovers. When the light hit it, the rodent looked up at me, its eyes glinting in defiance. I kicked a beer can in its direction and it ducked through a hole in the fence. Various other clumps of trash made me step lightly as I came to the corner of the building. I stuck my head around the corner, then the light, but couldn't detect anyone camping out.

I tried the knob on the door. Locked. Holding the end of the flashlight in my mouth, I pulled out my set of picks. With less light, I wasn't as handy as before, so it took me a little longer to open both locks. I slowly turned the knob and pushed. Something was on the other side of the door. I peered around the edge and saw a five-gallon can of paint pushed up against it. The obstacle made more noise than I would have liked as I pushed the door open and slipped inside, then shoved the door shut behind me. I stood still for a moment, listening. The interior was dead quiet and dark except for the ambient light coming through those glass block windows. I thought about calling out for Carla but decided against it. No telling who else could be inside.

I shined the light to my left, down the corridor where the hot water heater sat, and put my eye to the gap in the wall that I'd used before to see Curran and Scarborough pushing those false-bottomed crates. I didn't see any movement or hear any sounds. Going back to the end of the false wall, I peered around the corner, then shined the light at the cot pushed up against the wall. It was empty, and showed no signs of anyone having used it. My hunch was wrong; they'd taken Carla someplace else. I stepped farther inside and swung the light over the table and chairs and into the corner where the prop room was. No evidence of anyone here.

I stuck the flashlight inside the prop room, found nothing. Sitting in front of the metal roll-up door were three of the wooden crates on casters. I opened one, but it was empty. So was the false bottom. The other two were locked. I started to make my way back into the corner where the two men had pushed the other crates, but suddenly I stopped.

The back door had opened and banged against the five-gallon pail of paint.

CHAPTER THIRTY-EIGHT

———◆———

CURRAN AND SCARBOROUGH WOULD HAVE USED the roll-up door, so someone else had obviously seen me come in here. I doused the flashlight and started toward the corner where the rest of the crates sat, but not before stepping on a piece of 2x4 lying on the floor. I picked it up and set it on one of the crates in front of the main door, then darted to the end of the row of shelves sticking out from the rear wall of the room.

The intruder didn't have a flashlight, but in the ambient light coming through those glass block windows, I could see that the figure wore a hoodie and dark trousers. I peeked around the corner of the shelf in front of me and saw him slinking into the center of the room. I didn't have a clue who this guy was, but with all the trash strewn around the warehouse, I had to assume it was a street person.

I watched him as he moved to his left and eventually to the safe and pulled on the handle. It didn't open. He walked over to the three crates sitting in front of the main door and opened one. He had his back to me. I pulled out my Beretta and took a position about ten feet behind him.

"Very slowly, turn around and face me," I said. "And then drop to your knees and hug some concrete."

"I ain't looking for trouble," he said.

"Same here. Do what I say and we'll talk about it."

The guy put down the lid of the crate he'd opened and started to drop to one knee. As he did so, he grabbed the piece of 2x4 I'd put down, swung around, and threw it at me. I ducked and saw him grab two sides of a crate and shove it in my direction. I dodged the piece of lumber, but the crate collided with one of my shins. Pain shot up my leg. I saw him grab a second crate and push it in my direction.

He made a break for the back door. I stopped the second rolling crate with an outstretched hand and took off after him. He reached the door just as I grabbed his hoodie and pulled him backwards. He grabbed the paint pail and our feet got tangled up with it. As we both stumbled and crashed to the floor, my gun fell from my hand. He struggled to get to his feet, but I swept his legs out from under him and he collapsed.

I jumped on him and tried to pull off the hoodie, but he squirmed too much for me to succeed. Straddling his back, I pinned him to the floor. He managed to get to one knee but I punched the base of his skull and he fell back. He grunted as I put one knee on his back and pushed his head down against the hard concrete.

"Stay put, goddammit," I said. "What the hell are you doing in here?"

"I could ask you the same question," came the muffled reply. He flailed around, trying to latch onto something that could give him leverage.

I grabbed the hoodie and smashed his head into the concrete floor. He stopped squirming.

"All right, all right! Jesus Christ, you made your point."

I felt him relax and let go of his head. "You gonna stay put?" I said.

"Yeah, yeah," he moaned.

My gun had fallen only a yard away from me. Reaching over, I grabbed it, replaced my knee in the middle of his back, and started patting him down.

"Are you Collins?" he said.

He'd caught me by surprise. I was further thrown off guard when I felt a handgun in a holster under his left arm. I reached under the hoodie and took the gun.

"Yeah, I'm Collins. Who the hell are you?"

"I'm the guy you've been looking for."

"Frankie Rizzoli?"

"You got it."

"Why the hell are you packing?"

"Check my back pocket."

I reached into his hip pocket and pulled out a leather wallet. I flipped it open and caught a glint of metal in the dim light.

"What the hell is this?"

"A badge. I'm an undercover cop."

I handed him the wallet and his gun, then helped him to his feet. He dabbed a handkerchief against his cheek. It was bleeding slightly from having been scraped against the concrete floor.

"Sorry about that," I said, "but I owed you one for roughing me up last week."

"How'd you figure out that was me?"

"The tattoo," I said as I pointed to his arm. "Carla told me about it."

"Is she all right?"

"She's been kidnapped."

"Goddammit!" He punched the end of the shelf next to him. "Curran and Scarborough?"

"Looks like it."

"Fuck," he said as he replaced his gun in its holster and dusted off his clothes. "I knew that was going to happen."

"Why would they take her?"

"They're after me."

"Why?"

"Long story. Let's get the hell out of here first."

We replaced the wooden crates in some semblance of their original order, then locked the door behind us. Frankie said his pickup was around the corner but suggested we sit in my car. After we climbed in, he cracked a window and lit up a cigarette. I'm not too keen on anyone smoking in my car, but given what I'd just done to him, I didn't make an issue of it.

"When did they get her?" he asked.

"Tuesday. Curran waylaid her after she wrapped the day's shooting on this picture she was filming."

"Ah, shit, her and her damn acting bug."

"Better than Feline Follies, don't you think?"

"Yeah, I guess." He blew a cloud of smoke out the window and turned to me. "How much have you learned about those two guys?"

I told him what I knew. The false-bottomed crates, Enigma Productions, Foxtrot Enterprises. I asked him if both Curran and Scarborough were in the MPs with him. He said they were.

"So why the hell are they after you?" I said.

He took a drag on his cigarette, flipped it against the wall of the building, and looked behind him. "I have to keep moving," he said, as he looked at his watch. "And I also need to eat. You know Philippe's?"

"Can't live in LA and not know Philippe's."

"I'll meet you there."

He got out of the car, peeked around the corner of Crocker, and disappeared.

CHAPTER THIRTY-NINE

———— ♦ ————

I WASN'T SURE IF FRANKIE INTENDED TO meet me at the restaurant. His rusted-out pickup wasn't in the parking lot when I drove up, but it had been a while since I'd had my chicken whatchamacallit at the movie location, so I parked and went inside.

Legend has it that in 1918, Philippe Mathieu was making a sandwich for a cop when he accidentally dropped a French roll into the beef *au jus* of the roasting pan. The cop decided to take the sandwich anyway, and liked it so much he came back the next day for more. Thus the French Dip came into being, and Philippe's remains a Los Angeles culinary landmark. As with all legends, time has a way of distorting facts, but nothing can diminish the reality that several thousand pounds of meat are served in this place during the course of a week. That's in spite of the floors being covered with sawdust.

Usually lines are long in front of the ten carvers, but at this time of day, business had ebbed. The aromas hadn't. Opting for a roast pork with slaw and a bottle of beer, I took a booth in the corner and had just finished checking my cell for messages when Frankie came in. He ordered and brought his tray over.

"Switch places with me," he said. "I gotta see the front door."

I did as he asked and started in on my sandwich. "Why the paranoia?"

"Curran and Scarborough have been trying to find me for the past couple weeks. I wouldn't call that paranoia."

"I'll ask again. Why are they after you?"

He ripped open two packets of sugar, dumped the contents into his iced tea, and sized me up as he swirled his straw in the plastic glass. "Can I count on you to keep this between the two of us?"

"It goes no further," I said.

He sipped from the straw and said, "I'm on a task force that's investigating them."

"For what?"

"Smuggling drugs across the border."

I swiped at some mustard at the corner of my mouth. "So let me guess. That's the reason for the false bottoms in those crates?"

"Exactly. They've got other means too." He took a bite of his sandwich and eyed me as he chewed, probably still wondering if he could trust me. "You know about that TV show Enigma has got down in Mexico—*Flashpoint*?"

"Yeah. It's folded into Foxtrot Enterprises."

"Right. They shoot it east of Ensenada." He filled a fork with potato salad. "They're running trucks and vans across the border all the time. Sets, lights, props, cast and crew, the whole nine yards."

"Seems like they'd be easy to spot," I said.

"Normally you'd think so, but they're so used to seeing the vehicles, the guards don't pay much attention. Besides, Foxtrot has got both the Mexican and U.S. border patrols in their pocket. Not only with cash, but with product." His cheek had begun to ooze and he picked up a napkin and dabbed at it. "Dammit, Collins, I should arrest your ass for assaulting an officer."

"You shouldn't have thrown the two-by-four at me."

He grinned and gnawed on his sandwich. "Tell me. How did Carla come to hire you?"

"We worked together a few years ago."

"Where?"

"On a television show."

"So you're an actor besides being a PI?"

I nodded. "She told me she saw my ad in the Yellow Pages."

"And she hired you because of that damn note I sent her?"

"That's right. She said she hadn't seen you in a while."

"Yeah, I know. Dammit, I shouldn't have bothered her." He took another bite of the sandwich. "Does she know Curran and Scarborough?"

"They came into Feline Follies a few times and tipped her pretty good. She remembered them."

"I knew she got a permit to carry. So how the hell did they get ahold of her?"

"I got booked on the film as an extra and ran into Curran. He told me he was involved with the film. Apparently, he stopped her on her way home. He probably said he wanted to talk to her about the job." I sipped on my beer and watched him shake his head. "Where do you suppose they've taken her?"

"I don't know."

"You're going after her, right?"

"Of course I am. I'll take it to my bosses. See how they want to proceed."

"I want in when you do it."

"We're cops, Collins. We'll handle it."

"I still want in."

"Look, this is—"

"Frankie, you're not listening to me. She's my client. I feel responsible for her. I will be included."

He took a bite of his sandwich and looked at me for a long moment. "Somehow I get the impression that there's more than a client relationship going on here."

"You can assume what you want."

"You sleeping with her, Collins?"

"That's none of your goddamn business."

"Hey, chill, man. I got no beef if you are."

I put away the last morsel of my pork sandwich and wiped my mouth with a napkin. "We're friends, okay? Let's leave it at that."

"Fair enough." He slurped from the bottom of his glass of iced tea. "You want another beer?"

"Sure," I said as I reached into my pocket.

"Save your money." He grabbed the glass and slid out of the booth.

I upended my bottle of beer then picked up both our plates and dropped them in a plastic container against the wall. I'd surprised myself a bit by being so adamant with regard to Carla, but she had struck a chord in me, and I wasn't going to leave it to someone else to find her, even if he was a cop and her brother.

Frankie came back with a fresh iced tea and another bottle of beer. He slid into the booth and stirred more sugar into the plastic glass. "I didn't mean to ruffle your feathers, Collins. Who my sister sees is up to her."

"No worries," I replied. "We saw each other for a while after we did that television show. Another guy who'd been in her life showed up. She thought she still wanted to be with him, so she left. When she went looking for a PI, she walked into my office and I guess we reignited a spark."

"I hear you," he said. He sipped his iced tea and pushed up the sleeves of his hoodie, revealing the lightning-bolt tattoo on his arm.

"Scarborough's got the same ink as you. Curran as well?"

"Yeah. Our whole MP unit had them. Got to be sort of a camaraderie thing."

I pulled out the picture of him and Curran in their desert fatigues and showed it to him. "This look familiar?"

He glanced at the photo and chuckled. "Yup, there we are. My second tour. Curran was my CO."

"We've got something in common," I said. "I was an MP too."

"Really? Where?"

"Korea. In the eighties." He extended a fist and we bumped knuckles. "So tell me … how the hell did these two guys get mixed up in drug smuggling?"

Another long look from him before he said, "I'm still not sure how much I should tell you."

"One MP to another," I said.

He nodded and then proceeded to tell me a tale whose parameters fell far outside those of a Hollywood PI and a dancer and would-be actress.

CHAPTER FORTY

———◆———

As I sipped on my beer, I watched the kitchen help busing the odd dishes from tables. Frankie was in the john. It was almost ten o'clock, closing time for Philippe's. He came back wiping his hands on his hoodie and slid into the booth across from me.

"That place needs some serious attention." He pulled a couple of napkins from the dispenser and finished dabbing at the water. "Where did you do your MP training, Collins?"

"Fort Leavenworth. You?"

"Same place. Basic at Fort Lewis, then Leavenworth and a few weeks at Benning before Iraq."

"What were you doing before you enlisted?"

"I was getting ready to enroll in the police academy."

"Really? Carla didn't say anything about that."

"That's because I didn't tell her, or my folks. We weren't getting along. They hit the roof when I told them I was going to enlist."

"Why?"

"Aw, my old man didn't jump on the bandwagon after those Twin Towers came down. We had an argument and I just left."

"So when did you get in country?"

"Not long after the invasion. Bush had just dismantled the Iraqi Army and the fucking place was chaos."

"How so?"

"No army, no law enforcement. The borders opened up and drugs started flowing. Man, it was something."

"The MPs couldn't do anything?"

"We were told not to. The Army didn't have the personnel or the wherewithal. And they didn't have the interest. They looked the other way. It was a mess."

I nodded and sipped on my beer, mentally agreeing with Frankie's assessment. The years since then have borne out the contention that the whole damn war was a colossal mistake.

The cashier walked over. "Sorry, gents, but we've got to close up."

"No problem," Frankie said. "We're outta here."

I finished my beer and we stepped onto the sidewalk. Frankie immediately lit up another cigarette. "I've had all the iced tea I need. There's a little hole-in-the-wall a few blocks up Sunset. Wanna get a real drink?"

"Sure," I said, even though I was starting to feel the effects of the early Magic Mountain call time. He told me the name of the place and I followed him out of the parking lot.

THE WATERING HOLE WAS DIMLY LIT, small, and quiet. No jukebox, pinball, or pool table. Serious drinkers only, please. A muted television set above the bar had a basketball game on that was being watched by three middle-aged guys snuggled up next to the brass rail. I ordered a Bud draft and a double Beam, neat. Frankie opted for a bottle of Corona and two shots of tequila. I slapped some bills on the bar, told the man behind the stick to keep the change, and we found a booth in the corner. We clinked glasses and I asked him if he'd done only the one tour in Iraq.

"No. Even though the place was fucked up, I thought we could make a difference and I did a second deployment. That's when I met Curran and Scarborough."

"They came over with you?"

"Both of them were already there. Curran was my CO and Scarborough was a second lieutenant. I think he was also Curran's lapdog. Didn't have an original thought in his head. Still doesn't."

"Were the drugs still flowing?"

"Like water. Nothing had changed. Except for one thing."

"What was that?"

"Curran started to develop this fascination with the whole smuggling operation. We used to sit around getting shit-faced, and he kept saying we could do the same thing back here. I thought he was nuts, but I didn't say anything."

The front door opened and we turned to see an elderly man and a woman enter. From the way they walked, it looked like the party had started somewhere else. The bartender leaned on his elbows and glared at them, said something I couldn't hear, then reluctantly poured them a couple glasses of beer.

"They're in here all the time," Frankie said.

"Looks like some other places as well." I had a taste of the bourbon and followed it with a sip of beer. "So from what you've told me, it sounds like Curran turned his fascination into reality."

"That's exactly what he did. His old man has been with Foxtrot Enterprises for years. That *Flashpoint* television show isn't the only filming they've done in Mexico."

"So how the hell did they start running the drugs?"

"We're not entirely sure. But somehow or other, Curran's old man got in bed with one of the cartels. They saw how easy it was for Enigma to move across the border, and *voilà*, the deal was sealed."

From across the room, we heard a shout, and turned to see the elderly man fall off his stool. His companion laughed and pounded a fist on the bar. The man got up, steadied himself by leaning on the stool, and then straddled it.

I turned back to Frankie. "There's an argument for stools with backs on them."

"I guess."

I sipped on my Beam and said, "So how did you get involved with Curran and Scarborough?"

"After my discharge, I went through the academy and the department put me in plainclothes. I suppose my being an MP had something to do with that."

"Yeah, it helped me get my PI ticket," I said.

"Right. Anyway, it wasn't long before Scarborough came knocking on my parents' door looking for me. Of course they had no idea where I was or that I had become a cop. But my mother had my phone number and she left me a message. She must have given the number to Scarborough as well. He called me and I went up my chain of command and told the department what I thought the two of them were up to."

I sipped on my beer and glanced up at the television set. "Tell me something. What happened over on Crocker that night?"

"I'm not sure," he said. "Someone may have dropped a dime on me. In any case, Curran started asking questions I couldn't and wouldn't answer. Then Scarborough, the dumb shit, drew down on me. When I bailed out of their SUV, Curran took a shot at me, but missed and hit Scarborough. Just as I landed on the pavement, an unmarked cop unit drove up. The cops pulled me in and took off. That pretty much blew a hole in my cover."

"Even though they beat the shit out of you?"

"How do you know about that?"

"Willie told me he was in the Dumpster and saw it go down."

Frankie chuckled and took a hit off his beer. "Good ol' Willie. Yeah, the guys in the unmarked unit thought it would make it look like they'd arrested me. It didn't work."

"So you think the investigation is botched?"

"From my end of it, yeah."

"And in the meantime Carla is left as one hell of a pawn."

"Yeah, I know, goddammit." He slapped the table with his left hand. "I don't know if I can go to the department about this."

"Why not?"

"The smuggling ring is still being unraveled. I'm not sure the task force wants to blow the lid on the damn thing over a kidnapping."

"Even though it's your sister, for crissakes? What the hell happened to protect and serve?"

"Yeah, yeah, I know." He yanked a napkin out of the dispenser and dabbed at his cheek. "I'll take it to my bosses. See what they say."

"If they wash their hands, what does that leave?"

"Me," he said, "and you. You wanted in, right?"

"Hell, yes. How do you want to proceed?"

He pulled out a flip-phone. "This is a burner I use to communicate with Curran and Scarborough. I've got to assume they'll call me."

"Why don't you call them?"

"That'll tip them off that I know Carla's been taken. Better it comes as a surprise to me." He put the phone back in his pocket and drained his bottle of beer. "It would also tell them that I know you."

"How do you figure?"

"You said Curran saw you on the film shoot looking for her. They know you've been trying to find me. Seems to me they'll connect the dots."

He was right. As much as I wanted to charge off in search of Carla, my efforts would be useless without a plan. "Have you got any idea where they would stash her?" I said.

"Well, it's obviously not the place on Crocker. I know they've got another warehouse up in Valencia. Curran lives down in Chula Vista. Not exactly sure where. Have you been to Carla's house?"

"Twice after she disappeared. Her car was gone, and there was no indication that she'd been there. The house was undisturbed."

"As much as we may not like it, Collins, we're going to have to wait for them to play their hand."

"Yeah, I can't argue with you on that score."

"I'll go up the chain and we'll see where we're at." He took a smartphone out of his pocket. "I've got your number in this thing. Since you've been sending me texts, I assume you've got it in your phone."

"Should have," I said, as I pulled out my cell and looked for it. "Yeah, I've got it." I handed him one of my business cards. "Here's where my office is."

"Okay," he said. "I'll talk to you when I know something." We finished our drinks and shook hands. "Despite getting my face rubbed in the concrete, I'm glad you found me, Collins."

"More like you found me."

"Yeah, right." I finished my drink and we crawled out of the booth. "We'll get her, Collins. And don't forget ... I'm here to tell you Carla's one tough girl. She kicked my ass enough when we were growing up, I ought to know."

We left the bar and got into our cars. I sat for a moment, replaying the events of the day. I was beat. The early Magic Mountain call seemed like an eternity ago. I turned the ignition and started working my way up into Hollywood. While I appreciated Frankie's assessment of his sister's fortitude, I was worried. Worried that the two of us wouldn't be enough to rescue Carla.

CHAPTER FORTY-ONE

———— ✦ ————

E VEN THOUGH I'D BEEN READY TO drop by the time I got home last night, I hadn't slept well. What started out as a routine task of locating an errant brother had turned into something far more complex. I kept blaming myself for causing Carla's disappearance, but knew deep down that was harebrained thinking. By association, she had become enmeshed in a larger scenario, and it still left me wondering how this rescue was going to be accomplished without causing her or Frankie harm.

My morning lethargy prevented me from brewing a fresh pot of coffee, so I warmed up a cup of sludge left over from yesterday and immediately rued the decision. A hot shower perked me up and I opened the French doors and gazed out onto my front yard, Hollywood Boulevard. All seemed well without further attention, and I eventually plopped down behind my desk. Most of yesterday's mail went into the circular file, and I leaned back and stared at the poster of Bogie and Bacall above my desk, wishing they'd give me an answer to what the hell was bothering me.

The front door opened and Mavis came in. "Good morning," I called out. After a moment she appeared in the doorway with a paper bag in her hand.

"Hey," she said. "How was your day on the movie set?"

"Long," I replied. "What's in the bag?"

"Well, considering that kitchen of yours is usually a wasteland of nutrition, I figured you needed something to get you going." She set the bag down on the corner of my desk and put an aluminum foil-wrapped cylinder in front of me. "That's a breakfast burrito," she said, as she again reached and pulled out a plastic bottle and a cardboard to-go cup. "Also some OJ and coffee. If you keep zapping the contents of that pot of yours back there, you're going to short-circuit your microwave."

"Are you sure you weren't a nurse in your former life?"

She laughed and pulled out another cup of coffee, crumpled the bag, then sat down in front of my desk. "Lay it on me, boss man. Tell me what happened yesterday."

So I did.

The look on her face must have resembled the one on mine when I'd first listened to Frankie's revelation. She sipped on her coffee and said, "So what do the two of you think you're going to do?"

"Not sure. I'm waiting to hear from him."

"Far be it from me to give you advice, Eddie, but don't you think you're getting into something a little above your pay grade?"

"You could be right," I said, "but I'm not going to just stand by and hope for the best. Carla deserves more than that." I bit off a chunk of the burrito and chewed, looking at her. I can usually read Mavis pretty well, but I wasn't sure what she was thinking.

"She obviously means a lot to you, huh?"

"I'm afraid so, kiddo."

"You don't have to apologize. I'm glad." She grabbed the crumpled paper bag, got up from her chair, and started for her office. "Part of me says you should leave it to the cops, but I know how stubborn you can be. So just be careful, okay?"

"Always."

She disappeared into her office and I could hear the computer booting up. I reached into the center drawer of my desk for my checkbook and paid a few bills. The phone rang and Mavis answered it. I stopped what I was doing and listened, then heard her end the call.

"Who was that?"

"A reminder of my doctor's appointment on Monday." She stuck her head around the corner. "That Rizzoli guy wouldn't call here, would he?"

"Probably not. But I gave him my card, so he's got all the numbers. What are you going to the doctor for?"

"Some questions don't need answering, Eddie. That's one of them," she said, and went back to her desk.

I wouldn't exactly say I felt rebuffed, but I had no idea what the hell she was talking about. I picked up my cell and went into the apartment to answer a call of nature. When I came back, I finished my coffee and sat. And stared at the cellphone, like it was a pot coming to a boil. Finally it did. In the form of a text message. It read, *Pershing Square. Noon. Can do?* I replied that I could, made a golf ball of the aluminum foil holding the burrito, trashed it, and grabbed my hat.

"Was that a text?" Mavis asked.

"Noon at Pershing Square. I'm off." Pulling the office door open, I added, "I'll check in later, kiddo."

PERSHING SQUARE IS AN OASIS OF splendor smack-dab in the heart of downtown Los Angeles. Named for old Black Jack himself, the patch of landscape includes an orange grove, venues for the performing arts, and supposedly, from November through January, an outdoor ice rink, as anomalous as that may be.

As I circled looking for a parking spot, I wished I had taken the Red Line downtown. I could have stepped off the train and strolled right into the square. The subway. Another anomaly we Angelinos are having trouble getting used to.

I finally found a small lot that wasn't going to set me back a month's rent, got a cup of coffee to go, and walked a block back to the downtown oasis. Frankie hadn't said where he'd be, but I headed toward a large expanse of lawn that had several tables scattered around with umbrellas over them. I spotted a hand waving and headed toward it. He had a cup of Starbucks in front of him and was writing something in a small spiral notebook. His two phones also lay on the table.

"Morning," he said.

I nodded and settled into a plastic chair. "Do you live downtown?"

"Yeah, but I'm not going to tell you where."

"I wasn't expecting a dinner invite." He chuckled as I lifted the cover off my coffee to let it cool. "So, what were you doing at that flea-bag with the 'e' gone from the sign above the door?"

"Meeting with my guys. Trying to avoid you. Obviously it didn't work."

"Obviously." I sipped some coffee. "Question. How did you know Carla was working at Feline Follies?"

"I heard Curran and Scarborough talking about the place and this dancer called Velvet La Rose. They said her last name was Rizzoli and asked if we were related."

"So you had to tell them?"

"Right. Then they bugged me about going into the place with them, but I told them we were estranged. The DEA got on board, and as the task force dug deeper, I decided to send her that note in case things went belly up."

"But you didn't tell her that you knew Curran and Scarborough?"

"No."

"So when things went to shit over on Crocker, she was ripe for the picking."

"I guess that's one way of putting it."

"Why didn't you just go and see her?"

"I didn't want her to know where I was. For the same reason you're not getting a dinner invite."

"Aw, that's bullshit."

I shook my head and sipped on the coffee. Three young black men two tables over started arguing. One of them stood up, kicked his chair across the lawn, then stomped off. One of his companions picked it up and hollered at him but couldn't persuade him to come back.

"You should have gone and seen her, Frankie. You know the Follies is involved in some money laundering through Foxtrot, right?"

"We know." He lit up a cigarette and tossed his lighter on the table. "Look, Collins—"

"Why don't you try Eddie?"

"All right. Look, Eddie. In hindsight, I probably could and should have done things differently. Carla's a tough kid, and this task force has got some serious stuff on the burner. I didn't think those two assholes would pull something like this."

"Which brings us to your bosses. You hear from them?"

"I did."

"And ...?

"Well, like I thought, they weren't too happy to hear of the kidnapping."

"Well, bully for them. The question is, are they going to do anything about it?"

"They've detailed three guys to work with us."

"Is that going to be enough?"

"It depends on what these two yahoos are going to do."

I swallowed some coffee and watched the other two black guys start their own argument. My attention shifted to Frankie's burner when it suddenly started to ring.

He flipped it open. "Rizzoli." I watched him as he listened. "Eddie Collins? Who the hell is that?" He scrawled something on his notebook and showed it to me. It said "Curran" and for me to "be quiet." Then he wrote "speaker phone" and showed it to me.

He punched a key and laid the phone on the table. "Okay, go ahead."

"Collins?" I couldn't tell for sure whose voice it was, but when I looked at Frankie, he put his finger to his lips. "Collins, are you there?" came from the phone. After a moment, the voice said, "All right, Frankie, you want to be cute ...." We heard a slight rustling and a woman's voice came through the speaker.

"Frankie?" It was Carla. A lump formed in my throat and I clenched my fists.

"Yeah, sis, I'm here," he said. "Are you all right? Have they hurt you?"

"I've got a little bit of a black eye, but it cost the scraggly little shit a kick in the nuts."

Frankie leaned over the phone. "Curran, if you touch her again, you are dead."

"Hey, that was Phil, Frankie, not me. You know him. He saw her at the Follies flashing her tits. He can't help himself." In the background, I could hear a raucous laugh and I made a vow to myself: if that was Scarborough, I was going to do everything possible to make sure he never laughed again.

Frankie pulled the phone closer to him. "It's me you want, Jimmy, not her. Let Carla go, and we'll talk about what went down the other night."

"Oh, we will, Frankie. We'll talk. I'll get back to you. Phil's got that look in his eye again."

Curran broke the connection and Frankie closed the phone. A scowl burrowed its way into his face. "Goddammit!" he said as he slammed the phone down on the table. He jumped to his feet and upended his plastic chair.

I pushed myself away from the table to escape the spilled coffee. "Jesus Christ, Frankie. What's Scarborough capable of?"

"The man's a fucking psychopath."

"And you didn't tell Carla about him?" I said, anger welling up in me as I got to my feet and moved toward him.

"I already told you. I—"

"You told her to 'watch her back.' What the hell kind of a warning is that? She's performing almost naked in front of a psychopath and you tell her to 'watch her back'? That's bullshit, Frankie."

"Yeah, well, she should have thought about that when she started working at the fucking place."

"Oh, no, you don't put this on her," I said as I shoved him. He stumbled backward and tripped over his upended chair. "The minute you knew that Feline Follies was a target in this goddamn task force of yours, you should have marched your ass over there and told her to quit the damn place."

He got to his feet and came at me. "And you should have followed my advice when I told you to tell her I was dead. But no, you gotta go sniffing around both Curran and Scarborough, putting her in even more jeopardy." He shoved me backward and I careened off the table and landed on my ass.

As I scrambled to my feet, one of the black guys at the adjacent table walked over. "Hey, man, what's wit you two?"

"Nothin', pal," Frankie said. "Just butt out, okay?"

"Yeah, well, fuck y'all," the guy mumbled to himself and walked off.

Frankie picked up his chair, set it by the table, and leaned over it. "All right, look, this isn't doing either of us any good, let alone Carla."

I picked up my hat and brushed some grass off the brim. "Yeah, you're right. Sorry I popped off."

"Me too," he said. He stuck out his hand and I shook it.

After picking up the coffee cups that had fallen off the table, I sat down and said, "What now?"

He retrieved his phones and notebook off the ground and sank down in his chair. Flipping open a page of his notebook, he showed it to me. "You've seen both their vehicles, right?"

I nodded.

"Do these descriptions sync with what you know?"

I looked at the notes on the page. He had descriptions of both Curran's red Toyota RAV4 and Scarborough's black Hyundai. I checked my notebook and the license plates I'd written down.

"Those are right," I said.

"Okay," he replied. He picked up his smartphone and punched some numbers on a speed dial. "Dwyer, it's Rizzoli. I want a unit at these two addresses and put a tail on these vehicles."

He rattled off both Curran's address in Chula Vista and Scarborough's on Larch Street, along with the license plate numbers, then hung up.

"Nick Dwyer is one of the guys the department gave us. Stan Forbes and Al Medina are the other two. I don't know where those two assholes have stashed Carla, but until Curran tells us what he wants, we've got to put eyes on where they live."

"So we wait?"

"We wait, Eddie. Just remember, they want *me*."

"Yeah, well, you better remember something else."

"What?"

"They might want her too."

CHAPTER FORTY-TWO

———— ◆ ————

WAIT. THAT'S WHAT I DID FOR the rest of the afternoon after leaving Frankie in Pershing Square. I paced around my apartment and tried to keep myself busy, rolling around in my head titles like *Waiting for Godot, Waiting for Lefty,* even "Waiting for the Robert E. Lee."

While I appreciated Frankie's bravado regarding our efforts to get Carla back safely, I couldn't help but feel apprehensive. True, four cops were going to be involved, but I, for one, didn't know the resources Curran and Scarborough could bring to the table.

After I replaced CDs and DVDs in their jackets and dusted every surface I could find, I'd succeeded in driving Mavis nuts, so I took my cellphone and headed out onto the Boulevard, thinking a walk might settle my mind. I knew seeing a movie wouldn't do any good, primarily because I wouldn't be able to concentrate on the story, and secondly because of the ever-present admonition to silence all cellphones.

So I walked. And sat in a coffee shop and watched tourists take pictures of the stars on the Walk of Fame. At four thirty the cell went off. I picked it up off the table, expecting Frankie to be on the other end of the line. He wasn't. It was a number with no caller ID.

"Hello," I said.

"Is this Collins?"

"Yeah. Who's this?"

"Phil Scarborough. Remember me?"

A lump formed in my throat and I squeezed the cellphone. "I don't have a problem forgetting assholes like you." A guttural laugh oozed from the other end of the line. "Where's Carla?"

"She's sitting here looking at me like she wants me."

"Don't flatter yourself, pal."

"She talks about you a lot. You been dippin' your wick, Shamus? I bet it was you chased us down her driveway the other night, wasn't it? Come on, Collins, sounds like she's more than a client."

"What the hell do you want?"

"We know you finally found Frankie. You better call him. He's got something for you to do."

"What?"

"He'll fill you in. See you soon."

Scarborough broke the connection. Just as I started looking for Frankie's number, the cell rang again. It was him.

"Frankie, what's going on? Scarborough just called me. He said they know we're connected."

"Yeah, I figured that. I just got off the phone with Curran. We're on for tomorrow at noon. At the Farmers Market, of all places."

"On a Saturday? Why?"

"Beats the hell out of me, but we gotta talk. You know where LAPD's Olympic Station is?"

"Someplace on Vermont?"

"Right." He gave me the address and said, "Get here as soon as you can. Ask for me at the desk. Dwyer, Medina, and Forbes are on their way."

He hung up and I scribbled the Vermont address in my notebook, swallowed the last mouthful of coffee, and headed for my car.

The Los Angeles Farmers Market is a landmark that has sat at the corner of Fairfax and West 3rd Street for decades. Over a hundred shops give you everything from Marconda's Puritan Poultry to Magee's House of Nuts. On a Saturday the place would be teeming with people, not an ideal place to stage this Carla-for-Frankie swap. I hoped he had a plan.

I parked in a strip mall across the street from the LAPD's Olympic station. A uniformed cop sat behind a reception desk.

"Can I help you, sir?"

"I'm here to see Frankie Rizzoli."

He looked at a computer screen, picked up a telephone receiver, punched some buttons, and said, "Someone to see you." As he hung up the phone, he nodded at me. "He'll be right out."

After a few minutes, Frankie came through a glass door and handed me a lanyard with a visitor's pass on the end of it.

"Follow me," he said. We walked along a corridor with cubicles on one side, some of them occupied, most not.

"Why the Farmers Market?" I said.

He shook his head. "The only thing I can figure is they think there's less chance of something going haywire."

He pushed open a door and we entered what appeared to be a break room. Coffee pots and cups sat on a counter beside a sink. A telephone hung next to it. There were two vending machines against the far wall, one for drinks, another for snacks. A round table with five chairs occupied the center of the room. Behind it sat three men who got to their feet when we came in.

"Guys, this is Eddie Collins," Frankie said.

A tall, muscular man with a round face and blond buzz cut stuck out a huge hand. He looked like he could have played some football in his time.

"Nick Dwyer," he said. "Word is you're a PI?"

"That's right. Carla hired me to find him," I said, pointing to Frankie.

"So you know these two, Curran and Scarborough?"

"Yeah, I've talked to both of them."

A short Hispanic man with a mustache in the middle of a long, wrinkled face leaned over. "Hi, Eddie. Al Medina."

"Good to know you," I said.

The third man had long reddish hair tied back in a ponytail and a neatly trimmed goatee. He wore a black leather vest over jeans, a plaid shirt, and a tweed flat cap. "Stan Forbes," he said as he shook my hand and pulled out a chair for me.

"Okay," Frankie said. "Here's the deal. Curran called and said they want to make the exchange tomorrow at noon at the Farmers Market. He wants to hand Carla off to Eddie here. In the middle of the damn place, no less."

"Jesus," Stan said. "On a Saturday? It's going to be a zoo."

"I think that's what they're banking on," Frankie replied. "If they decided on someplace out in the boonies, they'd probably think it would be easy to get ambushed. This way they're assuming we can't control the location."

"And they're right," Al said.

"You've all been there, right?" Frankie said. "Fairfax and West Third?" The four of us nodded. He opened a Manila folder and slid maps of the Market across the table to each of us. "Try to get as familiar with this as you can."

"What else did Curran say?" Nick said.

Frankie sipped on a cup of coffee. "To come alone, except for Eddie here. He said if either of us is strapped, the deal is off."

"What, is he going to pat you down?" Stan said. "In the middle of a crowd?"

"I doubt it," Frankie replied. "Maybe I can get away with an ankle piece."

"So let's say this goes as Curran says," Al said. "Carla is handed off to Collins. What happens to you?"

"That's where you guys come in," Frankie answered. "With that many people around, we can't afford gunplay. Besides, the department needs them alive. I want you to get there early. Curran told me to come in at Gate Number Two. We can meet up in the East Patio." He referred to his map. "You see it there?"

"Got it," Nick said.

"Since he said Gate Number Two, I have to assume they'll park in the lot on the north side of the Market. There's tables out in the open by Bob's Coffee and Doughnuts. Nick, you place yourself someplace in the patio. Al and Stan nearby. You'll all be on radios."

"And you won't?" Nick said.

Frankie shook his head. "No. Curran also said if I had a wire, the deal goes south. He could poke around looking for one, so I better not risk it."

"Okay," Stan said. "We assume they leave your sister with Collins and take you out of there, right?"

"Right," Frankie replied as he again pointed to the map in front of him. "Like I said, I assume they park in the north lot. If they don't and leave by another gate, the three of you have to follow. Get close and we'll take them before they drive away."

"Provided they don't use you as a hostage," Al said. "They've got leverage as long as they've got you."

"But they're outnumbered," Frankie said.

"Where does that leave me?" I chimed in.

"Your main concern is Carla," Frankie said. "Stay put with her. Al, Stan, and Nick will have your cellphone number. Wait until you hear from them. You okay with that?"

"Yeah," I said, "provided you let me pound on Scarborough after you've got him in custody." Nick chuckled and Stan clapped me on the shoulder.

"You got a deal," Frankie said. He sipped more coffee and looked around the table at each of us. "Questions? Ideas?"

The three cops were silent and I gave them my cellphone number. They punched the number into theirs and after a moment Nick said, "Damn, I don't know, Frankie. What if they lose the three of us? How are you going to handle the two of them? And what the hell are they going to do with you once they've got you?"

"You three are the best plainclothes I know. I'm not planning on your first question happening, Nick. As for the other two, I'll cross those bridges if I get to them."

Nick shook his head and leaned back in his chair. "We're with you, man, but we're going to have to catch some breaks."

"Another thing," Stan said. "Collins knows these two guys. What happens if they all of a sudden decide not to let him go? I mean, they've got to think he knows something about the task force."

"But I'm not a cop," I said. "I don't know that I pose a threat to them. All I was hired to do was to find Carla's brother. I did that. As Frankie keeps telling me, he's the one they want."

Al leaned his elbows on the table and cracked his knuckles. "All well and good, but we don't know that for sure."

"I hear you guys," Frankie said. "It may look like we're flying by the seat of our pants here, but they've got me by the short hairs. I have to do what they say." He scrunched up his lips and took a swallow of coffee, then pinched the bridge of his nose. "She's my kid sister, guys. This needs to be done."

The four of us watched him pull a handkerchief from his pocket and wipe his nose. Finally Al reached over and grabbed his forearm.

"We've got your back, Frankie. Don't worry about it."

Frankie finished off his coffee, rinsed the cup in the sink, and wiped his hands on a paper towel. "Okay. That's it until tomorrow. Eddie, why don't I meet you at the clock tower by that old-time filling station? Say, eleven fifteen? The three of you should get there earlier. Grab some breakfast. Get some produce."

"Yeah, I'm out of eggplant," Al said.

The rest of us laughed and Nick punched him on the arm. "You wouldn't know an eggplant if it bit you on the ass."

"The three of you have done shit like this before," Frankie said. "You know the drill. So, we good to go?"

Stan, Nick, and Al nodded and got up from the table. They rinsed their cups, shook hands with me and filed out of the room. Frankie leaned on the sink cabinet and looked at me. "So, what do you think? Will it fly?"

"It has to, doesn't it?" I replied. "How much do you think Curran and Scarborough told Carla?"

"How do you mean?"

"They suspect you're a cop. You think they told her that?"

He looked down at the floor and said, "I honestly don't know, Eddie."

I shared Frankie's assessment, which now joined a growing list of uncertainties that lay before us tomorrow at the Farmers Market.

CHAPTER FORTY-THREE

———◆———

I DON'T USUALLY STAND IN FRONT OF my closet deciding on a wardrobe for the day, but this morning was different. Frankie's discussion yesterday of carrying weapons into the Farmers Market had prompted sartorial concerns. I decided I was going to arm myself, clip a holster to my belt at the small of my back. I hoped I wasn't wrong, but I couldn't see any reason for either Curran or Scarborough to frisk me. Consequently, I opted for a corduroy sports jacket that fit loosely enough to conceal a bulge.

Satisfied, I donned a porkpie and made my way to the front door of the office. This being Saturday, Mavis's presence was unusual. Some mailing had to be done. She looked up from packaging a four-piece set of coffee cups featuring the likenesses of *Bonanza*'s Ben Cartwright and his three sons.

"Hey, a spiffy private eye," she said. "Did you decide to take your gun?"

I turned my back and buttoned the coat. "It's on my belt. Can you tell?"

"Not unless I'm looking for it. You sure it's the right thing to do?"

"Yeah, those two goons are unpredictable. Besides, it's not like I'm breaking the law."

"Let's hope the goons don't have the same idea."

"Right," I replied, and opened the front door.

"Good luck, Eddie."

"Thanks, kiddo," I said, as I closed the door behind me and headed toward an encounter that filled me with more apprehension than I had experienced in recent memory.

THE DAY WAS FILLED WITH SUNSHINE and the traffic south on Fairfax was light. I hoped those were signs pointing to today's events going smoothly.

I passed CBS Television City and turned left into Farmers Market Place, adjacent to the north parking lot. After a couple of passes I found a parking spot, locked the door, and headed for the clock tower. Frankie sat on a stone bench in front of the landmark structure.

"Morning," he said as I sat next to him.

"You hear anything from the other three?"

"Texts. They've snooped around a little, but there's no sign of either Curran or Scarborough."

"So your people know what they look like?"

"Oh, yeah. All three of them have been on the task force from the beginning."

"Would Curran and Scarborough recognize your guys?"

"Nope. I'm the only one from the task force that's been one-on-one with them."

"You think they've brought reinforcements?"

"No way of knowing for sure," he said. "I still think they're relying on the presence of lots of people to help them."

"Did you decide on an ankle gun?"

"I did."

I glanced down at his legs but couldn't detect any evidence of it.

"And you?" he asked.

"I've got a piece clipped to my belt at the small of my back. I don't think they're going to go looking for anything."

"Let's hope you're right," Frankie said, as he got up from the bench. "Time to saddle up."

We headed for Gate #2. A trolley car runs between the Market and the Grove shopping center to the east. The mall opened in 2002, and some thought it would compete with the Market, but the opposite proved to be true. Now you park, catch the trolley to the shopping mall, get yourself a hundred-dollar Tommy Bahama shirt, then ride back and treat yourself to a Fritzi Dog. I've availed myself of the latter, but the day I spend a hundred bucks on a shirt has not yet dawned, nor ever will.

The trolley was just shoving off for its return trip as we walked up. We stepped over the tracks and entered Gate #2. On our immediate right was a newsstand and lottery booth.

Frankie pointed to it and said, "Feeling lucky, Eddie?"

"Not really. But be my guest."

He clapped me on the shoulder and we continued on. I'd been in the Market on numerous occasions over the years and was always spellbound by the diversity of produce and specialty foods available in the place. I immediately caught the scent of the Pampa Grill to my right, offering Brazilian food. We veered off to our left and saw a cluster of tables in front of Bob's Coffee and Doughnuts.

"I'll get us a couple of cups," Frankie said. "Might as well blend in. How do you take yours?"

"Black," I said as I pulled out a chair from a round table with seating for six. As Frankie walked off, I glanced behind me and saw Nick Dwyer at a table in the corner, reading a newspaper. He caught my eye and gave a slight nod.

Frankie came back with napkins and the coffees and sat. "Dwyer's behind us," I said.

"Yeah, I saw him when we came in." He sipped on his coffee, pulled out his cellphone and began punching keys. After a moment, he said, "Forbes is browsing in the newsstand we just passed."

"Christ, I never saw him," I said.

"He's good. All three of them are. Medina's behind Dwyer, down that aisle."

"Probably getting his eggplant," I said.

Frankie chuckled. "Yeah, right."

I sipped on my coffee and Frankie looked at his watch.

"Eleven forty," he said.

Nick Dwyer had a cellphone to his ear. I glanced to my right and saw Stan Forbes enter the east patio, a rolled-up magazine tucked under one arm. He also had a cellphone to his ear.

"Do those guys have radios in their sleeves, by any chance?" I asked. "You know, like the Secret Service?"

"That's exactly it," Frankie said. "With a cellphone you fool anybody."

I had another taste of the coffee and looked at Frankie as he kept glancing around the Market. I was a bit on edge, but he looked like it was just another day on the job.

"Level with me," I said. "What if this doesn't go off without a hitch? How are you going to deal with Curran and Scarborough on your own?"

"I'm counting on that not happening," he said, as he picked up his smartphone. "But if it does, there's a GPS in this phone. Our three amigos will follow me."

"I gotta admit, Frankie, I feel kinda like a third leg here."

"Well, that's bullshit. This whole deal is about getting her back. Once I take off, she's your responsibility. Not something you're going to be unhappy about from what you've told me."

"Can't argue with you there," I said.

"Try to get her to quit dancing at that goddamn meat market."

"I might have better luck buying one of those lottery tickets."

He chuckled and sipped on his coffee. "If this task force eventually takes down Foxtrot Enterprises, the damn place may be shuttered anyway."

"True that," I said as I started to take a sip of coffee. I stopped when I saw Curran and Scarborough come through Gate #2 with Carla between them. I gestured with my head and Frankie turned in his seat. My heartbeat noticeably quickened when I saw her. As they got closer, I could see the trace of a black eye, which only bolstered my urge to make mincemeat out of Phil Scarborough.

Frankie stood up when they got to our table and I followed suit. Curran wore a bulky black leather jacket and Scarborough had on a khaki safari number with all kinds of pockets. Plenty of space for concealed weapons.

Frankie pulled Carla into an embrace. "You okay, sis?"

"I am now," she said. "These two jerks have been telling me you're a cop, Frankie. Is that true?"

He shook his head. "Nah, of course not. We've just had a little misunderstanding."

She ran her hands across his cheeks and kissed him. Then she came around the table and I wrapped my arms around her and held her tight. I kissed her and said, "You sure you're okay?" She nodded. "Did they …?" I left the sentence hanging and she shook her head.

"God, I've missed you, Eddie," she said as she laid her head on my chest and tightened her arms around me. "What is happening here?"

"Don't worry," I said. "Everything's going to be okay."

On the other side of the table, Curran pulled Frankie into an embrace. "Hey, gimme a hug for old time's sake," he said. The hug turned into what amounted to a pat-down in search of a weapon. "I hope you're not strapped, Frankie."

"I'm clean," he replied. "I assume you're not?"

"You assume right," he said. "Both of us. You bring anybody with you?"

"Just Collins, like you said."

As if on cue, Scarborough moved toward me and said, "Come on, Collins, show me a little love here." He opened his arms and started to embrace me as well.

I stuck a finger in his face. "You lay a hand on me, mutt, it's going to be in a cast by the end of the day."

"Whoa, touchy," he said. "Are you carrying, Shamus?"

"No." I opened my jacket as proof, at the same time noticing that a couple of people at an adjacent table were looking at me. "Satisfied?" I said. "Or do you want me to draw more attention to myself?"

"Sit down," he said.

I did so, with Carla to my right. Frankie and Curran took seats on the other side of the table. He looked at us for a couple of minutes and finally turned to face Frankie.

"So, Rizzoli, seems like you've got some explaining to do about what happened on Crocker the other night."

"That was then, Jimmy, this is now. Let's do this swap and we'll talk."

Curran stared at me for a long moment and said, "You gonna forget you ever ran into us, Collins?"

"With pleasure," I said. "The farther we get from you two clowns, the better."

Scarborough took his hands off the table and leaned toward Carla. "But I bet you'll miss me, won't you, sweet thing?"

Carla flinched, then reached over and slapped his face. "You keep your goddamned hands off me," she said.

He let out a yelp and reached for her. I caught him by the wrists and twisted a thumb, which provoked a shout and some loud cursing. Curran grabbed Scarborough by the nape of his neck and slammed him back into his chair. "Knock it off, Phil," he said. Scarborough rubbed his cheek where Carla's slap had landed and slumped down in his chair. Curran glanced at the patrons looking at our table, then turned back to Frankie.

"Why did the cops show up on Crocker the other night, Frankie?"

"Beats the hell out of me."

"I think you dropped a dime on us."

"That's bullshit. They picked me up, knocked the shit out of me, and then threw me out of their car. I wouldn't exactly call them friends."

"Why didn't they arrest you?"

"For what?"

Curran glared at him, his look qualifying him for Mount Rushmore. "When we were over in the sandbox, I always figured you for a standup guy. That's why I wanted you on my crew. Now all of a sudden I'm having doubts. What did you tell the cops, Frankie?"

"I didn't tell them a damn thing."

"Then why have you been running from us?"

"Because this asshole pulled a gun on me," he said, as he gestured to Scarborough. "I didn't exactly think I was welcome."

"I drew down on you because I didn't believe a fucking word you were saying," Scarborough said.

Frankie leaned on the table and tossed a wadded-up napkin in Scarborough's face. "You're just damn lucky I didn't make you eat that gun," he said.

Scarborough started to get to his feet again and Curran pushed him back into his chair.

"Keep him on a leash, Jimmy," Frankie said.

Curran stuck a finger in Scarborough's face. "Phil, I don't want to have to tell you again. Shut your fucking mouth."

The two men glared at each other until Scarborough muttered something under his breath and leaned back in his chair, arms folded over his chest.

"Give me your cellphone, Frankie," Curran said.

"What for?"

Curran shook his head. "Jesus Christ, is anybody listening to me around here? Give me the goddamn cellphone."

Frankie glanced at me, then took his burner phone out of his pocket and slid it across the table. Curran looked at him and snapped his fingers.

"C'mon on, Rizzoli. The other one too."

"That's it," Frankie said.

Curran let out a huge sigh and shook his head. "Do you want Phil to frisk you?"

Frankie paused, then reached into his pocket, took out his smartphone, and slid it across the table. "What the hell is this, Jimmy?"

Curran shut down the burner and put it in his pocket, then picked up the smartphone. "You've probably got some kind of fuckin' tracking device on this thing," he said as he powered it down. When it was off, he stuck the phone in his pocket. "We're going to take a little ride and I don't want company. That includes texts and phone calls."

"I told you it's just me and Collins, Jimmy."

"Yeah, well, call me superstitious, but I think you've got a couple of buddies in here poking around the peaches and pears." He extended his hand in my direction. "Now yours, Collins."

Frankie and I looked at each other, not sure where this was going.

"Mine?" I said. "Why?"

"You and your girlfriend here are going with us."

"Whoa, whoa, whoa, Jimmy," Frankie said. "That wasn't the deal, man."

"The deal has been changed. Collins and the girl are coming with us."

"What the fuck for?" Frankie said.

"Insurance."

Carla gripped my hand. "Hey, you guys," she said. "I don't know what's going on between you and my brother, but it's got nothing to do with Eddie and me."

"That's where you're wrong, sister," Curran said. "I think your brother and your boyfriend here have been talking about Phil and me and what we're doing. Loose lips sink ships, as the saying goes. Collins and you are on the rocks, sweetheart."

"Let Carla go," I said. "She's no threat to you."

"I don't see it that way," Curran said. Carla gripped my hand tighter and

I looked across the patio in Dwyer's direction. He still had his cell up to his ear, and I could see his lips moving. I hoped to hell he was talking to the other two amigos.

"You never intended to make this swap, did you, Jimmy?" Frankie said.

"I did initially," he replied. "Not so sure now. We'll take a little ride and you can try and change my mind. Now, this is what's going to happen ...." He stuck his right hand into the pocket of his leather jacket. "I've got my fingers wrapped around a Glock. I don't know about Phil here. He's—"

"A Walther P99," Scarborough broke in. "And I've got me one itchy trigger finger."

"So listen up, you three," Curran said. "The five of us are going to get up from the table and slowly go out the same way we came in. We're going to walk toward the parking lot. If either of you doesn't follow directions, this swap for damn sure isn't going to take place."

He and Scarborough stood up. Carla, Frankie, and I did the same. Out of the corner of my eye, I saw Al Medina standing in front of a display of oranges, cellphone to his ear. When we started moving, I glanced back and saw Dwyer on his feet, watching us.

The three amigos had their antennae up. I hoped it was enough.

We walked outside to bright sunshine. Shoppers swarmed over the parking lot. I couldn't help but think this encounter was going to create problems. With this many people in a public space, the three cops faced the danger of innocent bystanders being at risk. But with Frankie's GPS disabled, Dwyer, Forbes, and Medina were going to have to make their move before we got into Curran and Scarborough's vehicle. I had a hunch they were going to come up on us from three different directions.

Carla was between Frankie and me. She gripped my hand, and I squeezed it as a sign of reassurance. Scarborough and Curran were a step behind us. To the right, the trolley car headed in our direction from its stop at the Grove. As we stepped across the tracks, I glanced to my left and thought I saw Medina moving among the cars. He obviously had come out of the Market through either Gate #3 or 4.

Curran poked me in the back. "Eyes front, Collins."

We walked down a lane and had to move to our left as a Subaru came toward us.

When we passed the next to the last row of cars, Curran said, "To the left, folks. Nice and easy."

I didn't see any vehicles that resembled Curran's Toyota RAV4 or Scarborough's Hyundai. Al Medina leaned against a car about thirty yards in front of us, the ever-present cellphone pressed up against his ear. I knew he was on the radio to both Dwyer and Forbes, wherever they were.

We came to the rear of a black Chevy Suburban and Curran told us to stop.

Scarborough stepped up next to Carla. "You ride shotgun, sweet thing. I want you close to me." He grabbed her elbow and started to pull her toward the front of the vehicle, but she wrenched her arm away.

"I told you to keep your hands off, asshole," she said.

Scarborough uttered a guttural laugh in reply.

"Dammit, Phil, you're driving, and that's all. Got it?" Curran said.

Scarborough put his hands up in surrender. The right one was filled with the Walther.

"Here's the seating arrangement," Curran said. "Phil opens the door for the girl, then gets behind the wheel with his gun on Collins and Frankie as they crawl into the backseat. I get in the third seat behind you. My gun is on your head, Rizzoli. If anybody moves, they're history. Got it?"

Neither Frankie or I said anything. Curran poked Frankie in the back with his gun. "You hard of hearing, Rizzoli?"

"We got it," Frankie said.

As we started to move toward the passenger side of the Suburban, I heard footsteps behind me. I turned and saw Dwyer approaching, weapon up and pointing.

"Everybody freeze, right now!" he shouted.

Medina also came running, hands in the classic cop stance, weapon drawn, yelling, "Hands in the air. Now!"

"You son of a bitch, Rizzoli," Curran said as he pulled out his Glock and fired at Medina. A round caught the cop on his right hip and he went down. Curran then grabbed Frankie around the throat and backed up so the two of them were flat against the rear of the Suburban.

When Scarborough heard Dwyer's command, he yanked Carla toward the front end of the vehicle. She stomped on his foot and followed up with an elbow in the face. He let out a bellow, lost his grip on her, and staggered back a step or two, but managed to fire a shot. Carla went down. My gun was out of its holster and I shot him in the chest. Before he could bring up his gun and aim, I fired again and a second bullet plowed into his chest. He staggered back and collapsed.

To my left, I saw Forbes also running and shouting instructions. Curran had Frankie around the neck up against the rear of the Suburban. He fired at the two cops, but Frankie struggled and the shots hit only cars and windows. Glass exploded, alarms blared, and screams from shoppers filled the parking lot.

I crouched down and peered around the end of the vehicle, thinking I could get a bead on Curran, but Frankie was in the way. He rammed a fist into Curran's face, then kicked him in his shin. Curran yowled in pain and relaxed his hold. Frankie stumbled forward and bent over to draw his ankle gun. Before he could get it loose, Curran fired twice.

Both shots hit Frankie. He fell to the concrete and lay still.

Dwyer and Forbes unloaded on Curran, hitting him several times and caving in the rear window of the vehicle. Curran jerked like a puppet on a string from the force of the bullets and collapsed at the rear of the Suburban.

In minutes it was over.

Brushing shards of glass from my head, I crept back to Carla and knelt down beside her. She gripped the hamstring of her left leg. Blood oozed from between her fingers. I yanked a handkerchief from my pocket and pressed it against the wound.

"Keep pressure on it. You're going to be all right," I said, as I cradled her head against my chest.

"My brother?" she said.

I looked behind me and saw Dwyer hunched over Frankie, yelling "Officers down!" into his radio and requesting an ambulance.

"He's been hit, Carla, but I don't know how bad. You just lie still. Help is on the way."

"And those two jerks?" she said.

"They're both down," I said. "Lie still and keep pressure on that leg."

"God, Eddie, I was so scared."

"Me too," I said, having no problem admitting it. I looked down at her and grinned. "Shut up, now, okay?"

She returned my grin and gripped my hand. "Yes, sir."

I glanced back at Dwyer, then turned and looked at Scarborough, the man I had just killed. He lay motionless, blood pooling beneath him.

CHAPTER FORTY-FOUR

———◆———

THERE MUST BE A REASON HOSPITALS offer the most boring periodicals known to man, but I can't tell you what it is. I made an effort, but couldn't concentrate on any of them. Nor could Nick Dwyer and Stan Forbes. I had wanted to climb into the ambulance with Carla, but since I was involved in a crime scene, the cops nixed it. When the detective in charge finally released us, Forbes and I piled into Dwyer's Range Rover and hightailed it for Cedars-Sinai.

We now sat on three sides of a coffee table strewn with magazines, waiting. Dwyer was in the middle chair and Forbes and I flanked him. Every squeak of rubber-soled shoes on tile caused our heads to pop up, in case the source would be someone with information.

James Curran was dead. So was Phil Scarborough. Killed by me. I had difficulty processing that fact. Numbness washed over me. I can count on one hand the times I've fired that handgun of mine, let alone killed anyone. Self-defense, yes, but that didn't dispel the sight of a man being gunned down by my own hand.

Al Medina was in fair condition, and a doctor had told us the prognosis was good. The bullet hadn't damaged anything vital. Carla was in good condition, and her prognosis was likewise favorable.

Frankie's condition was the problem. The initial report we'd received listed him as critical. He'd suffered two gunshot wounds, one in the chest and the other in the abdomen. He'd gone into surgery, and we were awaiting further word.

Dwyer stood up and made another circuit of the waiting room. I'd lost count of how many this was. He plopped down in his seat, crossed his legs in front of him, and let out a huge sigh.

"Nick, you're driving both of us nuts," Forbes said.

"Sorry."

He reached over and squeezed Dwyer's arm. "Hang in. Frankie's one tough bird."

I tossed a copy of *Scientific American* on the table and buried my face in my hands.

"How you doin', Eddie?" Forbes said.

I shook my head. "Can't get rid of the picture. The kick of the gun. Blood spurting out and the guy reeling backward."

"It was you or him."

"Yeah, I guess."

Dwyer sat upright and leaned in my direction. "You wanna know something?"

"What?" I said.

"At least one of my shots brought Curran down. I've been on the force twelve years. It's the first time I've fired on another person."

"What about the Army? You were in Iraq, right?"

"I was a clerk typist."

"How you going to handle it?" I said.

He shrugged his shoulders. "The department offers counseling. They strongly urge us to take advantage of it."

"If you want, Eddie, I can talk to someone on your behalf," Forbes said. "I mean, you were there with us."

"Might be a good thing," I said.

"They'll put us through the ringer for a couple of days, asking the same damn questions, but when that's over, we'll see if we can get you someone to talk to."

"Appreciate it," I said.

We looked up as a tall doctor with a neatly trimmed beard and rimless glasses approached. He wore a white coat, and a surgical cap still covered his head. A stethoscope was draped around his neck.

"Mr. Collins?" he said.

"Right here," I replied.

"Ms. Rizzoli is resting comfortably. You can see her, but try not to stay too long."

"Thanks," I said as I stood up.

"What about her brother?" Dwyer said.

"Mr. Rizzoli is critical, I'm afraid. Those two bullets did some damage. He's still unconscious."

"And Medina?" Forbes said.

"He's resting comfortably, but he's still in ICU. We'll want to keep him there for a bit longer. But it looks good."

The doctor gave me directions to Carla's room. Dwyer said they'd come and find me if there was any more news about Frankie. I walked past a nurse's station and turned left. Her room was on the right, halfway down.

I tapped on the door and went inside. She was propped up in bed, her eyes closed. A metal stand on wheels sat next to her right arm. A bag of what I assumed was glucose or antibiotics dripped into a plastic tube leading to an IV protruding from her arm. On the other side of the bed, a glass of water and a box of tissues sat on a table.

I grabbed the big toe of her right foot and wiggled it. Her eyes popped open and a huge smile broke out, one of the more pleasurable sights I'd seen in recent memory.

"How ya doin', Velvet La Rose?" I said.

"Better now that you're here." She held out her arms. "Come here, Shamus."

I went around the bed, leaned over, and was smothered in a hug that seemed to go on for a wonderful eternity. She finally released me and I kissed her and smoothed a strand of hair from over one eye. I perched on the edge of the bed.

"Frankie?" she said.

"Still in surgery. That's all we've heard. He was shot twice. The doc said they did some damage." She bit her lip and her eyes filled with tears. "He'll make it, kiddo," I said. "You Italians don't quit." She squeezed my hand and nodded, then yanked a tissue from a box on the table and took a swipe at a tear.

"How's the leg feel?"

"A little sore. But the doctor said there won't be much of a scar. When I get it back in shape it'll be as good as ever."

"Velvet La Rose with a scar? How's that gonna play?"

"No, I've figured it out, Eddie. I'm going to put a tattoo over it. And then one on the other leg to match it."

I rolled my eyes. "Oh, jeez."

"Maybe you should get one too."

I did the eye roll again and she laughed. I kissed her and she looked into my face. I could sense she knew something was weighing on me.

"Are you okay, Eddie?"

"Ah, it's been a rough day."

She laid her hand on my cheek. "You know it was self-defense, don't you?"

I nodded. "Don't ever let yourself think otherwise. I won't let you."

"Even if I don't get the tattoo?"

"Yeah, even then."

She wrapped her arms around my neck. I started to kiss her, but stopped when I heard a tap on the door. Dwyer and Forbes stood in the opening. They shuffled in and came up to the bed.

Carla gripped my arm and put her other hand to her mouth, biting on a knuckle.

"We're sorry, Carla," Dwyer finally said, his voice choking him.

"They did everything they could," Forbes added.

"Oh, God, no," Carla moaned and started sobbing uncontrollably.

I held her in my arms. "Let it go, honey," I said. "Let it go."

The sobs continued. I stroked her hair and held her close.

Dwyer walked around the bed and laid a hand on my shoulder. "Tell her the department will notify his parents. They'll make all the arrangements."

"Right," I said.

"We'll talk soon, Eddie."

I nodded to both men and they walked out of the room. Gradually, Carla's sobs ebbed and she lay back on her pillow. I handed her the box of tissues. She grabbed a handful and dabbed at her eyes. We looked at each other, our hands entwined. After a moment, a wan little smile crossed her face. I answered with one of my own. That's all I had for her. At least for now.

But there was tomorrow. Lots of tomorrows.

Photo by Larry Rosengren

CLIVE ROSENGREN IS A RECOVERING ACTOR. His career spanned more than forty years, eighteen of them pounding many of the same streets as his fictional sleuth Eddie Collins. He appeared on stages at the Great Lakes Shakespeare Festival, the Guthrie Theater, and the Oregon Shakespeare Festival, among others. Movie credits include *Ed Wood, Soapdish, Cobb,* and *Bugsy.* Among numerous television credits are *Seinfeld, Home Improvement,* and *Cheers,* where he played the only person to throw Sam Malone out of his own bar. He lives in southern Oregon's Rogue Valley, safe and secure from the hurly-burly of Hollywood.

Rosengren has written three books in the Eddie Collins Mystery series: *Murder Unscripted, Red Desert,* and *Velvet on a Tuesday Afternoon.* Books one and two were both finalists for the Shamus Awards, sponsored by the Private Eye Writers of America.

Visit him at his website, www.cliverosengren.com.

EDDIE COLLINS MYSTERIES
BOOKS 1 AND 2

PI and part-time actor Eddie Collins is hired to investigate the death of his ex-wife, Elaine Weddington, on the set of her latest B-movie. As Eddie follows the trail of clues, he realizes how little he knew about his ex, who was surrounded by jealousy and intrigue. And now the killer wants him dead too.

Hollywood PI, sometime actor Eddie Collins receives an SOS from Mike Ford. His Oscar has been stolen during a home invasion and his girlfriend drowned in the swimming pool. Did she surprise the burglar? All the dots connect around a movie Ford directed and acted in: *Red Desert*. Is a person associated with the shoot harboring a deadly grudge?

From Coffeetown Press and Clive Rosengren

———◆———

Thank you for reading *Velvet on a Tuesday Afternoon*. We are so grateful for you, our readers. If you enjoyed this book, here are some steps you can take that could help contribute to its success and the success of this series.

- Post a review on Amazon, BN.com, and/or GoodReads.
- Check out Clive's website (www.cliverosengren.com) and send a comment or ask to be put on his mailing list.
- Spread the word on social media, especially Facebook, Twitter, and Pinterest.
- Like Clive's author page (CliveRosengren43) and the Coffeetown Press page (CoffeetownPress).
- Follow Clive (@CliveRosengren) and Coffeetown Press (@CoffeetownPress) on Twitter.
- Ask for this book at your local library or request it on their online portal.

Good books and authors from small presses are often overlooked. Your comments and reviews can make an enormous difference.

Made in the USA
San Bernardino, CA
14 October 2017